Miss Perfect Meets Her Match

Wellywood Romantic Comedy Series

- Book 2 -

Kate O'Keeffe

Wild Lime Books

Miss Perfect Meets Her Match is a work of fiction. The characters and events portrayed in this book are fictitious. Any similarity to real persons, living or dead, is purely coincidental and not intended by the author.

- Formerly known as *The Heartbroker* -

ISBN-13: 978-1540366306
ISBN-10: 1540366308

Published by Wild Lime Books

CHAPTER 1

EVERYONE THINKS I'M A total hard-ass. No, really, they do. And if you met me, I bet you would too. But I'm not. *Honestly*, I'm not. I'm just a woman who knows what she wants and goes out and gets it.

You know how they say Cancerians are like crabs, with their hard outer-shell but totally soft insides? Well, I don't think it's any coincidence I was born under that sign. Not that I go in for that mumbo jumbo sort of stuff.

Really, at the heart of it all, I'm just a big old softie. It's just I don't need the world to know it.

And you know if you have a hard outer-shell you can deal with anything, right? Or at least *look* like you can deal with anything. And dealing with things is what I do, professionally.

And I'm damn good at it.

"He's here."

I look up, hit by a sudden surge of nerves. I see my assistant, Jocelyn, standing at my office door.

"Shall I bring him in, chook?" she questions, failing to suppress an excited grin.

"Yes, please. Thanks, Jocelyn." I take a deep breath as I get up from my chair and smooth out my skirt.

She shoots me an encouraging look. "Go get 'em, love. Do us proud."

I give her a nervous smile, pulling back my shoulders.

Jocelyn is the sort of assistant every manager dreams of: she's competent, organized, and, above all, a total Rottweiler when it comes to getting things done. She's got my back, and everyone knows it. What's more, she regularly dishes out 'fix-all-your-problems-in-one-squeeze' hugs.

She's the mother I wish I'd had.

"Thanks, Jocelyn. I'll do my best." The butterflies in my stomach start an exuberant dance party.

I check my reflection in my compact mirror. It's 7:30am and I've already been for my ten kilometre morning run, had my veggie-packed protein smoothie, and slipped into my favourite power suit, sweeping my long blonde hair into a classic French twist. I'm on top of my game.

And the man I'm about to meet could change my life forever.

The thought of how important this meeting could be to my business, to my *life*, makes my heart thump hard in my chest. *I have to kill this.* I take another deep breath in an attempt to settle those persistent butterflies in my belly.

You see I've been running my company, *Live It*, a personal growth business, for about five years now. I know, it sounds a bit hippie or New Age, but it's not in the least. Believe me. We help people unlock their true potential by showing them how they hold themselves back.

It's all based entirely on science, you know, and our customer survey results show ninety-two and a half per cent of our participants believe their lives have been changed for the better as a result of attending one of our seminars.

I figure the other seven and a half per cent of people who didn't think it helped them were probably forced to attend by their mother/ girlfriend/ boss/ long lost cousin, so they really don't count.

I started *Live It* with a boyfriend, Jonathon Melec, who was a clinical psychologist. He was a bit older than me—okay, a lot older than me—and had years of experience in counselling people in a group environment.

My background, on the other hand, was a business degree from a local university and a couple of years' experience selling software storage systems: not exactly 'touchy-feely-change-your-life' stuff.

Jonathon often talked about how successful his group therapy sessions were and how he'd like to expand them to help more people. Recognising a good business idea when I saw it, I did some research, discovered how popular these sorts of seminars are overseas, quit my job, got a business loan, and hey presto, *Live It* was born.

Of course we started out on a very small scale, holding our seminars in a back room we hired out for the day at Newtown Community Centre, a predominantly working class area of Wellington. But over time, word got out, and soon we needed bigger and bigger spaces, full weekend seminars, and a more central and upmarket location to accommodate the waiting list of people dying to do our courses.

We expanded into working with the government and corporates and our business took off like a NASA rocket ship on a mission.

I was able to pay off my loan within a matter of months, and we started to make some decent money in just over a year.

Not quite an overnight success, but pretty meteoric for a woman still in her twenties.

My relationship with Jonathon didn't fare quite so well. He decided to go back to the wife he had left a few months before we met.

Unsurprisingly, his wife wasn't thrilled at the idea of him continuing to spend all his time with his twenty-four-year-old ex. Go figure.

In the end, it worked out just fine for me: he got his wife back, and, for a guilt-ridden bargain, I got *Live It*. My baby.

Five years on and I have the most profitable personal growth business in the country.

I smooth my hair down one last time as I wait, standing nervously by my desk. The image I've seen of the man I'm about to meet enters my head: Logan McManus. He's one of the top executives of the wildly successful American-based *You: Now* personal development and coaching company.

The image is all chiselled jaw, brown eyes, and mischievous smile, and I smirk to myself; he looks more like a cover model for a romance novel than a high-flying corporate type here to discuss business opportunities with me.

Well, I for one won't be swayed by his Hollywood good looks. I've been down that road before and it's nothing but trouble, believe me. No more sexy American men for me. They're nothing but trouble with a capital 'T'.

Having only seen his doubtlessly photo-shopped picture on the *You: Now* website, I expect he'll be much less attractive in person.

In the George stakes he'll certainly be more Costanza than Clooney. I let out a chuckle, momentarily looking away from the door my eyes have been trained on.

"Found something amusing, Ms Mortimer?" a smooth American voice drawls.

"Umm, I—" I begin, only to be utterly fazed by just how gorgeous this guy actually is. He's tall, broad, and athletic, with tanned skin, dark brown hair, and eyes a girl could easily get lost in.

I can't help but drink him in. He's textbook handsome, even better looking than his online photo.

Now I know you haven't known me for long, so you'll have to take my word for it I'm not usually like this. I am a confident twenty-nine-year-old woman for whom the power of speech is readily available. At all times. A woman with poise, class, and sophistication, totally rocking a power suit, every bit the successful businesswoman.

A woman who can say more than 'umm' and 'I' to a man on first meeting, even if that man is mesmerizingly hot.

Sensing my discomfort, he reaches out to shake my hand, never once taking his eyes away from mine. "Brooke Mortimer, I presume? I'm Logan, Logan McManus. From *You: Now*. It's great to meet you."

His voice is like a river of slowly flowing rich, mellow chocolate, with more than just a hint of spice. Mm, utterly delectable.

"Logan McManus," I repeat, as I take his hand in some sort of hot-guy-induced haze.

I've been hit by a sledgehammer, right between the eyes.

"Yes. And please, call me Logan." His lips quirk, the skin around his eyes crinkling. I swear my heart skips a beat.

Definitely Clooney, without even a hint of Costanza.

I pull my hand away from his in order to break the spell. This is *work*, Brooke, not a blind date. He's here to do business with you, nothing more.

Oh, but it's been so long since I've been in the presence of a cute guy who makes my heart race. Not since the good-for-nothing love rat Scott two-timed me a year ago, shattering my heart in the process.

Yes, I'm Brooke Mortimer, and I'm now a fully carded member of ARA—Asshole Recovery Anonymous.

If I'm to be totally honest here, a year is a long time to go without any romance in your life. Although I love my work more than I can say, it doesn't keep me warm at night.

And if my obsession with rom coms is anything to go by, my heart is definitely beginning to miss it.

But really—love? Come on, what's the point? It's so messy, so time consuming. Quite frankly, I've got better things to do. Like clean the toilet.

I've got my family, my wonderful friends, and a life I adore. I live in one of my favourite cities in the whole world: Wellington, New Zealand's cool little capital city. Life is good.

Why would I want to go doing something stupid, something totally ridiculous, like falling in love?

I've been down that road before and I can tell you there's nothing fun about falling for someone only to have your heart ripped out of your chest, chopped into little bits, and scattered to the wind. No thank you.

I can most definitely do without 'love'.

And anyway, my life is perfect just the way it is. Well, almost perfect.

"Of course. Logan," I reply, calling on some previously unknown super human strength to regain my composure. "And I'm Brooke. Shall we take a seat?"

I gesture to the table in the corner of my office.

"Sure, thanks," he replies.

I watch him walk towards the table. I take a few deep breaths to steady my nerves before following him.

Jeez Louise. It's bad enough this man holds the future of my company in his hands, it's hardly fair he's hotter than The Sahara in summer.

Before I can stop him he pulls my chair out for me, and I have no choice but to plonk my aerobicized butt down on the seat as he waits to push it in for me.

It's like we're on a date in Nineteen-Sixty-Three.

"I'll get back to it, then. Leave you two to crack on with the hard yakka," Jocelyn says, barely suppressing a grin.

I realise with embarrassment she's been standing at my office door this whole time, observing me reduced to a gibbering wreck.

I steal a glance at Logan and take in a thoroughly baffled look plastered across his handsome face. I'm guessing he's struggling to understand a word Jocelyn said.

"Oh, what a silly chook. I almost forgot. Can I bring you both a cuppa?" she asks brightly.

I smile at her like a demented beauty pageant contestant, preparing to comment on my desire to bring peace to our world. "Thank you, Jocelyn. That would be great."

I'm wondering whether I really need any additional form of stimulation right now: Logan McManus seems to be doing caffeine's job just fine.

And then some.

Jocelyn smiles quietly to herself as she darts a quick look from Logan to me and back again, before winking at me and leaving the room. Winking? Really?

"A cuppa?" Logan questions once Jocelyn has left the room. "Is it like a cup of Joe?"

Having watched more than my share of American movies, I know what a 'cup of Joe' is.

"Probably more like tea, but I'm sure Jocelyn would be happy to get coffee for you. I'll just ask." I get up from my seat.

"It's fine, Brooke. Really. Tea would be nice." I stop in my tracks. Literally.

"Are you sure? It's no problem." I half sit, half stand at the table, giving my quads an unscheduled workout.

He chuckles gently and the most delicious heat spreads through my body and down my limbs.

"Really," he confirms with a smile. "I'm in New Zealand, I should do what New Zealanders do, right?"

"Well, actually, we're really big coffee drinkers here," I begin, returning to my seat, my quads silently thanking me. "Wellington in particular. We're kind of the coffee capital of the world, or something, I think. Whatever it is, we're big on coffee here."

I'm aware I've begun to ramble as I glance at Logan, noting the amused smile on his face.

"Is that so?" he asks. "I didn't know that. But I'm happy to have tea."

I smile at him, trying to regain the air of professionalism I can usually muster with very little effort, but which appears to be playing some kind of game of hide and seek with me right now.

Why does this guy have to look like a combination of every rom com hero out there? Part Ryan Gosling, part Ryan Reynolds—all the Ryans, it would seem—with a touch of Channing Tatum thrown in for good measure.

Oh, mercy!

"It's great to finally sit down with you, Brooke, the über-successful face of *Live It*."

"Thanks." I'm flattered, blushing like a thirteen-year-old girl.

I'm finding his foppish hair à la Hugh Grant in *Four Weddings and a Funeral* really distracting, as I imagine raking my fingers through it as he kisses my lips, his tongue finding mine as he... *STOP!*

Focus, Brooke, *focus*.

And note to self: stop watching rom coms. They're clearly not good for my professional health.

"Here we go. Two lovely cuppas," Jocelyn says, placing a tray of tea and pastries on the table.

"Cheers, Jocelyn." I'm thankful for the interruption her presence brings.

"Baked goods? Wow, you're amazing," Logan says, smiling up at Jocelyn.

She flushes with pride, winking at me again before beating her retreat.

I take a sip of my tea as Logan bites into his pain au raisin, wondering why Jocelyn has taken to all this winking today. It's not exactly her usual form of communication. I'm finding it a little disconcerting to say the least.

Logan takes a bite of his pastry. "Mm, this is so good. You should try one."

"Thanks, but I'm fine," I reply. I work hard to look good and eating carb-intensive pastries, although tempting, is a luxury my thighs frankly can't afford.

"As you know, we're very interested in finding the synergies I'm sure exist between our companies so we can forge an effective and mutually beneficial partnership agreement," Logan says, getting straight down to business.

As he talks I find my eyes drifting to his lips. I wonder what it would be like to kiss those lips, like Isla Fisher kisses Ryan Reynolds when they finally get together in *Definitely, Maybe*?

"—still good for you?" he asks, bringing me back to reality.

Err, what? I've been too busy fantasizing about him to know what he's just said, and now I need to respond? The safest thing to do is to simply agree with him.

"Yes, absolutely." I put on my best 'I'm-a-serious-professional' face. Which I am, but you would never know it by the way I'm behaving.

By now the heat from my face is creeping towards my hairline. It's so hot I could probably fry an egg on it: hand and cheese omelette, anyone?

Logan looks at me and nods, clearly happy with my reply. I heave a metaphorical sigh of relief. Got out of jail on that one.

"Great! I know our assistants set this up, but I'm also aware we work in a dynamic business and things can change. So shall we get down to it?" he asks, pulling up the calendar on his phone.

"Sure," I reply.

This is so unlike me! Ordinarily I'm the queen of control: work comes first, second, and third in my world, with no room for anything else. You've heard of A-type personalities? Well, when it comes to work, I'm an A-plus-type, that's how single-minded I am.

And hot guys with thick, floppy hair, square jaws, and playfully twinkling eyes barely manage a footnote.

I must be ovulating or something. Yes, that must be it. This is all down to my hormones.

Or, the thought strikes me with a sickening blow, my biological clock has suddenly kicked in and my eggs have decided to scream at me. *'Fertilise! Fertilise!'* I shudder.

No, just ovulating. I'm only twenty-nine, after all. And twenty-nine is still biologically young.

Isn't it?

"I want to see how you work, your culture, how you run things. What Brooke Mortimer and *Live It* is all about. As I mentioned on the phone, you run a really successful enterprise, Brooke. We're impressed at the depth of your market share here in New Zealand: a country, as you know, we don't currently have a presence in. If we are to progress this thing, I need to spend some time with you, with your team, to really get to know the 'ins and the outs' of your operation."

'This thing', as he calls it, is the very reason Logan McManus is here in Wellington with me and not in his native San Francisco, doing whatever it is native San Franciscans do.

Thoroughly handsome and sexy things, by the looks of it. Sigh.

You: Now and has expressed an interest in working with us to expand into the New Zealand market. It would mean selling fifty per cent of the business to them and going into equal partnership. I would have to relinquish the complete control I have right now, of course. But it's an incredible opportunity for *Live It* to work alongside his company and reap all the rewards associated with their global presence.

It could help us expand into Australia and even South East Asia, which we've been trying to do with little success for some time now.

It really is the opportunity of a lifetime—of *my* lifetime—and I need to give it my full attention. Not let my rom com-addled brain run away with foolish notions of being swept off my feet by some matinee idol American.

I take a sip of my tea. "I've got it all set up, Logan. This is very important to me, so absolutely nothing has changed," I reply. "We're meeting the head of sales and marketing next. First I want to present our approach and structure, which we can do now, if you like?"

I've prepared a fantastic presentation showing who we are, where we came from, and what we want to achieve, complete with video footage of some of our participants' more dramatic self-discovery moments. No matter how long I've been doing this, I'm always amazed at the way some people leap at the opportunity to share their heartache with the world. I keep mine firmly under lock and key, that's for sure.

As I launch into the presentation I've prepared for him on how *Live It* came about, our ethos and approach, thoughts of Logan's hotness mercifully float out of my mind. I'm so passionate about what I do, what we've achieved as a company, I almost forget about how intently he's looking at me, how he makes my heart race. Almost.

"You've achieved so much in such a short time, Brooke. It's fantastic to see." He looks directly at me and I find myself struggling for air.

Without wanting to boast, he's right. I've taken this company and made it into what it is today. And I'm damn proud of it too. But there's so much more I could do with it. With Logan and *You: Now*'s help, that is.

Keeping my mind on the work, rather than on Logan McManus, is going to be one tall order. But it's one I have to fill if I'm going to change my life forever.

CHAPTER 2

LOGAN AND I WALK out of my office together. It's only just before eight in the morning and already the place is a hive of activity.

We all know you can't discriminate against anyone based on age, race, gender, and religious beliefs: you know, all the big ones. However no one ever said you can't choose only to employ morning people. Being a morning person myself, I prefer my team to be up and at it before most of the city has hit the snooze button. Voila, an office full of hard working, focused early birds.

It makes me feel all warm and fuzzy inside, just looking at them.

As we walk into the open plan office every eye turns in our direction.

"Morning everyone. I'd like to introduce Logan McManus from *You: Now* in San Francisco, and, well—" I shrug and smile at him "—everywhere."

Logan shoots me a sexy smile and I swallow hard.

He turns to face the team. "Good morning, all. It's great to be here with you."

There's a general murmur of "Hi Logan" and "Welcome" from the staff.

"As you all know, he's come to New Zealand to spend some time with us, and I'm sure I don't have to say again what an honour it is to have him here," I add for good measure. "We hope you enjoy your time here with us."

See? You can do it, Brooke. Professional and in control: that's me.

"I'm sure I will, Brooke," he says with a hint of a smile teasing the corners of his mouth. Is it just me or did that come across as a little flirty?

"And hi everyone. I'm looking forward to spending some time with you over the next couple of days. But really, just forget I'm here."

Ha! As if.

I've known Logan McManus for—what? Half an hour?—And already I'm finding it hard to concentrate on anything but his dreamy eyes, his broad shoulders, the hint of stubble around his strong jaw... See what I mean?

"It's great to see you all here so early. I won't hold you up," he says by way of farewell.

"Oh, we like to be up at the sparrow's fart here, Mr McManus," Jocelyn replies, suddenly at my side without me noticing.

She's alarmingly nimble for a large woman.

"The sparrow's what?" he asks, that oh-so cute confused look spreading across his handsome face again.

"She means 'early'. It's a Kiwi expression," I explain.

Jocelyn is the best assistant I could imagine having, but she certainly favours the use of New Zealand slang. If you're not a local, I could imagine following what she says could be quite a challenge.

"Stefan's got the conference room sorted out and he asked me to come and get you," she says.

She takes Logan by the arm, walking him back to the conference room. I trail behind. "Now, I know you're the Yank here to suss us out, so you need to know we really bust a gut around here to put on a good show. Not that I want to skite or anything. I just thought you should know we really care about what we do."

Logan nods at her, smiling like a dimwit. "Yes. Good," he replies with clearly more conviction than he's feeling.

I suppress a smile. "Thanks, Jocelyn."

We reach the conference room door. I spot Stefan through the window, bouncing about the room like a kite in the wind, putting the final touches to his presentation. It's obvious to me he's nervous, and I say a silent prayer he doesn't fall apart in front of Logan.

Now that I think about it, perhaps I should throw in a prayer for me, too!

"No worries, love. Good as gold," Jocelyn says, closing the door behind her.

I glance at Logan, taking in his bemused look. "She's a little hard to understand if you're not from around here."

"You can say that again. I'm amazed Kristie could understand enough to organise our meeting."

I laugh. "Maybe she had a Kiwi-American dictionary on hand?"

I open the conference door and enter the room, followed by Logan.

"Morning, Stefan," I say. "Logan, this is Stefan Drake."

Stefan is my head of marketing, and one of my close friends. We met when he applied for the job three years ago and I liked him instantly. He keeps me entertained with his wicked sense of humour and his ever-eventful love life. And he's good at his job, too.

Logan walks over casually and shakes Stefan's hand. "Great to meet you, Stefan."

"Likewise," Stefan replies, his smile broadening as he gives Logan a none-too-subtle once over.

I dart him a 'keep-it-in-your-pants' look—ironic, I know—and he purses his lips at me in response as he checks the connection between his laptop and the projector.

What is it with this guy? He's got the two of us so hot under the collar I'm surprised neither of us has spontaneously combusted.

"Stefan has a presentation on our marketing strategy and successes for you today, Logan. He's been with us for some years now and has some real achievements under his belt."

"Oh, stop it, Brooke," he purrs, obviously thrilled by the compliment.

I pull out my chair and sit down before Logan has the chance to act like an American Prince Charming again. He takes a seat a couple of chairs away and I heave a sigh of relief: keeping some physical distance between us is just the ticket.

Turning to face us with the title of his presentation flashing up on the screen behind him, Stefan begins. "*Live It* is the personal development experience of choice for thousands of New Zealanders. With a satisfaction rate of over ninety-two per cent, what began as a small enterprise catering to only a few has expanded into the most popular group of seminars in New Zealand's main city centres and beyond."

Stefan flicks up slides covering our numbers throughout the country for both our government and corporate work and our weekend seminars, which are open to all. He's his usual efficient, knowledgeable self throughout, but has a stiff, formal air I've not seen before.

I catch Logan glancing at me a couple of times as Stefan talks through his slides, and I feel a little thrill in my belly each time.

"Can I interrupt?" Logan asks when Stefan pauses for breath.

"Sure." Stefan shoots him a steely look.

I glare at Stefan, wondering what's got into him. One moment he's undressing Logan with his eyes, and the next he seems irritated by his presence.

"Have you run seminars in Sydney or Melbourne? They're the largest cities in Australia, right?" he asks.

"Yes, they are," Stefan replies icily. "We've been trying to crack the Australian market for a couple of years now, although competition is high over the pond." He returns to his presentation, flicking to the next slide.

"Just a minute, Stefan," I say, interrupting him. "Stefan can show you some of our results and the tactics we've been using over there, if you're interested?"

"That would be great," Logan replies.

"Of course." Stefan brings up the relevant information and talks us through it, pointing to expected growth across six Australian cities. Growth we can only achieve with Logan's company's help.

"Okay, so I can see your market penetration has increased in the last fiscal year, which is great," Logan says after Stefan has completed his spiel. "Our research suggests this is just the tip of the iceberg in Australia."

"Exactly!" I reply with enthusiasm, glad we've reached the crux of the matter. "That's why we want to work with you, Logan. Your backing in Australia and beyond could increase *Live It*'s business tenfold."

I hope I don't come across as desperate. Truth be told, we've been working hard to crack the Aussie market, but so far there's been no pot of gold at the end of that particular rainbow. We may be New Zealand's current success story, but we've still got a long way to go.

There's a sudden beep and we all automatically glance at our phones.

"I do apologise. I'm going to have to make some calls," Logan says, still looking at his screen. "But I'm impressed with what I'm seeing here. You've confirmed everything we had thought about you."

I feel a surge of excitement and anticipation. Does this mean they want to do the deal? Wow, this could mean huge expansion for us.

"Brooke? Is there a private office somewhere I can make some calls?" Logan asks.

"Sure. Of course. Stay in here. We have lots of work to do for the seminar this weekend in Queenstown. Take your time."

As Stefan and I leave the room, closing the door firmly behind us, he corners me. "You should watch yourself with that one, Brooke." He's speaking in hushed tones.

"What? Why?" I snap.

"Mr America in there." He nods his head towards the conference room. "He's not to be trusted, Brooke."

"Why?" I ask, shocked. "What have you heard?"

I lean in conspiratorially. Alarm bells begin to ring out an unpleasant tune in my head. This deal could take *Live It* to the next dimension, and then some. It *has* to work.

"Nothing," he replies, shifting his weight from foot to foot again. "It's just he strikes me as dodgy."

"Dodgy? How?"

"I don't know, Brooke. Too smooth, I guess."

I narrow my eyes at him. "Too *smooth*?" I ask, incredulously. "We're trying to pull off a multi-million dollar deal here, and you're concerned that 'Mr America', as you refer to him, is 'too smooth'? Come on, Stefan, if you're going to raise something like this with me, you need to have some substantial evidence to back it up."

He bites his lip. "Look, Brooke. All I'm saying is there's something not quite right about him. And I care too much about this company to let it fall prey to some Flash Harry's personal agenda."

Deciding it's best to placate my over-sensitive head of sales and marketing, I give him the most sympathetic look I can muster, which probably isn't that convincing, really. "OK. Thanks. I'll do that."

As I turn to leave, he grabs me by the arm. "And one other thing," he continues.

I turn back towards him to listen, but I'm reaching the end of my tether with this malarkey now.

"What?"

"I saw the way he was looking at you in there. I know I'm *clearly* not his type, shall we say. *You* most certainly are, if you know what I mean."

"What?" I squeak, sounding like I've just sucked in a balloon full of helium. I try to hide the instant flush of warmth creeping up my face as my heart kicks up its pace. Stefan thinks Logan's attracted to me?

He laughs and it sounds a little bitter. "You must have noticed, Brooke. You might be acting like you're some sort of nun these days, but that guy would quite happily defrock you, given half a chance."

My stomach does a flip at the prospect of having my clothes ripped off me by the very sexy guy in our conference room right now.

Stefan darts me a knowing look. "See? You fancy him too. No, Brooke. It's dangerous territory. He's a total player," he advises, taking me by the shoulders. "I know one when I see one. Don't go near him with a ten-foot barge pole."

Why has he come over all concerned-big-brother on me? He wasn't like this while I was dating Scott Wright. And with the sorry way *that* one turned out, I could have done with it then.

"I'll do my best," I reply, trying to muster a most convincing 'what-the-hell-are-you-talking-about' look on my face. Ha! As if I didn't know.

Before he has the chance to see just how far my blush has reached, I turn on my heel and head to the sanctity of my office. I close my door behind me and throw myself onto the cool black leather sofa in an effort to stymie the heat in my cheeks.

Stefan's words ring in my ears. Logan McManus is a serious businessman, here to do a deal with us. He wouldn't have flown all this way to meet with us if he didn't have every intention of making our deal work. What would be the point?

And so what if he's a player? That's his business. He might be the hottest guy I've met in a year—perhaps ever—but I'm not looking for a relationship. Or even a fling, for that matter.

No. I'm in no danger of any kind here. None at all. He's just here to broker a deal with me that will make me—and him, of course—a lot of money. Nothing more, nothing less.

And I would do very well to remember it.

CHAPTER 3

"HOW DID IT GO?" two enthusiastic voices enquire as I sit down at a table at Charlie Noble, one of my favourite restaurants.

I'm meeting my two closest friends, Laura Moore and Alexis Callaghan, for the lowdown on my day with Logan McManus.

"Well," I begin, "I *think* it went well. Really well." I can't stop my eager smile spreading from ear to ear. Logan had been complimentary about my company and had certainly suggested *You: Now* would want to partner with us. Everything is falling into place, just as I have planned.

"Yippee!" Laura responds, clapping her hands together like an over-excited seal.

Laura and I have been friends since high school. She's sweet, kind, very 'down to Earth', as the saying goes, and has always got my back. Although we live completely different lives—she's a full-time mother of three under three—we've got serious history together, and I can't imagine my life without her in it.

"So what happened? We want details," she continues, as both she and Alexis lean in conspiratorially. Seriously, you'd think I was a world famous thief about to divulge the details of my latest heist.

"Okay. He said he was impressed with us after we delivered our sales and marketing plan," I begin, pushing Stefan's unfounded concerns out of my head, "and that it confirmed everything he had suspected about us." I smile.

"Well, *that* could mean anything," Alexis replies, ever the pragmatic businesswoman. She tucks one side of her sleek shoulder-length behind one ear.

Alexis is more like me than anyone else I know: we're both competitive and driven, each achieving what we set out to achieve through hard work and tenacity.

"I guess."

"What if he'd expected *Live It* to be in need of direction or lacking in expertise? It's a potentially misleading statement," she continues. "Perhaps his company just wants to buy you out? Maybe they're not interested in working with you at all."

I look at her in alarm. Perhaps she's right. Maybe Logan's the type of person to shoot off endless, meaningless compliments that don't mean a thing.

"Alexis!" Laura bleats, gently hitting our mutual friend's arm and shooting her a 'shut-the-hell-up' look.

"What?" Alexis asks innocently, oblivious to the impact her words are having on me.

"I don't think this is helping. Brooke thinks it went well, so it must have."

I shoot a grateful look at Laura.

Alexis looks mortified. "I'm sorry, Brooke. You go on. I'm sure I'm being unnecessarily sceptical."

I try my best to shrug off Alexis's concerns. "I guess it was the *way* he said it that made me think he wanted to work with us. I really do believe he wants to broker this deal."

He had definitely sounded positive. I'm sure I'm not just dreaming this: it's real.

"And, most importantly," Laura interrupts, with a devious smile on her face, "is he as cute as he looks online?"

I had shown the girls Logan's headshot on the *You: Now* website, a step I regret as the now overly familiar heat creeps up my cheeks.

"He's err—" I stutter.

"Are you blushing, Brooke?" Laura cries, raising her eyebrows at me, a look of amused incredulity on her face.

"Oh, my god, he *is* as cute as he looks online," Alexis chimes in.

"Well, he's a good-looking guy, sure. If you like that sort of thing," I sniff, hoping being off-hand will put them off the scent and my deepening blush will go unnoticed.

It doesn't.

"Oh. My. God. You *totally* fancy him!" Laura proclaims loudly, causing a variety of nearby patrons to turn our way, adding to my mortification. "Look at you, you're as red as a Santa suit!"

"No!" I reply, as my friends shoot one another a knowing—and thoroughly gleeful—look.

It's proving pretty hard to fool Little Miss Private Investigator and her sidekick here.

Alexis holds up her iPhone with the photo of Logan I know all too well, and I shrink down into my seat. "Well, he's definitely hot. You're only human, Brooke. And it's been, what? A year since Scott?"

Yes, a whole year since Scott. A whole year since my heart was broken, broken by the man I thought I would spend the rest of my life with.

So that must mean... no! I swallow hard. A whole year since I had sex.

I've become a reclaimed virgin.

As I glance between my friends I decide the best course of action is to placate and divert. "He's actually not as good-looking as his photo. It's been photo-shopped."

Again, it doesn't work.

"So why are you blushing so much, Brooke?" Laura asks, feigning innocence as she bats her eyelashes at me.

Laura is my oldest friend and I love her, but right now I could happily kill her, hide the body, and drive off into the sunset guilt-free.

"Well, I think he's just as handsome in person as he is in his photo," Alexis declares.

"How would you know?"

"Because," she begins, pausing for dramatic effect, "he's standing over there."

My heart skips a beat as I glance in the direction Alexis is nodding. Surely she's mistaken. There are so many restaurants in Wellington, what are the chances Logan McManus would be at the same one as me tonight?

But she's right. Logan is standing at the bar, on his own, perusing a drinks menu. He's removed his tie, undone his top button, and looks even hotter than he had at the office earlier in the day.

It's a Casablanca moment: "Of all the gin joints, in all the towns, in all the world, she walks into mine." The fact I'm not a washed up American bar owner in Northern Africa during World War II, pining after a woman in love with someone else, is beside the point.

Against my will, a thrum of exquisite desire course through my body, my heart rate increasing, as I watch him absentmindedly run his hand through his thick dark hair.

And, hello? What's this? My Girly Bits wake up and give me a nudge. '*Remember us?*' Hmm, I haven't felt *them* for a while. A long while.

Best to ignore them. I shift in my seat.

As he looks over in our direction I swiftly grab my menu, hiding behind it in a move I've seen in the movies. It's all I can think of in the heat of the moment, so it'll have to do.

Jeez Louise, I hope he didn't see me!

"It's him, isn't it?" Laura asks in hushed tones, leaning in towards me as she too holds up her menu.

We probably look like a couple of Roman soldiers defending ourselves with our shields against a foreign attack. I guess in some ways Logan's a bit like that—he *is* from another land, after all.

"Shhh." I hope against all things holy he hasn't seen me.

"If it's not him, Brooke, then why is he walking over towards us?" Alexis asks in mock naiveté, revelling in my discomfort.

"Is he?" I squeak.

In an ill-advised move, I lower my menu to determine whether he is in fact approaching our table or if Alexis is just ribbing me, which she has a long history of doing.

"Hi, Brooke?" a deep, rumbling American voice asks by my side.

And there's my answer.

I lower my menu, humiliated he's caught me out in such an obvious and childish attempt to hide from him.

"Logan." I try my level best to act as though I was simply reading my menu at close range, and that it's just fine to bump into him while I'm out with my girlfriends. "Nice to see you. How are you?"

"Great." He smiles broadly, amused by my antics.

"You're having dinner here?" I ask.

He's at a restaurant at dinnertime: fantastic question, Brooke.

"Yes. I'm meeting a friend soon. Seems like a nice place." He looks around the restaurant at its stylish décor.

His low voice brings my Girly Bits to attention and I squirm again, trying to ignore them.

"Oh, it is," Alexis replies for me. "We come here all the time."

She extends her had to shake his. "Alexis Callaghan, and this is Laura Moore."

"Hi," Laura says, clamouring over the table to grab his hand as well. "Great to meet you."

"Yes, sorry. These are my friends. This is Logan McManus, from *You: Now*."

That's right Brooke, move the tone of the conversation onto a professional footing.

Work I can do: romance I most certainly cannot.

"I may have mentioned Logan is here from the US to look into the viability of working with *Live It*," I say to my friends.

"Yes, you may have mentioned that, Brooke," Alexis replies, her eyes widening.

"Hmmm. Yes, now that I think about it, I do remember you saying something about that," Laura adds in, playing along.

I shoot an 'I-am-not-amused' look at the pair of them and decide it's best to change the subject. I'll deal with these comediennes later.

"We're here for dinner too," I state.

Why does this man rattle me so much?

"I can see that." He chuckles in a kind way, and I think I fall for him a little bit more. "Well, I hope you have a lovely evening, Brooke. I look forward to seeing you in a few days' time." He turns to my friends. "Ladies, it was great to meet you both."

"You too," they coo, as he retreats to the bar.

Once he's out of earshot I kick them both under the table. "Thanks a lot, you two."

"Hey, that's uncalled for!" Laura exclaims as she leans down to rub her shin.

"Oh, come on. I didn't kick you hard. Not as hard as you deserve, anyway. It was mean, teasing me like that."

"Oh, Brooke. It's only a bit of fun," Alexis replies. "I have to say, though, I think you're in trouble." She shakes her head at me as she grins.

"What? Why?"

"You've obviously got it bad for Mr McManly over there."

"Oh, yes," Laura confirms.

I swallow as I look at my friends. "He's nothing I can't deal with." I hope I sound more confident than I feel.

My friends think the only thing missing from my life is a man.

They're both loved-up and expect me to be too. Laura married her high school sweetheart and is now a proud mother of three, complete with mortgage and house with a white picket fence. And Alexis is madly in love with Tim, a gorgeous guy she met two years ago now.

And just because they're both fully carded members of Lovesville they think I need to be too. But I don't feel the need to have a man in my life for it to be complete. Or at least that's what I've been telling myself since Scott left and I picked up my rom com habit.

I steal a glance in Logan's direction and my heart does a quick squeeze. Although I don't want to admit it—even to myself—Alexis is right. Logan McManus is quite possibly my ideal man: he's strong, clever, successful, and confident. Add the fact he's the sexiest man I've met in way too long and even I would have to admit I'm in trouble.

I shake my head. Trust me to fall for the most unobtainable and inappropriate man within a five thousand kilometre radius.

So what if I'm like melted butter when he walks into the room? He's a man, I'm a woman: it's only natural. That doesn't mean I'm going to *do* anything about it.

"You two have sex on the brain, I tell you. He's here to do a business deal with me: nothing more, nothing less."

"Sure," Alexis replies, sounding unconvinced. "Keep telling yourself that, hon. But it's hard to deny he's a hottie. And for the record, he looks *just* like he does in his photo."

I roll my eyes. "Okay, I'll admit it."

"And he doesn't have a wedding band. I checked," Laura chimes in. She sounds smug.

"So he's not married. Big deal. That doesn't mean anything's going to happen between us. And anyway, Stefan thinks he's a player."

Alexis taps her chin, looking over at Logan, who is now deep in conversation with another man of about his age, sipping his beer.

"He might be. But I don't get that vibe from him. I mean he could be if he wanted to be, he's cute enough. I think he's just a nice guy who happens to be better looking than any one person ought to be." She flashes us a wicked smile.

Laura laughs, nodding. "Totally."

"When are you seeing him next?" she asks, thankfully moving on from the uncomfortable conversation of how attractive he is. Player or not.

"He has some other thing on for the rest of the week, but we're meeting him in Queenstown on Friday. He wants to experience one of our seminars first hand."

Logan's visit has been timed so he can see how we work 'in the field'. He'll be attending our seminar with another member of the *You: Now* executive team, Brad Stephenson. We're going to dazzle them with our approach—at least, that's the plan.

Although we've run events in Queenstown before, it never fails to take my breath away afresh whenever I visit it. It's a small town situated on a beautiful glacial lake, in New Zealand's Southern Alps in the South Island. It's a top tourist destination, and for good reason: it's stunning. Mother Nature sure can get it so very right sometimes. And we figured the amazing setting couldn't hurt our chances.

"What a *romantic* place to go," Laura gushes, nudging me with her elbow.

I'm beginning to suspect she's living vicariously through me. After all, she's the first to admit her life is pretty much baby poop, dishes, and laundry these days. My life must seem enviably glamorous in comparison.

I've reached the end of my tether. "Okay, I've played along with this for long enough now, girls." I try to give them my very best 'don't-mess-with-me' stare in order to get my point across.

"All right, we'll lay off, won't we Laura?" Alexis replies, laughing.

"Do we have to? It's so much *fun*," Laura complains.

"Just be careful," Alexis adds, turning to me. "Promise."

"Yeah, Brooke," Laura agrees. "He's pretty cute, and you're going to be working with him very closely."

I smile at the way in which my friends care for me. They may take great joy in ribbing me, but underneath it all they're the best friends a girl could have.

"Don't worry about me. I'm perfectly in control. All I want from Logan McManus is to broker this deal, nothing else. This is all on my terms."

"Hi there, girls," I hear a voice beside me coo.

I turn to see Lucinda Hargreaves, a girl I used to get up to no good with as a wild teenager, standing at our table. Whereas I've moved on from our outrageous adolescent behaviour, she's blossomed into Wellington's resident vamp, with her big boobs, big blonde hair, and, should we say, 'friendly' personality to match.

"Oh, hi, Lucinda," I reply in what I hope is a discouraging tone. The last thing I want is for her to join our little group tonight.

"Hi, Lu. Good to see you," Laura says as Alexis and I share a look. It's fair to say neither of us are big fans of Lucinda Strap-A-Mattress-To-My-Back Hargreaves, that's for sure.

"Budge up," she says to Laura, who obediently moves to the vacant seat on her right, despite Alexis's and my glares.

Laura slaps her little butt down. "What's up, ladies?" she asks, flicking her long, blonde hair over her shoulder. Extensions, for certain. Probably synthetic. Ick.

"Just chewing the fat, Lucinda. Catching up on the latest," Alexis replies coldly.

Alexis and Lucinda have 'history'. Alexis's boyfriend, Tim, had a short-lived fling with Lucinda before Alexis met him, much to her dismay. It took her a long time to come to terms with the fact her new boyfriend could be attracted to both her *and* Lucinda. His insistence it was 'just a sex thing' didn't help much. Men can be such idiots.

"Well, maybe I should share *my* news." She adjusts her strappy figure-hugging black dress so more of her DD's spill over the top. As if anyone needs to see more of *them*. "I've just won salesperson of the year. They're sending me off to Thailand for the week with a friend."

"Oh, how fantastic! You must be so proud. I know how hard you work. You deserve it," Laura gushes.

"Wonderful news. Isn't there a small problem? I mean do you have a friend to invite along?" Alexis asks sweetly.

Laura scowls at her and I can't suppress a snigger. It's fair to say Lucinda isn't overly popular with the females of the species, no doubt because she's slept with most of their men.

"She means, do you have a boyfriend to take, don't you Alexis?" Laura says in an attempt to smooth over the blatant jibe.

"Of course I do," Alexis replies. It's clear she doesn't.

"I'm between men, right now," she begins, playing with her hair.

"That's what they call 'single'," I can't help myself saying, adding air quotes for good measure.

"Oh, ha ha. A bit like you, Brooke? Tell me, when did you last have a man? Oh wait, that's right. Not since the hot tennis coach did the dirty on you with Jessica Banks. Right?"

I squirm uncomfortably in my chair. Being reminded of what Scott did to me is bad enough without the slut-a-licious Lucinda rubbing my face in it.

"I'm only joking, sweetie," she adds, rubbing her hand on my arm. It's all I can do not to recoil at her touch. "I'm sure you're completely over him now."

"She is. Absolutely," Alexis replies defiantly.

I dart her a grateful smile.

"Speaking of men, who was the delectable guy I saw you talking to before? The one over there at the bar?" she asks, looking over in Logan's direction.

I narrow my eyes at her, my heart hammering in my chest. I may have decided Logan is a no-go zone, but that doesn't mean I want Lucinda's mitts all over him. I shudder at the thought.

"His name is Logan McManus, one of Brooke's colleagues," Laura answers before I can shoot her a look screaming 'NO!'

"Really?" she replies, turning to me. "You've kept that one quiet, Brooke. A man like him?"

"Oh, he's only over from the States for a few days." I glance over at him. He catches my eye and smiles at me. I give a fainthearted smile back, feeling self-conscious.

Great. Now he knows we're talking about him. Again.

Like the eye of Mordor, Lucinda follows my gaze and, looking directly at Logan, tussles her hair as she pushes out her assets, shooting him a dazzling smile.

I swallow hard as I watch her advertise her impressive wares. Logan doesn't stand a chance.

If we had those yearbook captions graduates from high school get in the US, I wonder what her tag line would have been? "Most likely to bed half the city'?

"Well, I'll leave you girls to it. Lovely to see you all." She stands up, smoothing down the skin-tight dress that leaves nothing to the imagination. "Bye, girls. Don't do anything I wouldn't do. She saunters off.

That rules out running for prime minister and wearing comfortable sweat pants. I think we're good.

"She drives me *insane*," I complain once she's out of earshot. "She's so fake: fake boobs, fake hair, fake tan. Ugh. Men just don't see how manufactured she is. No one has hair that platinum blonde."

"Ahem," Alexis interrupts.

"What?"

"Something about a pot calling a kettle black? Or should I say the blonde calling the blonde blonde?" Laura says, ribbing me.

I let out a chortle. "I know. I'm not a natural blonde. But I like it. And it doesn't look all fake and cover-my-nipples long like Pamela Anderson's over there."

"But you had such gorgeous hair before," Laura protests.

"What was it like?" Alexis enquires. She's never seen my natural shade.

"Soft, light brown curls, Alexis. Just divine. And she dyes it and straightens it," Laura replies for me. "It's a crime against hair."

I shake my head at them. "Blonde makes more of a statement. I'm more confident as a blonde. I stand out more."

"Well you do it much better than Miss Sex On A Stick," Alexis comments, nodding in Lucinda's direction.

She's at the bar chatting up the barman now, by the looks of things. Poor guy.

"She's all right, you two. She's got a heart of gold," Laura protests.

"'A tart with a heart', is that the expression?" Alexis asks cheekily.

"I think that one refers to prostitutes, actually, Alexis. Now, I may not hold Lucinda in the highest of regards—"

Alexis snorts with laughter, interrupting me.

"—but, I don't think even she stoops quite that low."

"I don't know what you see in her," Alexis says to Laura. Laura has remained friends with Lucinda since high school, and by all accounts they're pretty close.

She shrugs. "I've known her for ages, and she's a really nice person, even though she has sex on the brain half the time. She's not all catty and competitive with me, like she is with you two. You bring out the worst in her, for whatever reason. And it's pretty clear neither of you like her."

"In Alexis's case, I think we all know why." I smirk at her.

"Oh, come on, you'd feel the same way if your boyfriend refers to her as 'the best sex I've ever had'," she replies indignantly.

Outraged on her behalf I exclaim, "Tim didn't say that, did he?"

"Well, no, not in so many words," she concedes. "But he may as well have."

"What does it matter? He chose you. She was just a flash in the pan fling. You're a proper relationship. Love is so much more than just sex," Laura states.

"Exactly," I agree. "She's a cheap takeaway and you're Cordon Bleu."

I look over at Logan and his friend and am startled to see them now standing with Lucinda, laughing at something she's saying as she flicks her hair, simpering at him. My belly twists as Lucinda places her hand on Logan's arm flirtatiously and he looks down at her, smiling.

I bury my head in my hands. We've just unleashed Wellington's weapon of mass destruction on the unsuspecting Logan McManus. He'll be left shattered and gasping for air before he even knows what's hit him.

A few moments of heinous flirting later, all three of them leave together. Logan looks in my direction. He has an expression on his face I can't quite read. Is it regret?

He shoots me a quick smile and wave as he walks out of the door.

Where can they be going? More to the point, do I want to know?

I sigh, turning back to my friends. What Logan McManus does with his life is no concern of mine. If he wants to spend time with one of the fakest, bitchiest, sluttiest women to ever waggle her butt across the face of the Earth in six-inch heels, who am I to judge?

I've made my decision: hands off Logan McManus. I'm just a business owner trying to broker a partnership deal with his company. Nothing more, nothing less.

So why should I feel such uncomfortable pangs of jealousy?

CHAPTER 4

A COUPLE OF DAYS later I'm at the family home in Brooklyn, a hilltop suburb close to the city with views over Wellington's beautiful harbour. As I work a lot of weekends, I tend to catch up with my family during the week. We've developed a bit of a regular Wednesday night dinner thing, which seems to work for us all most of the time.

When I say 'us all' I mean my dad, his wife, my stepsister, and my half brother. My full-blooded brother, Jeremy, lives in Auckland, so he doesn't count. Yes, we're quite the modern, blended family, us Mortimers.

My mum died from cancer when I was just a kid. We have loads of photos and videos of her, which I looked at again and again after her death. It got to the point where the line between the photos and videos and my actual memories blurred, and now I don't know what I remember of her and what's been put there.

What I do know for certain, however, is when I think of her I'm filled with love, followed by a deep sense of sadness she wasn't there to see me grow up, she wasn't there to be my mum. To begin with her loss was a piercing, agonizing sadness. Now it's more like a dull ache. It's never gone away in all this time, and I doubt it ever will.

Not being one to mess around, Dad started dating one of her friends, Jennifer, within the year, and they were married by the time I was ten years old.

Although I got to realise the common girlhood fantasy of being a bridesmaid for them, the pretty dress and flowers did very little to appease the despair I felt inside. It was about this time I learned how to look 'the part': to appear as though I didn't have a care in the world, even if I was dying a little bit on the inside. My trusty, tough, crab-like exterior was born.

Once Dad married Jeremy and I got a new mother, although we'd both just known her as Mum's tennis doubles partner for all our lives. She was divorced with a four-year-old daughter of her own called Grace, a girl who we now were told was our new sister. It was beyond weird.

Of course I love Jennifer—in reality she's been my mother for way longer than my actual mother was—but she's not Mum.

What's more, a few years after they married, they produced a half-sibling for us all: Dylan. He's in his final year at high school now and we get on pretty well these days, but things between us weren't always as rosy as they are now.

In fact, I felt like my life was over when Dylan was born. I was just about to turn thirteen, entering those weird and wonderful teenage years, when all attention was diverted from Jeremy, Grace, and me to this crying, pooping, vomiting little pink lump.

Jennifer was all-consumed by the newest member of our family, and it felt like Dad decided overnight I was no longer just his daughter, but also the live-in help, expecting me to do Jennifer's bidding any time of day or night.

Cutting a long, predictable story of teenage rebellion short, I started acting out. Big time. Over the coming years I did things like cutting school, getting in with the 'cool' crowd, doing drugs, sleeping around. That's when Lucinda and I became friends and, more often than not, she was my partner in crime.

I indulged in all the classic defiant behaviour any self-respecting teenager does. I got my rebellion badge and I wore it with pride.

It wasn't until I left school I realised what a waste of energy it all was: it only served to provoke Dad's anger, not his love. Which was all I wanted, after all.

"So what sort of deal do you think they'll offer you, kiddo?" Dad asks as he spoons out some minted peas onto his plate.

Whenever we're together Dad and I always talk work. He's a successful businessman, running a profitable property development company, and I love getting his advice and sharing my achievements with him. It's become 'our thing', something only we share, making it extra special to me.

"Well, I'm asking them to provide support, like finances and marketing, to help us move into the Australian and Asian markets. We'd be kind of like their Asia-Pacific face."

"And what do they get in return?" he asks, ever the savvy businessman.

"I've offered them an equal partnership. As you know, right now I own one hundred per cent of *Live It*. By selling them half of the business we'll have an equal say in the running of the company, and most importantly, they'll have a vested interest in making our deal a success."

Although I'm nervous at the prospect selling half of my baby, I realise it's the only way in which I can move *Live It* forward. Truth be told, our latest financials showed we haven't grown our markets, and are just stagnating. Something's got to change if I want to achieve my goals.

"You've been trying to crack into the Aussie market for a while, haven't you?" Jennifer asks, breaking my train of thought.

"Yes, we have. But it hasn't exactly gone to plan. That's where Logan comes in."

"Logan?" she asks.

I colour at my inadvertent mention of his name. I clear my throat in a vain attempt to divert attention away from my current imitation of a tomato.

This is getting annoying. If I insist on blushing at the mere mention of his name, how am I ever going to spend the weekend with him in Queenstown?

Honestly, it's getting ridiculous.

Jennifer shoots me an inquiring look. "Who's Logan?"

I feign nonchalance. "Oh, he's just the company representative from *You: Now*, that's all. Here to check us out."

"I see," she replies, smiling quietly to herself.

Due to his status as a male, Dad is thankfully oblivious to any unspoken communication between his wife and I. "Well it sounds like you've done your homework on this one," Dad says, tucking into his dinner. "Great potatoes, Jen."

"Thanks, darling," she beams back at him.

I watch the look they share and once again see how much in love they are. Despite my insistence I prefer to be single, I wonder if maybe one day I'll have that with someone.

Lately I've started to feel a little less anti-men. My hurt and betrayal when I broke it off with Scott is somehow less acute, less demanding Maybe I could have another relationship some day? Or maybe not. The thought of opening myself up to someone still gives me night sweats.

And of course, this possible change of heart has absolutely nothing to do with Logan McManus.

"And what have you been up to lately, Gracie?" Dad asks.

"Dad," she groans in frustration.

Jeremy and I have always called Jennifer 'Jennifer', but Grace called Dad 'Dad', rather than Roger, from day one. When she was old enough to decide, she changed her name to 'Mortimer' too. I guess it's because she was only little when our respective parents got married, and her biological father moved to Brisbane when she was about three. She sees him a couple of times a year, so he's more like a distant relation than a father to her.

"I'm a twenty-three-year-old woman, Dad. Please call me 'Grace', not 'Gracie'."

"Yeah, Dad," I chime in. "It's about time you did what she's been asking you for—oh, I don't know—ten years is it, Grace?"

"Exactly," she replies. "Thank you, Brooke."

"You're welcome, little sister."

"I know, I know. I keep forgetting. But you'll always be my little Gracie to me." Dad reaches over the table and playfully pinches her cheek like she's the little kid she was when he and Jennifer got married.

"Dad!" she exclaims, glaring at him.

"Oh, lighten up, honey. He's just messing with you," Jennifer chimes in. "How's work?"

Grace works as a fashion buyer for a chain of stores and loves her career. "Oh, it's great, thanks. We're looking at bringing in some new designers and Cybil wants me to check out their lines."

"That's wonderful, honey," Jennifer replies.

"Thanks. I'm so excited about it." She beams.

"Are you modelling much?" I ask before I take a bite. "Mm, this is delicious, Jennifer."

Thanks to winning the gene pool game and getting the best of both Jennifer's and her biological dad's features Grace is also a part-time model. She's one of those effortlessly beautiful women you grudgingly admire.

In stark contrast, *my* effortless beauty takes considerable effort.

"Just a bit, you know how it is."

Ah, no, I don't.

"Pass the peas, please."

"Sure." I pass her the bowl. She grabs the spoon to scoop some onto her plate, but manages to drop most of them onto the floor.

"Oops, sorry," she mutters.

She might look like Giselle, but she's a clumsy as a tap dancing elephant after a few beers.

"Can I be excused?" Dylan mutters, and we all turn in surprise to notice he's licked his plate clean—well, not literally, we have standards in our family, you know. Clearly bored by the conversation, he wants to go back to texting and Facebooking his friends. Or whatever it is moochy teenage boys do these days.

"Of course," Jennifer chirps. "Have you had enough, honey?"

"Yep," he replies in that wonderfully succinct fashion favoured by teenagers the world over.

Dylan is a great kid. He does well at school and seems to have a good group of friends he hangs out with. Maybe because he's a boy, my Dad and Jennifer are very soft on him and they let him do whatever he wants, whenever he wants. I could only ever dream of the freedom he takes for granted.

Luckily for me I was good at climbing out of windows or my high school social life would have been limited to my eleven o'clock Friday night curfew.

Up until recently he and I would hang out together—catching a movie, going for a run—but I haven't seen much of him in the last few months.

With Dylan leaving the table I spy the opportunity to head off myself. I want to get home, curl up under my duvet, and watch one of the rom coms I've got lined up for myself. Bliss.

I've been working my way through a list of the top one hundred rom coms of all time for a while now.

Have you ever wished life could be like a rom com? I don't just mean the falling in love, the dishy guys, the fabulous fashion, or even the happy endings. I mean knowing who the right guy is for you from the outset. I'll admit the heroine doesn't always know who she's going to end up with, but the audience does. And there's such a feeling of calm, of reassurance and satisfaction when the hero and heroine finally do get it together at the end of the movie.

I've had boyfriends in the past who've complained rom coms are too predictable, that the girl always gets the guy. But for me, that's the whole point.

If I knew who I was going to end up with I would forget my 'no men' policy and throw myself into the relationship with happy abandon.

Think about it: how easy would life be if you knew who the right person for you was? No stressing over whether he's the one, whether you should follow your heart or your head. Just straightforward, no mess, happy ending.

Bam. Perfect.

Laura's my partner in rom com crime. We've both been working our way through the list, although mostly alone as she's got three young kids to deal with. As she puts it, her outings are usually limited to visits to story time at her local library, playgroups, and the supermarket. A glamorous life indeed.

Occasionally though I will turn up on her doorstep with a movie from the list, a slab of Whittaker's milk chocolate, and a bottle of wine. Once the kids are tucked in for the night, we'll laugh and cry our way through a movie together, relishing every moment, right up to the predictable happy ending.

"So what are the next steps with the deal?" Dad asks me as we put the final clean dishes away.

"They're meeting us in Queenstown for our seminar this weekend. Logan and Brad Stephenson, one of the other executives, are attending as silent observers."

"Well I'm sure they'll love what they see, kiddo."

"Thanks, Dad." I beam at him.

I'm not ashamed to admit I love it when my dad compliments me, especially about something as important as my work. Whenever he does so I swell with pride, and tonight is no exception.

Floating on Cloud Nine, I head home to watch Molly Ringwald try to win the love of the rich kid in that 'Eighties classic, *Pretty in Pink*. And you know what? I bet my last dollar she does just that.

CHAPTER 5

I FLY INTO QUEENSTOWN on a stunning day, one without a breath of wind or a cloud in the sky. The purple-hued peaks of The Remarkables mountain range are covered with bright, white snow, adding to their majestic beauty, juxtaposed against the deep, dark blue of Lake Wakitipu below.

It's spring and the deciduous trees have blossomed into an array of whites and soft pinks, creating an almost impossibly gorgeous picture-perfect spot.

It's hard not to wax lyrical about the magnificence of this place, even if you're like me and have been coming here to ski every winter since childhood. Its beauty never gets old for me.

I've decided to fly down south before the rest of the team by about twenty-four hours so I can spend some quiet time preparing for my next meeting with Logan.

Logan. My conversation with Laura and Alexis the other night made me grasp just how dangerous it would be to act on my feelings for him. I know we're going to be spending a lot of time together this weekend, but I'm hoping I'll be so absorbed in the seminar it won't even occur to me to focus on how gorgeous he is.

Or on the way he makes me feel.

Not having seen him over the last few days has certainly helped diminish my attraction to him. Out of mind, out of sight. Well, almost.

I just need to be strong and focused: two things Brooke Mortimer is known for. It should be a total cinch, right?

After a quick taxi ride from the airport, I arrive at an imposing hotel on the lakefront where we will be both staying and holding the seminar.

I check into my room with its view of the calm, cool waters of the lake, and decide to settle my thoughts with a run. Running has always been my haven. It keeps me in shape, gives me time to think, and helps me stay calm throughout the day. I'm uptight if I miss my daily run, and try at all costs to get one in, even at my busiest times. I guess you could say I'm a run-aholic, needing my fix. And today is no exception.

Before even unpacking, I throw my running gear on, sweep my hair up into a ponytail, and head out the door.

Once outside I decide to turn away from the township, running along the road next to the lake. Despite the cold, the air is so crisp and clean and I want to stay out in it all day. I take one of the roads winding up the hill away from the lake. After running uphill for some time I stop to catch my breath and take in the view. The lake and surrounding mountains are bathed in the midday Spring sun and I take a moment to take a deep breath, appreciating Mother Nature's handiwork.

When I reach the hotel I'm hot and sweaty and in desperate need of a shower. I spy the sign for the hotel pool. A dip would be bliss right now. I decide to check it out on the off chance no one is around.

As luck would have it, the pool is deserted. Making a quick check around I strip off to my sports bra and cotton panties, loosen my hair, and dive in. The water is refreshing against my skin, cooling my exercised-induced flushed cheeks as I swim a couple of lengths before languishing in the cool water.

Despite my best efforts, my mind wanders to Logan. I find myself sighing as I think of him. Oh yes, he's definitely that kind of man: the kind women sigh over.

I try to snap myself out of it by reminding myself his attractiveness is merely an annoyance, one I can handle with ease. He'll be gone soon and I doubt I'll ever have to see him again.

Just get through the next few days, Brooke, that's all you have to do.

I duck my head under the water and swim across to the edge of the pool. As I climb up the steps I spot a pile of complimentary towels at the cabana.

I freeze as I hear a door close behind me.

Busted.

I swivel around, my embarrassment rising as I glance down my dripping wet body. What felt like acceptable attire when I was alone a few short moments ago, now suddenly feels completely *un*acceptable.

I decide to fake it and plaster a confident smile across my face as I turn to face my fellow swimmer.

Oh. My. Freaking. God. No no no no no. It *can't* be him.

"Brooke? Is that you?" Logan asks, sauntering towards me.

Rooted to the spot, I watch with growing mortification as his gaze sweeps my body, finally resting on my face. A smile teases at the corners of his mouth.

He's wearing swimming trunks and a white T-shirt, snug over his toned chest, a towel tucked under his arm. He's standing by my side in a few quick strides.

Why does it have to be Logan McManus? Why? *Anyone* but him!

I'm acutely aware I'm soaking wet, dressed only in a sports bra and undies. And they're white.

I'm practically *naked* in front of this man. The almost transparent material clinging to my body leaves little to the imagination.

It's like a scene from a tacky soft porn movie. In a moment Logan will come out with some cheesy line as he rips off his T-shirt and I'll fall into his arms in a sexy embrace . . . Or not. Sexy is the very last thing I'm feeling right now.

More like humiliated. Deeply, deeply humiliated.

I struggle to take in enough oxygen.

My eyes dart to the towels mere metres away. I decide to lunge for one in order to preserve what little dignity I still have, then turn to face him. I plaster a look of bravado on my face.

"Logan." I force a smile and ignore the acrobats doing energetic flips in my belly. "How nice to see you."

"Great to see you too, Brooke," he replies in his low, rumbling voice.

'*Hello there, Big Boy,*' my Girly Bits reply, clenching at the chocolaty, masculine sound of it.

I tighten my towel over my chest.

I want to dive back into the pool and hide there like an embarrassed mermaid. But then I'd have to flash him my undies again. I don't think I could face that level of humiliation once more.

"What are you doing here?" My eyes dart to his swimming trunks and towel as he stands next to the pool. "Other than going for a swim, that is." I laugh to cover my embarrassment, hoping he'll laugh with me.

I remind myself he's almost undoubtedly slept with Lucinda by now. He's damaged goods. Hot and sexy damaged goods, but damaged goods all the same.

"Yes. I'm going for a swim," he confirms, still smiling at me, holding my gaze. "And it looks like you've just had one." Once again his eyes slide down my body and back up again, causing me to catch my breath. "Water nice?"

I swallow. "Lovely. I needed to cool off after my run. But I'm going to get some work in now. So, I'll see you later?" I ask in a sing-song-y voice, inching away from him.

I'm so flustered by his unexpected arrival—and the fact he looks so darn gorgeous—I can't get out of here fast enough.

"Sure. Catch you later, Brooke," he replies, putting his towel down on one of the lounge chairs.

He pulls his T-shirt over his head, and I'm mesmerized by what can only be called a Magic Mike Moment. Only he's here, in the flesh. And my, what flesh!

I'm rooted to the spot, transfixed by his toned, tanned body. He's in great shape: broad shoulders, defined torso, and strong, muscular arms.

My body thrums at the sight of him. I tell you, it's all I can do to stop myself reaching out and stroking his chest there and then.

I shake my head to break the spell he's cast over me and walk as fast as I can towards the door. Just as I'm about to push it open, blushing fiercely, he calls out to me.

"Hey Brooke? What are you doing later? Do you have some time to get together, say after lunch?"

He's now standing facing me, wearing just his hip hugging trunks. I steel myself as I turn to face him. He's just a man, Brooke, like your brother. Yes, that's right, just like your brother. And seeing your brother in his swimming shorts is no big deal is it?

"Um, just working." I concentrate hard on looking at the spot just to the right of his head so as to control myself, causing him to look behind him to see what's attracted my attention.

"Everything okay?" he enquires, looking concerned.

"Ah, fine. Never better."

Just keep looking to the side, Brooke. Not at him, whatever you do.

"Okay. Good." He's clearly feeling awkward at my odd behaviour. "Can we get together then? At about two?"

"Oh, sure. Of course. Two would be great."

"See you in the lobby then."

I turn to leave, scuttling through the door as quickly as I can as I hear him splash into the pool.

How's that 'I-can-ignore-my-feelings-for-Logan-and-just-focus-on-work' thing working out right now, Brooke? Hmmm, yes, it's definitely a work in progress.

CHAPTER 6

I ARRIVE AT THE lobby a few minutes before two o'clock, aiming to be a little more poised and prepared than I was for our last encounter. Which, let's face it, isn't exactly hard, considering I'm pretty sure there's very little mystery surrounding my physical appearance for Logan after this morning's efforts at the pool.

I've agonized over what to wear to our meeting: too casual and I'll look like I'm not professional enough; too formal and I'll look like I can't relax. I settled on my favourite pair of skinny jeans, a white collared shirt, with a slim-fitting black merino V-neck, and a pair of black ankle boots with a low heel.

I'm carrying my laptop bag in case he needs to see any documents or I need to refer to anything, and I'm confident and prepared for our meeting.

I'm also trying to forget my complete mortification at the pool. Blocking it out of my mind is the best way forward, and that's what I'm going to do. I'll just act like it never happened.

I smile at the concierge as I take a seat in one of the lobby's plush chairs. Almost as soon as I've taken a steadying breath in anticipation of seeing Logan again, he appears at my side, looking down at me with a friendly smile.

"All set to go?" he enquires.

"Go?" I ask, standing up to face him, taking in his jeans, sneakers, and jacket, trying hard not to notice how hot he looks. Again. "Did you have another venue in mind? I thought we might just have our meeting here in the lobby, or over there, at the restaurant? We can order some coffee."

"Our meeting?" he asks. "No, I've got a much better idea."

He eyes my laptop bag, which I've leaned up against my seat in preparation for our discussion.

"We won't be needing that." He grins, his eyes twinkling.

"We won't?" I yelp, unsure what this afternoon is turning into. I've mentally prepared myself to discuss work, a sturdy table positioned firmly between us.

"Absolutely not. It will only be in the way. And it might get damaged."

Damaged?

"May I?" he asks and I nod in my confusion as he leans down to pick it up.

"Sure." I'm more than a little nonplussed.

"Campbell? Would you mind taking this to Brooke Mortimer's room?" he asks the concierge, as he places my laptop bag carefully on his desk. He turns to me. "It's room number—?"

"Ah, it's—" Do I want Logan to know my room number? The memory of his gaze sweeping over my body at the pool pushes into my brain.

'*Yes!*' scream my Girly Bits. '*Tell him!*'

Oh, that's *so* not a good idea.

Logan waits patiently.

"Err—" I stammer.

"It's alright, Miss. Tell me your name and I'll look it up for you," Campbell The Lifesaving Concierge offers.

He takes my bag and I give him my name, heaving a sigh of relief.

"Room Two One Seven," he announces a moment later in a booming voice. "I'll have it sent up right away."

"Thanks a lot." Thanks for nothing.

The bag dispensed with I turn back to Logan. If I don't need my laptop and this isn't a meeting, then what is it? A *date*? My heart rate increases at the possibility.

He places his hand on the small of my back and leads me out of the lobby and into the afternoon sunshine. I try to ignore how thrilling it feels, to be touched by him. As he turns and smiles at me I force myself to repeat the mantra I've been practicing in my head since I met him: 'It's just business, it's just business, it's just business'.

Now, if only my body would get the memo.

Instead his touch heightens my awareness of our dangerous proximity, and I find it almost impossible to focus on anything other than the way my body tingles for him.

I need to get a grip.

We walk together down The Esplanade, the road running alongside the lake.

"So what exactly are we going to do?" I ask, trying to ignore the exhilaration zinging around my body.

"I thought we could go have some fun." He grins at me again, raising his eyebrows.

"Fun?" I squeak, swallowing hard.

My mind darts to the fantasy I've been trying so hard to suppress about what 'fun' might look like with Logan McManus, and it's all I can do to put one foot in front of the other on the footpath.

"Yeah, fun. I'm sure even Brooke Mortimer has fun, every now and then."

I laugh nervously. "Of course! But I thought you wanted to discuss some items in relation to our deal."

"There's plenty of time for that. Did you know this is my first time ever in New Zealand? This place is so beautiful, and I really want to enjoy it before we get back to work. I figured you'd be a fun partner in crime. Okay with you?"

An involuntary smile spreads across my face. The thought of being out having some fun with Logan McManus in stunning Queenstown creates a sudden flurry of emotions: from nervous, to worried, to ecstatic, and everything in between.

He catches my smile. "I'll take it as a yes, then."

By now we're in the township and there are tourists and locals alike bustling around us.

"We need to hurry or we'll miss the bus."

Bus? He's taking me on a bus ride? Bus rides might be considered fun in San Francisco, but it's considered a dull activity here in New Zealand.

"Here we are. Just in time."

I look up at the sign above the storefront and I think my heart stops entirely. It reads, *AJ Hackett Bungy.*

Oh. My. God. He wants me to *bungy jump* with him?

I must have started hyperventilating as I see Logan's concerned look on his face, one of his hands on my shoulder. "You okay there,

Brooke?"

'Fine, fine." I'm *very* far from fine. My knees go suddenly weak, and for once it's not because of Logan.

Not convinced, he puts his arm around me. "Are you sure? Because you don't look so good." Concern is etched on his face, and I find myself relaxing a little in his embrace.

Taking a few deep breaths I manage to speak. "Are you planning on doing a b-bungy?" I don't want to know the response.

"Maybe," he replies, looking down at me. "I don't think you want to though," he adds.

"You worked that one out, did you?" I laugh self-deprecatingly. "Heights and me don't go together well."

"Brooke, I'm sorry. I had no idea. His arm is still around my shoulder, warming and calming me. His touch is so reassuring; I don't want him to let me go.

"So a bungy jump is out. Fine. There's this cool looking, low impact, not scary at all zip ride thing over the Kawarau River I thought looked good. Do you think you might be up for that?"

I'm not sure if he's pandering to me or not, but I leap at it nonetheless. "A not scary zip ride, you say? Sure, sounds good."

How bad can a zip ride be? Whatever *that* is. And whatever it is, it has to be less frightening than a bungy jump.

"I'll tell you what. Let's go into the store, check it out, and if you want to do it, we will."

I've calmed down enough now to know I need to regain some composure in front of Logan and appear to be unfazed by anything he could throw at me.

Although I suspect that ship has already sailed with a big neon sign screaming 'Brooke's-a-scaredy-cat' emblazoned on its side.

"Sure. Let's do that," I say as we walk through the door, his arm still wrapped around me.

A few moments later and feeling much more settled we're sitting next to one another on the bus, heading to Kawarau River. We've paid for two tickets on the sedate, non-scary zip ride.

"I know you were pretty freaked out at the idea of doing a bungy jump back there, but do you think you might be able to watch me do mine?" he asks gently.

I laugh self-consciously. "I'm not sure. I'm not good with heights." As though that wasn't obvious a few short moments ago.

"Or with hurling myself off a perfectly good bridge with an elastic band attached to my ankles, for that matter."

He chuckles. "Fair enough. I guess it is a pretty crazy thing to do, when you think about it."

"I don't even need to think about it to know it's at the top of the list of crazy things to do, Logan. Well, the top of my list, anyway."

He laughs and I can't help but allow a smile to spread across my face. I'm so at ease with him. He's sweet, kind, and funny, making my job of *not* falling for him harder by the minute.

I remind myself he's here to broker a business deal with me, and simply invited me along today as company. Sure, he's a nice guy; I could have been anyone. And his arm around me might have felt amazing back at the bungy shop, but he was just being kind, helping a mildly insane woman during an embarrassing panic attack.

Logan interrupts my thoughts. "I think you're going to enjoy the zip ride. I did one in the States a while back and it was real fun. You see the world from a different perspective from up there, that's for sure. And it's nothing like a bungy jump, so don't worry at all."

"You've done a jump?" I'm both impressed and appalled in equal measure.

"Yes, I did it with a group of my buddies years ago when I was a freshman in college. It was such a rush. I always vowed I'd do it in New Zealand at the original spot where it was invented." He shrugs. "And here we go."

"So that's where AJ Hackett comes in?" I may not be a bungy jumping aficionado, but I don't live under a rock, either. I know he invented the bungy and it all started on a bridge over the Kawarau River, the very spot we're heading to right now.

"Yeah. This is the pinnacle of my short, meagre bungy jumping career."

"You set your mind to a goal and achieve it," I comment, almost more to myself than to Logan.

"I suppose I do. A lot like you do," he replies and as I look into his eyes I think I detect something akin to admiration. Something moves in my chest. I turn away quickly, looking out of the window at the landscape whizzing by.

What was that mantra of mine again? Focus, Brooke, focus: 'It's just business, it's just business, it's just business'.

We arrive at the zip ride and my heart rate quickens as the staff talk us through the safety aspects of the ride and I spy the harnesses people are donning in front of us in the line.

Sensing my unease, Logan takes my hand. I look immediately up at him, enjoying the sensation of his skin on mine. "You're going to do great."

His presence is so reassuring, so calming. If he wasn't here with me now I know I'd be freaking out, making a total fool of myself.

Hang on a minute: if he wasn't here with me now, then *I* wouldn't be here at all. So, in fact, I should be freaking out at him! But just as this thought occurs to me, he squeezes my hand encouragingly.

"You ready?" he asks, grinning like an excited kid, causing me to let out a giggle despite myself.

"Sure," I reply, watching as his eyes crinkle into a fresh smile.

"All right, people," a staff-member says to Logan and me, breaking the spell. "Let's get you strapped in here."

Thanks to Logan my confidence is up a little. We reach the end of the platform, and then I make the classic mistake of looking down. I know this isn't the bungy jump, I know this is the sedate ride your grandmother might enjoy—non-scary, Logan said—but it sure is a long way down to the river below.

My instinct is to step back abruptly. I bang straight into Logan. He grabs hold of me before I can do any further damage.

"Look Brooke, I'm sorry. You don't have to do this."

My eyes dart nervously around the people watching me on the platform.

"Everything okay here?" asks a young guy holding some white helmets. Helmets? Why do we need *helmets*?

"Just give us a minute," Logan says to him. He puts his hands on my shoulders but it has no effect on me: there's no way there's anything zinging around my body right now other than sheer, unadulterated panic.

"I didn't realise this was going to be such an issue for you. Let's just go back to Queenstown. There's plenty for us to do there. Okay?"

He's so considerate, so understanding. I'm relieved and embarrassed, all at once.

"Hey, you know you can do a tandem if you want. You know, to make it easier? That way you can do it together," Mr White Helmet says to us, wanting us to make a decision either way.

Logan's face broadens into a grin. "Great idea. What do you say, Brooke? Want to do a tandem? I'll be there, right next to you, the whole way."

I feel so foolish and am trying desperately to overcome my fear as I turn from Logan to Mr White Helmet and back again, both of them with hopeful looks on their faces.

I know I desperately need to recover this situation: not just to regain my professional image in front of Logan but also for my own feelings of self-respect. A tandem ride might be a little less terrifying.

And hey, if the rope fails and I plunge into the icy depths of the Kawarau River below, at least I'll have company on the fall.

Not wanting to risk talking in case my voice sounds like Minnie Mouse, I nod and force a smile.

"Great!" I'm warmed by his enthusiasm—despite my anxiety.

Once we're helmeted up and strapped in, sitting side by side, Logan takes my hand once again, looks directly into my eyes, and smiles. I'm so diverted by him that we're suddenly zipping through the air before I realise we've even launched, the trees whizzing past us below.

It's an exhilarating feeling as we rush through the cool air, me screaming my head off in what I'm sure must be a most unladylike manner. I really don't care. This is *fun*!

We reach the end of the ride with a jolt, which makes my stomach do a flip, and are then transported back to our launching pad in a much more serene fashion.

As we climb out of our harnesses and remove our helmets, I know I couldn't wipe the smile off my face if someone offered me a million bucks. I'm not sure whether it's the zip ride, Logan, or a combination of the two, but I'm *invincible* right now.

"Oh, my god! That was amazing!" The adrenaline surges around my body, keeping me on my high.

Logan laughs. "It was, wasn't it?"

"Oh, let's do it again!"

"Maybe another time," he replies, eyeing the growing queue of tourists and thrill- seekers waiting their turn.

As we wander away from the platform, he wraps his arm around my shoulders, pulling me in towards him. I have enough presence of mind now to appreciate how it feels, but don't even bother trying to resist it. I'm in too much of a euphoric state to care right now, and being close to him is oh-so good.

"Hey, do you know what's so amazing about this? You were scared out of your brain doing that, weren't you?" It's clearly a rhetorical question.

I laugh out loud, remembering my very recent behaviour with a tinge of shame. "Oh, you noticed, did you?"

"Um, yeah. Kinda. But you did it anyway, Brooke. I'm impressed."

"Thanks." I'm pretty darn rapt with myself too.

"So, do you think you're up for a bungy jump now?" Hope flashes in his eyes.

I look up at the bridge above us as someone takes the leap off the edge, bungy cord strapped to his ankles.

I don't know whether it was the zip ride euphoria, the desire to impress Logan, or simply Logan himself, but before I know what I'm doing I'm strapped onto a bungy cord, standing at the edge of the bridge, high above the river, preparing to jump.

Continuing the theme of the day, Logan suggests a tandem bungy, and, if you'll excuse the weak pun, I leap at the idea. We're standing side by side, our arms wrapped around one another, as the instructor asks if we're ready.

"Hell, yes!" I exclaim, as we dart one another a quick look.

We take the leap together. As we go sailing through the air, I scream at the top of my lungs once again. The free fall is frightening, exhilarating and incredible all at the same time, and it goes by too fast as the bungy kicks in a mere handful of centimetres above the river's surface and we're bounced back up like fish on the end of a line.

We're both still buzzing from the jump as we shakily step out of the boat we were lowered into.

"I take my hat off to you, Brooke Mortimer," Logan says as we stand on the shoreline, looking up at the bridge we've just hurled ourselves off. "If I had a hat to take off right now, that is. Does a helmet count?"

I can't quite believe I've done it. I've been scared of heights since I was a little girl, finding even the jungle gym at school a challenge. I used to watch other girls my age climb fearlessly up it and dangle upside down from their knees. I pretended I preferred the swings and slides, but I was jealous of their bravery, of their ability to climb up high and to have fun while doing it.

For someone who thought her brain might explode at the suggestion of the calm, serene zip ride, I'm pretty amazed at myself for having done a bungy jump.

"You too, Logan," I reply, unable to resist the surge of pride from rising inside me. I give him a friendly punch on the arm. "I can't quite believe you got me to do it."

"It's all you," he replies, our eyes locking. I'm suddenly aware of our close proximity. "I'm so glad you came along for the ride."

As I look at his handsome face, a stray hair that came loose from my ponytail during the jump blows across my cheek in the gentle breeze. Logan reaches out and brushes it away, grazing my cheek. His touch causes a tingling sensation so intense, so intimate, my heart rate quickens as my Girly Bits clench in expectation.

I catch my breath and my gaze moves down his face to his lips, wondering how he would taste, how his lips would feel pressed against mine.

Before I know what's happening, his soft, sensual lips are on mine as we pull one another close, locking ourselves in an incredible embrace. And oh, it feels so good! As our tongues find one another his fingers slide up my neck and through my hair, tangling up in it, bringing my nerve endings alive. It's like an electric shock.

Instinctively my entire body responds to him, as I arch my back at his touch, my desire for him coursing through my veins, my knees turning to jelly.

Our kiss is ferocious and deep, full of the promise of fulfilment as it releases the sexual tension between us in an exquisite explosion. My whole body tightens with lust. My Girly Bits, now fully awake, scream for more.

Kissing him is better than anything I've ever done. Ever. In fact, I wonder why I've bothered doing anything else in my life. I could live and die here in his arms, kissing this sexy, strong, wonderful man.

I'm like a heroine in a Forties movie, swooning as the handsome hero takes me in his arms. It's so real, so right.

"Woo, yeah!"

A loud cheer interrupts our moment.

Suddenly realising my mistake, I pull away, shocked I allowed my feelings for him to sneak out. I look down at the ground, shifting my feet, smoothing my hair—*anything* not to look directly at him—as my cheeks redden in embarrassment.

"We get a lot of that after these jumps," the guy who had untied our ankles in the boat says to us.

I turn to him, grateful for the distraction. "Really? I bet you do. All that adrenaline and stuff, I guess?"

"Yeah, but don't let me interrupt. You can pash your boyfriend all you like." He grins lasciviously at me.

"Oh, he's not my boyfriend," I reply, hurriedly.

"Even better!"

I glance at Logan and notice he's enjoying our exchange, smiling to himself.

I clear my throat. "Logan, we should go."

"Sure," he replies, as I turn on my heel and walk away as fast as my trembling legs can take me.

CHAPTER 7

BACK IN MY HOTEL room, I try hard to concentrate on answering emails but can't stop my brain—and my body—from thinking of our kiss.

I can almost feel him pressed hard against me, our tongues entwined in our delicious, heat of the moment kiss. I'm virtually having a wet dream about this guy and it was just a kiss: an incredible one, granted, but just a kiss nonetheless.

I sit back at the desk in my room, looking out at the lake. It all happened so fast I can't work out who initiated it. Was it Logan? Was it me? God, I hope it wasn't me and he was just being polite by kissing me back.

Do people kiss like that out of politeness?

Oh, why did we have to kiss at all? Sure, we were on a high from our jump, the adrenaline was surging, and we did have a fantastic day together. But I had vowed not to let my feelings get the better of me.

No. It was a mistake, a mistake on an epic scale. Not only did I break my rule to stay away from men, I got myself entangled with the very man who holds the fate of my company in his hands.

The very hands that felt so incredible tangled up in my hair.

Talk about choosing the wrong guy.

And what's more, I saw him leave the restaurant in Wellington with Lucinda Hargreaves, and I can't imagine it was to go for a cup of tea and cucumber sandwiches. She would have offered it all up to him on a platter, and I imagine he would have found her and her overt womanly wiles hard to resist. Hell, he's only a man, after all.

The bus ride back to Queenstown was more than just a touch awkward, with me struggling to talk about anything other than what had just happened between us. I imagine I sounded like a demented parrot, squawking on about random things for the whole trip, my 'silence-is-power' approach well and truly flown out the bus window.

I put my head in my hands and groan to myself. Why does Logan have to be so freaking hot? And why can't I control myself around him? Seriously, I'm like some lovelorn pre-pubescent teenager, desperate for my idol to show even the tiniest bit of interest in me.

Right now I wouldn't put it past me to blow his profile picture up to poster size, stick it on my bedroom wall, and have fake conversations with him before kissing his papery lips each night.

I'm so angry with myself I could scream!

My phone rings, jolting me out of my thoughts. It's Alexis.

"Hey." I'm glad of the intrusion.

"Brooke! I'm so happy I caught you," she says with exuberance. Whatever's happening in her world doesn't involve the conflicting emotions I'm dealing with.

"You sound good." The understatement of the year.

"Oh, the most wonderful thing has happened! But I can't tell you over the phone. When are you back in Welly?"

"Monday morning. Why? You have to tell me what's going on."

"Let's meet for coffee at ten. Astoria? I'll tell you then."

"You can't do this to me!" It's only Thursday, Monday's days away.

"I just did," she trills cheerfully.

"Give me a hint?"

"No can do, Brooke. I've gotta go. See you Monday at ten." And then she's gone, leaving me wondering what's got her so excited. Maybe her company won some new big business? I guess I'll have to wait until Monday.

I almost feel lucky to have my current emotional turmoil as distraction between now and then. Well, almost.

"There's a tentative knock at my door. Housekeeping, probably. I glance around the spotless room; hardly worth it, I've barely used the room. Still pondering possibilities for Alexis's good mood, I open the door.

It's Logan, smiling sheepishly at me. "Hey."

The acrobats in my belly go at it again. "Hi, Logan."

We stand in my doorway uncomfortably. I don't know quite what to say.

Logan breaks the awkward silence. "I'm heading out for some dinner and wondered if you'd like to join?"

The self-preservation in my brain kicks in. Finally.

"Thanks. I've got quite a lot of work to do, Logan. I think I'll just get some room service and press on here."

Where was this resolve at the bungy jump this afternoon when I needed it most?

He grins at me playfully. "I think we can do better than room service, don't you?"

I bite my lip, thinking up another excuse. Truth be told, I brought *Sleepless in Seattle* on DVD with me, and I rather like the idea of curling up in bed and watching it on my laptop tonight with a glass of wine.

Before I have the chance to answer, he continues, "I hope you don't think I'm being presumptuous, but I've booked a table for two at a place in town the concierge recommended. It looks great."

What can only be regarded as my flaky resolve begins to waiver at the thought of hitting the town with Logan. Before our kiss complicated things this afternoon, we had an amazing time together, and I know we would have a lot of fun going out for dinner.

What's more, I remind myself, regardless of anything that may have happened between us, Logan is still *You: Now*'s representative. Without them my big plans to expand into other countries will be just that—plans.

I take a deep breath, relenting. "Okay. But it can't be a late one. I honestly do have a lot of work to get through."

Perhaps not the most circumspect decision, considering how I feel about him and the fact that we shared that incredible kiss just hours ago. But it's in *Live It*'s interests to keep him sweet in order to broker this important deal.

Well, that's the story I'm telling myself.

"Excellent."

"Can you give me ten minutes to get ready? I can meet you in the lobby."

"Sure. Of course. See you down there in ten."

* * *

"I hope you like Mexican," Logan says as we walk out of the hotel into the frosty evening air.

"Who doesn't?" I've had some legendary nights out eating Mexican food and indulging in the odd margarita or two in Wellington, and I certainly know my mole from my tamale these days.

He grins at me as he zips his jacket up against the cool air. He's wearing a collared shirt, jeans and boots combo, with a casual black zip-up jacket. Once again, he looks devastatingly handsome—almost too good to be true—and I repeat my mantra in my head: *'It's just business...'*

Forget the fact just a few short hours ago I was passionately kissing the man at my side on the banks of the Kawarau River. And loving it too.

The restaurant is decorated typically for a Mexican place, with large, bulky wooden tables and bright, colourful pictures adorning the walls. It's warm, smells amazing, and is completely packed. We're lucky Logan had the foresight to book or we would be turned away.

"Table for McManus, please," Logan says to a young, hip looking maître d' with a very low-cut top that leaves little to the imagination.

She looks him up and down, quite obviously checking him out. I'm mildly offended on his behalf.

"I'll just check." She winks and smiles at him as she runs her finger down the list of the evening's bookings. The cheek of her!

I glance incredulously at Logan and note he's barely registered her existence as anything other than a member of the restaurant staff.

"Come with me," she purrs, grabbing a couple of menus and sauntering off, hips swinging towards our table.

We reach the table and Logan pulls my chair out for me again before I can stop him. I take my seat.

"Your waiter will be here to take your order soon," she says as she passes us our menus.

She turns to Logan, leans in towards him and adds in lowered tones, "But you just let me know if you need anything. Absolutely anything."

As he gets an eyeful of her cleavage, I can't help but laugh at her outlandish come on, and she shoots me an evil look as she turns and saunters away, clearly for Logan's benefit, not mine.

"She was a bit much, huh?" Logan comments once she's on the

other side of the restaurant.

"Do you have this effect on every woman you meet?" I realise too late I've inadvertently given my feelings for him away. Not too clever, Brooke

"Oh, of course. They fall at my feet wherever I go," he replies, deadpan.

I let out a snicker. "That must be *such* a problem for you." I'm enjoying our easy repartee.

"Oh, it has its uses," he replies, raising his eyebrows at me suggestively, causing me to let out another laugh. "I find New Zealanders real friendly."

My mind darts to Lucinda Hargreaves and how he'd left the restaurant with her that night. 'Friendly' doesn't even begin to describe Lucinda's approach to tallying up the men.

I must have a sceptical look on my face as Logan asks, "What? You don't agree? I've found all the Kiwis I've met on my trip here really great. Are you telling me I've been fooled and you're all just a pack of assholes at heart?"

He grins at me and I shift uncomfortably. An image of Lucinda and her buxom, bouncing assets flashes before my eyes.

Even though it shouldn't be of any concern to me—I've made the decision Logan is a no-go zone, after all—part of me needs to know whether he did in fact go home with Lucinda that night.

Before I can stop myself, I ask, "Can I ask you something? I mean, feel free not to answer, because it isn't any of my business or anything."

"Ask away." He smiles, indulging at me.

I'm suddenly very nervous. "Did you have a nice time with Lucinda?"

"Who?" he asks, sounding surprised.

"Lucinda. You met at Charlie Noble, the restaurant I saw you at in Wellington? You left with her."

"Oh, Lu." My heart sinks at his use of her nickname.

"Yes, sure. We did. She was real friendly."

I bet she was.

I let out a bitter chortle and he darts me a quizzical look. "What's Lu got to do with anything?"

"Did you sleep with her?" I whisper, not sure I want to hear his response.

"*Sleep* with her? No! What makes you think I did that?"

A wave of relief washes over me. Lucinda failed to catch her prey? That must have been a first. I bet she's spitting tacks over letting Logan slip through her fingers.

I shrug. "I just thought—" I stop before I incriminate myself any further.

As far as Logan is concerned, I'm the woman he's brokering a partnership deal with. I can't go acting like a jealous girlfriend now. I haven't earned that right.

"I'm sorry. I thought you might have, but it's none of my business if you did."

I watch as his smile spreads from ear to ear. "She offered to take Chad and me to a bar we'd heard of, so we left. We just had one drink and then we said goodbye to her and came back to the restaurant."

"You did?" I ask in surprise.

"Yeah, but you must have left already."

"Oh." The girls and I had a quick bite before heading to the movies. We must have just missed him. I wonder why he came back?

"You know, her type is a dime a dozen where I'm from."

"I bet." I return his smile, my head buzzing with a cocktail of emotions: from relief to embarrassment, with a growing urge to reach across the table, pull him to me, and kiss his sweet, soft lips right off his delectable face.

"So," he begins, changing the subject as he peruses his menu. "What looks good to you?"

I resist the urge to say 'you', and instead look over my menu, settling on a sizzling chicken fajita.

"After the excitement of today, I'm going to order a frozen margarita. Will you join me?" Logan asks, and I'm unclear whether he's referring to our jumping adventures or our post-bungy activity.

I clear my throat, pushing thoughts of the incredible way his lips felt on mine out of my mind. "Sounds good. Although just the one for me tonight. I need to work later."

I sit back in my chair, satisfied I'm setting the tone for the evening: this is a dinner between colleagues, after which I will be returning to work. I think that's clear.

"Sure." He smiles and orders our drinks.

"This place is so beautiful. You sure live in an amazing country."

"Yeah, I guess."

"You guess? It's incredible! I've just seen mountains, lakes, fiords, geysers and boiling mud, all within a sixteen-hundred mile radius."

"Wow, you've been busy since I last saw you. Where have you been?"

He looks a little bashful. "I'll tell you, but you can't breathe a word to anyone else, okay?"

Wondering what weird and wonderful things he's been up to, I lean in conspiratorially. "Agreed."

"Well, I've been on a tour."

"Well that's nothing to be embarrassed about. Why the secret squirrel act?"

"It was a tour for fans of, umm, The Hobbit."

"Oh, I see," I murmur, smiling. "So you're telling me you're a sci fi geek."

He laughs his warm, comforting laugh. "I guess I am, then."

"Well, each to their own. Just as long as you don't run around wearing pointy elf ears with long cloaks, or re-enact violent battle scenes or something."

"No, I don't do that," he chuckles. "Definitely not. Although I am a big fan. I've read all of the books, seen all the movies, and I have to admit I put my hand up for this trip as I've been keen to visit New Zealand ever since I saw the first Lord of the Rings movie years ago. My buddy Chad, who was with me at the restaurant, travelled around with me. In fact, that's why we left with Lu that night. She showed us a bar we'd heard the stars in the movies used to drink at."

"Oh, I see." I know full well she would want to show him a lot more than some bar. "Where did you and Chad go on your travels?" I ask, thanking the waiter for my margarita as he put it on the table in front of me.

"Well, before I came to Wellington to meet you I did the tour around Hobbiton in the North Island. They shot a lot of Middle Earth scenes there. I also went to Roto-ah—" he struggles with the name.

"Rotorua? Where all the thermal activity is?"

"Yes, that's the one. With all the geysers, hot pools, and the boiling mud. It was all so amazing. Stinky, but amazing."

I laugh. Rotorua's thermal activity makes the whole place smell a little like a rotten egg, but once you've been there for a while, you barely notice it.

"And then before you got here I did a tour of all the sites they filmed around Queenstown. There are loads of scenes shot here for The Hobbit, Lord of the Rings, as well as others, like The Narnia movies. It is such a beautiful place. You have no idea how lucky you are to live here."

Although I've enjoyed The Hobbit and The Lord of the Rings movies, I wouldn't call myself a big fan, and I can't imagine ever taking a tour of the filming locations. But his enthusiasm is so cute, making him even more attractive: something I thought wasn't humanly possible until this moment.

Any second now I'm going to melt into my chair so I change to a neutral, non-melty subject. I choose a topic close to my heart: our potential partnership deal. "What do you think of our operation so far? I know you haven't seen us in action yet, but you've had a chance to look through the material we provided and get to know us a little, right?"

"Yes. I have. And I have to admit, *Live It* is one inspiring organization. You've got quite the business there, Brooke."

"Thank you. We think so too." I swell with pride. It's been hard work and years in the making, but I have to agree with Logan: we've built a fantastic little company. It's up to him and *You: Now* to help us get to the next level.

"Brad Stephenson is arriving in the morning. He works closely with our seminar leaders and is excited to meet you and attend the seminar."

"Yes, I'm looking forward to meeting Brad. I've only ever talked with him on the 'phone."

"Brad's great. He's been working for us for a few years now and has an amazing rapport with our attendees. He started out as a leader, but now is in a senior management role. He can't help but get involved, though. I guess it's in his blood."

Brad Stephenson is the final piece in the puzzle. If we get his thumbs up as well, our partnership deal is all but signed.

"It all kicks off tomorrow afternoon?" he asks, draining his margarita and signalling to the waiter to bring us each another.

"It does. The attendees are set to arrive at the venue at four and we start at four-thirty sharp. It's important we stick to our schedule, I'm sure you'll agree, as we have so much to get through. The Friday session runs until ten with a dinner break about half way through. I like the Friday sessions as we introduce what we're going to do for the rest of the weekend, and get people fired up about it. There's always lots of excitement and energy in the room."

"I bet," he replies. "What's your involvement?"

"I'm the first speaker of the seminar. I welcome everyone, tell them what *Live It* is about, what they should expect from the weekend, that sort of thing. I'm not a seminar leader, so it's my main contribution to the attendees over the weekend."

"Your work is done after the initial session tomorrow?"

"Yes, my official work is done. But I like to be on hand, in case I'm needed."

I'm very comfortable in talking about my work, and find myself waxing lyrical about the different elements of our programme, the way in which our attendees respond, and the successes we've been involved in. I'm pretty sure my eloquence has been lubricated by the margarita that's been going down rather well. The evening zings by.

"It is such a privilege to be able to help someone see the negative thought patterns they've been imprisoned by for so many years, and to help them form new ways of thinking," I say after we've finished our delicious meal.

"I can tell you're passionate about what you do, Brooke." His face creases into his oh-so-sexy smile, and I have to avert my eyes to avoid becoming lost in them.

I clear my throat. "Speaking of work, I need to get back to the hotel and finish up some things before tomorrow. Shall we get the bill?"

"By which you mean 'the check'?" he asks with a chuckle. "Of course," he replies, as I get our waiter's attention by doing the international hand sign for the bill.

We amble back to the hotel together, taking in the twinkling lights surrounding the lake. It's impossibly romantic, and if Logan McManus didn't hold my future in his hands, I would be in very real danger of falling for him tonight.

"Okay, it's your turn. What else do Kiwis say differently from Americans?" I ask as we amble back to the hotel by the shore.

"We say 'trunk' and you say 'boot', right?"

I nod.

"You have to admit, that one is weird. A boot is something you wear on your foot, not put your groceries into."

"I'll give you that one, but *you* have to admit saying 'lift' for 'elevator' is so much more efficient."

"Well, if your goal is efficiency, then yes, I guess it is," he says with a chortle. "Jocelyn uses some odd expressions. Sometimes she says something and I seriously have no clue she's even speaking English."

I laugh. "You need a degree in Kiwi slang to understand her half the time. Don't worry, I'll translate for you."

He stops walking and turns to face me. "Hey, I have another one. A smile twitches at the corners of his mouth. "'What's a 'pash'?"

I swallow hard as my mind shoots to our tonsil activity this afternoon.

"Oh, umm—". I look down, suddenly self-conscious as I try to think of how to answer.

"The guy in the boat at the bungy jump used it." As though our kiss isn't seared into my memory.

He takes a step closer to me. I look up at him and notice he has that mischievous grin on his face again: he's thoroughly enjoying teasing me.

"Brooke. Our kiss was unbelievable." His voice is sexy and gruff as he gazes into my eyes.

As I look at him, something moves in my chest.

I clear my throat and look away, my heart quickening. Damn this man! Just when I think I'm back on top of my feelings for him, he reels me back in with expert ease.

"I can tell this is making you uncomfortable, Brooke, and I'm sorry. But I was kind of hoping we might be able to... '*pash*' again." He raises his eyebrows at me.

My body betrays me once more, and my Girly Bits begin that humming they seem to love to do whenever Logan's around. '*Oooh, the things we could do with him,*' they coo.

To my eternal gratitude my rational brain—which seems to have been on holiday since I met Logan, lazily sipping cocktails by the pool—kicks in. "I don't think that's a good idea. This afternoon was a heat of the moment thing, you know? Kind of like the adrenalin from doing the jump made us act in a way we wouldn't usually. I mean, we had both just cheated *death*, when you think about it. Hadn't we?"

"I guess." He looks dubious.

"So let's leave it at that, okay? Can we just say it was a 'bungy thing'?"

"A 'bungy thing'," he repeats.

"Exactly." I'm awe-struck by my strength in the face of such unbelievably sexy odds.

"Well, if that's the way you want it," he begins as I chance a direct look up into his eyes, "can we go do another jump right now?" He grins from ear to ear, and my Girly Bits scream at me again. *'Come to mama!'*

This man was sent to test me. Of that I am now certain.

I laugh and shake my head at him. "You're nothing if not persistent, Mr McManus. I'll give you that." My tone belies the lust for him seeping out of my every pore.

With willpower of steel I turn away from him and begin walking somewhat shakily towards the hotel.

"Well, you can't blame a guy for trying," he replies, hooking his arm through mine.

My body stiffens at his touch. I want him so much I have to resist the urge to rip my panties off and throw them in the air, groaning *'take me now, tiger!'*

What's more, my heart feels something else. And I don't like it. No ma'am, I most certainly do not.

We arrive back at our hotel. Knowing my resolve is on shakier ground than during a magnitude seven earthquake, I decide it's safest to bid Logan goodnight in the lobby and most certainly not at my bedroom door.

"I'll see you tomorrow, Logan. And I look forward to meeting Brad then, too." I smile my most 'I'm-a-successful-and-focused-businesswoman' smile at him and put my hand out to shake his.

He takes my proffered hand, leans in, and kisses me on the cheek. His breath is warm against my face, sending shivers down my neck.

"You know, I think we both missed a real opportunity here." His voice is quiet.

I look into his eyes and hold his gaze for a moment too long as my heart hammers in my chest. My mind darts to *Four Weddings and a Funeral*, when Andie McDowell says that very thing to Hugh Grant. And we all know they were destined to be together.

I shake the image out of my head. I know I've made the right decision.

"Goodnight, Brooke. Thank you for a great day."

Time to turn around and head to your room, Brooke. Alone.

As though on autopilot, I blink several times to break his hold on me, turn on my high heels, and walk towards the lift. I hold my head high, knowing I have shown impressive determination in resisting his deeply alluring charms.

As I close my bedroom door behind me, I lean against it, my head abuzz with thoughts of him. I take a steadying breath, my reinstated rational brain telling me I've done the right thing.

But my heart—and my body—unquestionably disagrees.

CHAPTER 8

I'M UP BRIGHT AND early the next morning, out on my regular morning run. It's another stunning day, crisp and cool, with a smattering of clouds hanging low around the mountains, serving only to make the view even more picture perfect than it was yesterday.

As usual, my run helps me clear my head and prepare for the day. The introduction evening is always a big event. There's so much to do to prepare for it and we all have a few pre-seminar nerves.

But today my mind is full to the brim with more than just the upcoming seminar. Thoughts of Logan keep invading my every thought. And he's a persistent man, I can tell you: no sooner have I dragged my brain away from thinking about him to concentrate on what I'm planning to say in my opening remarks, something cute or amusing he said the night before barges back in, taking over again.

It's like he's infiltrated my every thought, short-circuiting any hope of conducting a productive day.

I arrive back at the hotel after my run and think better of diving into the pool in order to cool off, remembering the cringe worthy 'Almost-Naked-Gate' incident yesterday morning.

Instead, I make it back to my room, where I jump into the shower, hoping to wash away my desire for him, the desire that could be my ruin.

After I'm dressed I begin the transformation required to make my hair look effortlessly done. I spritz it with product, blow dry it in sections, then apply my trusty hair straighteners. It's quite the process.

I'm not the kind of girl who can get dressed, throw on a bit of lipgloss and head out the door, confident I look a million bucks. Sadly, no. That's more my sister Grace's style, not mine. This takes time, people.

Stefan, Jocelyn, and the team arrive mid-morning, and the rest of the day is spent organising the final details for the seminar.

As head of promotion and marketing, Stefan doesn't need to be here, but he offered to come along for the weekend to act as support, tagging on a trip to see his family in Dunedin on the way home.

"You look great, Brooke. The southern air must be good for you." Stefan gives me a quick hug.

"Thanks." I blush, thankful Stefan can't read my mind.

He shoots me a quizzical look and I turn away from him and begin to busy myself with the seminar paperwork.

"And how *is* The Player? Managed to keep his hands off you, has he?"

"What?" My voice is possibly more than a fraction high. "You're dreaming."

"Come on, Brooke. You're a hot chick and he's up for it: it's a match made in one-night-stand heaven."

I'm a little grossed out by Stefan's less than delightful turn of phrase. "As I've said before, we're trying to broker a deal that will benefit all of us—" I prod him on the arm "—and that's all there is to it."

"Well, if he does try anything, you just let me know and I'll sort him out, okay?"

"You'll *'sort him out'*?" I laugh. "What are you, a gangster all of a sudden? Are you going to have him 'whacked' or something if he comes near me?" I joke, trying to put him off the scent.

Not that there is a scent, I remind myself: we've established the ground rules now, and we can all get on with the business at hand.

"He's been a gentleman," I add. Well, that is, if you count kissing me like his life depended on it followed by a late night proposition as being a gentleman.

"And here he is. The man himself: Hugh Hefner," Stefan says frostily, looking towards the door, his arms crossed as he purses his lips.

I half expect to see an elderly man in his dressing gown shuffling towards us as I turn. Logan walks into the conference room and my heart does a flip. He's accompanied by another man, almost as handsome as he.

The two men walk towards Stefan and me, both of them smiling.

I am in control.

"Logan," I say in a professional tone, taking the upper hand. "How nice to see you again."

"You too, Brooke," he replies as he shakes my hand, seemingly taking my cue.

My Girly Bits clench. I may have successfully delivered my 'let's-keep-our-relationship-on-a-professional-footing' speech to him last night, but my feelings for him haven't magically vanished just by saying the words.

More's the pity.

"This is Brad Stephenson. Brad, this is Brooke Mortimer, chief executive of *Live It.*"

"Great to meet you in the flesh, Brooke," Brad enthuses as he pumps my hand with vigour.

"Great to meet you too, Brad," I reply, resisting the urge to pull my hand away from his extremely firm grasp.

With his wide grin, enthusiastic personality, and impossibly square jaw he bears more than a passing resemblance to the game show host from Sesame Street. Now what was his name? Guy Smiley, that's right. I half expect him to burst into song about the wonders of the alphabet at any moment.

I have to exercise considerable self-control not to burst out laughing at the thought.

"This is Stefan Drake, *Live It*'s head of sales and marketing," I add, thankful when Brad releases my hand in order to shake Stefan's.

"Stefan, hello. Great to meet you, too." Brad shakes Stefan's hand equally eagerly. "I'm so excited about this," he exclaims to no one in particular, looking like he might pop.

Oh, yes, he's definitely from the Street.

Stefan beams at him. "We are too. We're happy to have you here. Aren't we, Brooke? Really happy." He's still holding onto Brad's hand, smiling at him like a love-struck fool.

Subtlety thy name is not Stefan Drake.

"Thanks. I'll a——" Brad begins, clearly trying to pull his hand away from Stefan's grasp.

"Oh," Stefan replies. "Am I still shaking your hand?" he asks, still not releasing it.

"Ah, yeah," Brad replies, pulling it from him.

Realising an intervention is required, I place my hand gently on Stefan's arm, diverting his attention from Brad, who looks like he's beginning to sweat.

"Stefan," I say out of the corner of my mouth.

"Oh!" Stefan reluctantly pulls his hand away. "Silly me. What must you think of me, Brad?" He chortles, blushing every shade of red in the colour wheel as he gazes at him.

I guess Stefan must have a thing for puppets.

Observing the awkward exchange, Logan raises his eyebrows as he shoots me a half smile and I close my eyes in embarrassment. Not only did I throw myself at him following our bungy jump yesterday, now Stefan's doing the same sort of thing with Guy Smiley. He must think we're a bunch of idiots with sex on the brain.

He might be right.

Turning to Logan, Stefan says coldly, 'Hello, Logan," adding an unconvincing, "It's nice to see you again."

Taking a mental note to deal with Stefan's all too obvious preferences later, I invite Logan and Brad to join us as we run through the specifics of the upcoming seminar.

"—and we wrap it all up on Sunday night at about nine," I say, having gone through a detailed breakdown of each session, its goals, and expected outcomes.

I'm impressed with the way I've managed to stay calm and professional while sitting opposite Logan. He looks good enough to eat in his suit jacket and open neck pale blue shirt, showing off his tanned skin to perfection. Maybe delivering my 'back off, buddy' speech to him last night has done the trick?

I feel a small twinge at the thought.

"Just stick with me, Brad. I'm happy to be your shadow for the weekend," Stefan purrs, sitting so close to Brad he's almost in his lap.

"Sure. Thanks," Brad replies uncertainly, his ever-present smile drooping around the edges.

I spy Jocelyn entering the room with Michael Cray-Smith, the seminar leader who's worked at every *Live It* seminar since Jonathan and I set the business up years ago. He's enthusiastic and inspirational with a proven track record: the key qualities we look for in our leaders.

Wanting to divert everyone's attention away from Stefan's

increasingly lurid behaviour, I say, "Look, there's our seminar leader for this weekend, Michael." I stand up and motion for him to join us, which thankfully he does after a few quick words with Jocelyn.

"Hi Brooke! Ready for another amazing event?" he asks as he hugs me. "Hi there. I'm Michael." He turns to the group of men, all of whom are now standing.

There are handshakes all around and I suggest Logan and Brad spend some time with Michael while I get on with the seminar work at hand.

I nearly have to pull Stefan away. He reluctantly leaves the men, throwing in another icy look at Logan for good measure, much to my continued embarrassment.

"Settle it down a bit, will you?" I stage whisper once we're out of earshot.

I'm painstakingly aware I've behaved a little like a love-sick teenager over Logan in the very recent past, but that doesn't mean he should come on to Brad so very blatantly.

And, yes, I do see the irony.

"What?" Stefan replies, grinning, as though butter wouldn't melt. Brad's an all-American looking guy: healthy, tanned, with white pearly teeth. Totally Stefan's type. His last boyfriend bore more than a passing resemblance to Chris Hemsworth in his role as Thor— without the big hammer and Norse costume, that is.

"You know exactly what." I shoot him my best 'don't-play-dumb-with-me' look. "Let's keep this professional. Okay?"

"Sure, okay." He looks like a child who's had his favourite toy taken away. "You have to admit though," he adds, gazing over at Brad, who appears to be in full flight about something with Michael and Logan, "he's dreamy."

I watch Brad wave his arms around animatedly, imagining what he's saying. *This just in. Ernie has found his missing rubber duckie!"* I chortle to myself: definitely Guy Smiley. Whatever floats your boat, Stefan.

I clear my throat.

"And you're a fine one to talk," he accuses.

I shake my head. "This is too important for us to let lust for some guy who's only in the country for five minutes mess things up. And yes, I know: that goes for me too."

Stefan crosses his arms, glaring good-humouredly at me. "Good."

"And you have nothing to fear on that front," I add, sounding a whole lot more confident than I feel.

I simply need to stick to my guns. Either that or hope Logan is abducted by aliens who take him back to their planet, never to return to Earth.

We walk into the conference room and begin the process of setting it up in preparation for the seminar. We're scheduled to have just short of eighty people in this room tonight, which is both thrilling and daunting in equal parts.

"How's it going with brokering the deal, Brooke? Made any headway?" Stefan asks as we line up rows of seats.

I glance around the room, satisfied no one else is within earshot. "Logan seems positive about us, which is great. I'm not sure who the decision maker is here, so allowing Guy to see just how great we are is equally important this weekend."

"Guy?" Stefan questions, looking puzzled. "Who's Guy?"

"Oops, I mean Brad. Hey, don't you think he looks like Guy Smiley? You know, from Sesame Street?"

"No." Stefan looks indignant.

"Hmm, I do."

"Brooke, Guy Smiley's a puppet." He gets a misty look in his eyes. "Brad Stephenson is a man, a flesh and blood man."

"Settle down there, tiger. Do these chairs look straight to you?"

He squints his eyes, looking down the row from one end. "Looks good to me. I'll get another stack."

"It needs to be perfect, Stefan. A lot's riding on this weekend."

* * *

Several hours later the rooms are all set up, every last detail has been attended to, and a full audience sits facing me as I prepare to deliver my welcoming speech before handing the seminar leadership over to Michael Cray-Smith. There's an almost tangible feeling of expectation in the room. It's my job to set the scene for what will hopefully prove to be a life-changing experience for each and every one of our seminar attendees.

I love this part of my job, and it's where I think I shine. I love being able to get an audience excited about what they are about to learn and how we can help them change their lives. I'm so proud of what *Live It* can do—and has done—for our attendees, and that pride swells in me as I speak tonight.

Music is pumped out through the PA, setting the scene for my arrival. I walk up onto the stage, smiling at the audience as they cheer and clap. What a rush! This is what rock stars get addicted to, and I know why: it's nothing short of amazing.

As I talk, I'm aware of everyone's eyes on me, especially Logan's. He's sitting in the front row, listening intently to what I have to say. Every now and then he catches my eye and flashes me an encouraging grin, and I feel a small but perceptible surge of exhilaration.

I introduce Michael, after sharing some of the incredible work he's been involved in in his career, and exit the stage to a flurry of applause.

"Great work," Jocelyn says as she helps me unclip my headset outside the conference room. "You gave it heaps tonight. Good on ya, love."

I'm still on a high, a kind of post-speech euphoria I'd like to bottle and crack open whenever I'm in need of a boost. "Thanks so much."

"Yeah, you were awesome," I hear Logan's voice say behind me as I hand Jocelyn my headset. "At least, I *think* that's what you just said, Jocelyn."

I turn to him and smile. Despite my decision to keep him at arm's length, I'm glad he was there to witness my presentation, which seemed to have been well received by the Queenstown attendees.

"Sure did, Mr McManus. She's a real corker," Jocelyn gushes, winking at me. Winking? Again? I flush with pride.

A mother's approval—even if Jocelyn's just a surrogate version I acquired in adulthood—is always wonderful.

"I think a 'corker' is a good thing, right? Nothing to do with a bad bottle of wine or anything?" he asks, looking between the two of us.

"Too right," Jocelyn replies with a grin.

"Well then, I have to agree with you, Jocelyn: Brooke *is* a real corker, and she did a wonderful job tonight."

I flush at the compliment as my heart squeezes in my chest.

"We use some different terminology from you and there are some subtle differences in our approaches, but in essence I'd say our philosophies are pretty well aligned. I can see what a great fit we would be."

He gazes directly into my eyes, and I'm aware he's talking about more than the 'fit' between our respective companies.

"Fantastic!" My voice is a full octave higher than my usual pitch.

"Are you heading up to the suite?" he asks.

We always book a suite for the *Live It* staff to eat and relax in during a seminar. It means everyone gets a break away from the attendees to recharge. There's a buffet, tea and coffee, and people come and go as they need. As I'm not required again tonight, I had planned on heading there now.

"Sure am," I reply in a slightly manic tone of voice, knowing we're likely to be the first ones there. Which means we'll be alone.

In a hotel suite.

With a bed.

Lord, give me strength.

"Great. I'll walk with you."

"Are you coming, Jocelyn?" I ask, hoping she'll agree to act as a buffer between Logan and me. There's safety in numbers, as they say.

"Oh, you two go on ahead. I'm needed here," she replies, smiling sweetly at me.

I shoot her a look of suspicion, not sure what she could need to do now that she hasn't done already. Jocelyn is efficient with a capital 'E'. She has everything organized down to the smallest detail before a seminar. I wonder what she's up to?

As I walk out of the conference room, a fresh wave of nervousness hits me. Having been in Logan's presence without melting to butter so far today—okay, there's been some melting going on, but come on, I'm not made of wood—I have some confidence I can resist his charms.

But if, for some unforeseen reason, there's a repeat of our amazing kiss yesterday, I know for certain I'm a dead woman.

"Do you follow the same format for all your seminars?" he asks as we exit the lift together.

"As you know, we've got a variety of courses people can choose from, starting with the beginner's and going right through to advanced, as well as our corporate offerings, which we tailor for each company we work with."

I open the door to the suite. I give the room a quick once over. We are, in fact, alone.

I continue to ramble. "We tend to start with a scene-setting

70

introduction for all of them. The advanced courses are smaller, with people who've attended a number of our other courses. A more intimate atmosphere develops fast. Which is great, of course."

I'm powerless to stop myself.

"One introductory course we ran a few months ago in Auckland had nearly one-hundred-and-twenty people. Which was amazing, but kind of unwieldy, you know?"

I pause to take a breath and Logan uses the momentary silence to take a step closer to me. I'm acutely aware of his close proximity, as my breathing becomes fast and shallow.

His face creases into a smile, causing a zing of pleasure through my body.

As he looks down at me, I can't help but gaze up into the deep pools of his brown eyes. My body responds to him, reminding me with a jolt how much I want him, the determination I had literally moments ago slipping all too easily off the cliff and splashing into the deep waters below.

"Brooke, I—" he begins. He reaches across to me, looking deeply into my eyes, only to stop before his hand reaches me, pausing mid air, before he returns it to his side with a heavy sigh.

"No," he utters in his deep, rumbling voice, seemingly changing his mind. He looks away and shakes his head, breaking the tantalising spell.

He turns abruptly away from me and walks to the other side of the room. I notice his hands are clenched into tight fists at his sides, hinting at the feelings he's holding deep inside.

Confused, I watch him leave, my chest sinking. I know we agreed to stay away from one another—hell, it was my idea—but my heart clenches as I think of what may have been.

I'm rooted to the spot, unable to speak or move as I watch him stare out the window at the twinkling lights surrounding the pitch-black lake.

I want to scream at him, force him to come back to me, feel his body next to mine. I know he's wrestling with his obligation to follow my wishes, and his desire for me, and all I want is to give myself to him.

Before I have the chance to utter a word, I hear a knock at the door and a moment later a key card inserted outside the suite. The door swings open.

It's Jocelyn.

"I thought it best to knock, love, in case I was interrupting anything." Do I detect a hopeful look in her eye?

She stands in the doorway, holding the door ajar, taking in the scene: the tormented look on my face and Logan's tight back and clenched fists. "Everything all right here, love?" she asks, a look of disquiet flashes across her eyes.

Through some sort of miraculous intervention, I find the ability to speak. "It's fine. Really. Everything's fine."

She raises her eyebrows in disbelief.

"And you're not interrupting at all. Is she, Logan?" I say, forcing him to turn around.

When he does, I catch a fleeting look of thunder on his handsome face before his mouth creases into a smile, directed at Jocelyn. "No. We're all about the work, aren't we Brooke?"

I look at him uncertainly. Is there a hint of bitterness in his voice?

"Righto," Jocelyn replies. "Anyone for a cuppa?" She breezes in the room, closing the door behind her, and heads to the catering.

I say a silent prayer for Jocelyn. If it wasn't for her, who knows what I would have done? Watching Logan wrestling with his emotions like that stirred something deep inside me, something I haven't felt for a long, long time.

And it scares the living daylights out of me.

CHAPTER 9

DESPITE TOSSING AND TURNING all night, I rise early the next morning. I have a job to do, and it needs to take precedence over anything else this weekend.

If I'm honest, there's nothing much else I can do now as Michael is leading all the full group sessions and the smaller breakout groups are all up and running. Nevertheless, *Live It* is my baby, and I'd be a bad mother indeed if I didn't at least keep an eye on it.

It's yet another striking Queenstown day—this could get boring—and as I run along the shoreline my mind inevitably turns back to Logan. The look on his face haunts me and I know what we feel for one another is more than lust.

I don't know whether I'm thankful Jocelyn interrupted us or not. Her arrival in the room meant I didn't act on my instinct to go to him, to comfort him. To give myself to him.

It also gave us the opportunity to keep things on a professional level, to ignore any inappropriate, messy feelings we may have for one another, and focus instead on brokering our deal.

I can almost feel the angel sitting on my right shoulder dancing with glee at Jocelyn's timely arrival, almost as though she had willed her into the room herself. The devil on my left? Well, I think she's a bit miffed - she had other things in mind, things I force myself to push from my head as I quicken my pace, trying to outrun my feelings.

Back in my room I shower and dress, and style my hair to within an inch of its life. Checking my image in the mirror prior to leaving the room, I notice how tired I look: not my usual energetic self.

That's what men do to you.

It's best to not get involved with one. Life is so much easier without them.

I dab some concealer under my eyes in an attempt to disguise last night's lack of sleep.

After a quick debrief with Michael and a few moments to ensure the conference and breakout rooms are readied, I walk with a sense of trepidation to the staff suite, the scene of the almost-crime last night.

My body is shaking so much I feel as though I'm strapped to one of those old fashioned machines people thought would wobble your fat off——if only—as I place my key card into the slot to open the door.

The room is deserted. I heave a sigh of relief.

Moments later I settle into a sofa, hot coffee steaming in my mug on the table, and check my phone for messages. I realise I've had my phone on silent since my presentation last night, and notice there are three missed calls from Grace but no message. Puzzled, I begin to type out a text to her, and fail to notice Logan sit down in the chair opposite me.

"Morning, Brooke" he says breezily. "How are you today?"

My heart begins to hammer in my chest as I peer into his smiling, handsome face, looking as though he doesn't have a care in the world.

He smells freshly showered, a hint of aftershave hanging in the air around him. An image of a wet, naked, soapy Logan flashes into my mind and I dig my nails into one of my hands. No, I don't want to think about him in the shower right now.

How can he look so calm, so happy, so *normal* after what happened last night, while I'm stuck sweating it out as I wrestle with my feelings for him?

Perhaps I read it all wrong?

"Hi Logan," I manage to utter. "Did you ah, s-sleep well?" I stutter.

Which, on reflection, is not the best question to ask the guy you're trying desperately hard not to think about: an image of him asleep, bare-chested, a sheet just covering his modesty, flashes into my mind. I'm forced to look down at my screen and re-read my text to Grace in order to steady it.

"Yes, thanks. Slept like a baby. You?"

"Oh, me too," I lie. I narrow my eyes at him. "You're very happy this morning."

He shrugs. "I made a decision. It made me happy," he replies mysteriously. "So, what are you up to today?"

"Me? Oh, I'm doing some work right now, catching up on a few things."

"You're not needed here for the seminar, are you?"

"Oh, umm, no. But I do like to be available, of course, just in case."

"I'm sure you do." He raises his eyebrows as his smile widens. "I was thinking of heading out, though, and wondered if you might be able to come with me?"

Memories of the last time we went out together blaze through my mind.

I shake my head. "No, I think I should stay here. But thanks. You go ahead. Queenstown's a beautiful place."

He nods, looking at me. I squirm under his gaze.

"It would help me if we could talk more about working together. I have a few questions."

I narrow my eyes at him. Questions? What is he up to? The contrast between the Logan from last night, all brooding and angry, and the man in front of me today is stark.

I wonder what his decision was? It sure does seem to have put him in a good mood.

Come on, Brooke. He probably does need to talk to you about the deal. In which case you'd be a fool the size of Africa not to take him up on his offer.

"Sure." I put my phone into my handbag. "I'm more than happy to discuss any aspect of our business with you. I can give you an hour?"

His lips curve into an easy smile. "Great. Grab your jacket, it's cool out there."

A few minutes later we walk through the lobby and out of the front door. I take a deep breath, enjoying the crisp, clear mountain air, hoping it will fortify me for whatever Logan has in mind for us today.

I can do this. Whatever it was that was going on with him last night seems to be completely gone today. I must have misread the situation. Logan wasn't wrestling with his feelings for me at all.

Perhaps he'd eaten a dodgy prawn?

I say a silent prayer for Jocelyn: if she hadn't walked in on us I would have totally embarrassed myself.

Logan pulls a key fob out of his pocket and I hear the 'bip bip' of a car as he unlocks it and opens a door, clearly meant for me.

I regard him quizzically. "You have a car?"

"Yeah. I hired it. For us."

I balk at his confidence—he knew I'd say yes to coming out with him today—but am also secretly flattered. "And you want me to drive?" I ask.

"No, why?" he replies, confused.

"Because you're holding the driver's door open. The driver's side is on the right here."

"Oh. Damn." He closes the driver's door, scoots around the car, and opens the passenger's door for me.

"Let me get this straight: you want me to get in the car so you can drive me to who-knows-where, and you're not even sure which side the steering wheel is on? You know we drive on the other side of the road too, right ?"

"Yes?" he replies, uncertainly, his lips quirking into a self-deprecating smile.

Despite the tension I've felt all morning, I laugh. "How about I drive and you just tell me where you want to go?"

"Sure!" he replies, holding the keys out to me.

I take the proffered keys, jump into the car, and buckle up. I smirk to myself as I realise quite how ambitious he had been in hiring this car: not only is it a right-hand drive, but it's a manual as well, or 'stick shift', as he might say.

Whatever you want to call it, for someone used to driving on the other side of the road, it's a double whammy.

"Where to?" I start the engine.

"Arrowton. I hear it's real pretty."

"It's Arrow*town*," I correct him. "And you're right, it is pretty, and it's also about a twenty-minute drive. We've only got an hour."

"I was kinda hoping that was open to negotiation."

I purse my lips. "Look, we'll go, have a look around, then come straight back. Deal?"

"Deal," he replies. "Now drive, woman."

I let out a laugh despite myself and pull out from the curb.

We drive through the magnificent mountain scenery, out onto the long stretch of road next to the mirror-like Lake Hayes, and finally into the small township of Arrowtown, an enchanting village of charming old buildings, set on the River Arrow, nestled into the hills.

To keep conversation light during the trip, I've been telling Logan about places we've passed along the way, acting as his personal tour guide.

I park the car by the river. Once out, I turn to go up the small hill onto the main street, but Logan has other ideas.

"Let's check the river out first. It's so pretty here."

The trees are in blossom, rendering the town with an otherworldly, fairy tale quality anyone may be tempted to regard as irresistibly romantic.

Thank goodness I've been listening to my shoulder angel.

"This place started out as a mining town?" he asks as we wander up the riverbank.

"A gold rush town. Prospectors came here in the Eighteen-Sixties, found gold, and the place took off."

We walk through the Chinese Settlement, laughing as we crouch down to get in and out of the small buildings. I'm about average height for a woman, but Logan's pretty tall, so he clunks his head more than once.

"Oh, you poor thing." On instinct, I reach up and rub his forehead where he had clocked it on the doorjamb.

"I'll survive," he replies, looking deeply into my eyes, a half smile dancing on his face. "But you rubbing me sure does help."

At the hint of what could be in his words, my Girly Bits remind me with a pulsating clasp they want Logan and me to be more than work colleagues.

It takes a moment for me to snap myself out of it, and I pull my hand away from his forehead, clearing my throat as I do.

"I know Arrowtown quite well," I say in a brisk tone, trying desperately to ignore the buzz building low in my belly. "My family came here to ski every year. Two weeks in the winter school holidays, without fail."

I turn to walk down the hill towards the township. Logan walks beside me.

"Really?" He turns to look at me. "What an incredible place to have on your doorstep. I bet you're a great skier."

I shrug modestly. "I'm okay."

"I never learned to ski myself. My family was more into summer vacations. It's weird as I grew up in San Diego, which is like being on a permanent beach vacation."

"Oh, that must have been so hard for you," I tease. "All that warm sun, the beaches? Sheer torture."

"I know, I know. But I wanted to have what my cousins in Colorado had: seasons. I wanted to make snowmen in winter, to play in the leaves in fall."

"Seasons are not all they're cracked up to be." I think of the crazy winds Wellington gets in spring, the freezing southerly storms that chill you to the bone in winter.

I smile to myself, thinking how easy conversation flows with him—and how nice and safe talking about the weather is. Much better than all that eye gazing malarkey that could get me into serious trouble.

"Well," he begins as he stops walking and turns to me. "I guess you want what you don't have. Or at least, *I* want what I don't have."

There goes the weather talk safety net. My senses go on alert. I'm aware of our proximity, how his eyes shine at me, how the butterflies in my stomach have decided to have a disco.

I swallow hard and turn away, doing my best to break the spell. "Let's head to the main street," I suggest, walking away from him, back down the rise.

"Sure," he replies, trailing behind me.

It's crazy, I know, but quickening my pace is like I'm out-walking my desire for him. Although to do that, I imagine I'd have to run a couple of marathons in record-breaking speed.

We reach the crowds on the main street and I heave a sigh of relief: there's *got* to be safety in numbers here. Right?

We wander through the shops, looking at locally-produced woollen and possum fur clothing, tourist shops, wine shops, and finally into the most amazing old fashioned sweet shop—or 'candy store', as Logan puts it—I've been into.

We marvel at the array of glass jars full of any type of sweet you can imagine. Logan grabs a bag, piling in about ten different types. I abstain, confident in my commitment to my diet. I work hard at being fit and healthy, and know very well just one sweet can become a slippery slope.

People are impressed with my dedication, but for me it's just part and parcel of the way I live my life: I do everything one hundred per cent. Go big or go home, that's always been my philosophy. What's the point in doing something half-assed?

"So you're telling me you never eat candy?"

"No, I don't. Well, very occasionally."

"You don't like it?" he asks in disbelief.

"Of course I *like* it. Who doesn't? It's just all that sugar is bad for you."

He pushes his open paper bag towards me. "Come on. Have one. Make this one of those occasions."

I look from his face to the bag, trying to decide whether I should stick to my guns or take one out of politeness towards the man who holds my future in his hands.

"You have to try one of these ones in the green wrapper. They're delicious." His mouth is full of sweets.

Politeness—and perhaps something else—wins over, and I take a sweet from his bag. It's a sticky toffee, and tastes wonderful. I smile at him as I chew, a little rebellious as I break my diet.

"Good, huh?" He takes another. We've wandered further down the street, finding ourselves in a more residential area.

I glance at my watch. "We should probably get back to Queenstown."

"How about we agree if you check your phone and you don't have any work-related messages, we'll stay for lunch, and then head back."

Expecting to have at least a handful of messages I happily agree. "All right, then."

I pull my phone out. Angel Brooke is hoping for several messages requiring my immediate attention. Devil Brooke is jumping about on my shoulder, yelling at me to forget about work and instead throw myself at Logan. The things she wants me to do with him right now are making me blush. I'm blocking her out as best I can.

As it turns out, the decision is made for me because, to my surprise, I have no messages.

Logan glances at my phone. "Excellent. Brooke gets the morning off. Are you hungry? I sure am. How about we go to that little place we just passed back there? It looks nice."

"Sure," I reply in resignation, part of me thrilled our fun morning is being extended. "But please, can we talk about the contract over lunch?"

"Of course."

After a short stroll we arrive at the quaint Postmasters Restaurant. It's a sweet former cottage, complete with white picket fence, and wisteria around the door. We take a table by the open fire, warming ourselves up after our walk in the cool air.

The atmosphere is warm, cosy, and oh-so-romantic. As I look around the room I take a deep sigh. Those matchmaking gods are pulling out all the stops today. Devil Brooke is delighted.

We order the sharing platter and Logan suggests a bottle of local pinot noir wine, the varietal this area is famous for. Concerned that alcohol will erode my defences, I suggest a sensible cup of coffee instead.

"How about just a glass, then? I mean, it's not every day you get to dine in Arrowtown with a handsome American." A smile teases at the edges of his mouth. "Or, at least, I hope it's not."

"Sure, why not." I laugh as Devil Brooke does star jumps in the air.

Our wine and food delivered, I realise with a start we've spent hours together already and, other than checking for messages, not once have I thought about work.

"So, you said you had some questions for me, Logan. To do with *Live It*?"

Hi grins. "Actually, I don't. I just said that to get you to come out with me. My bad."

My mouth forms an 'O' shape as I gape at him in disbelief. "You sneak! So you don't want to talk about work things at all?"

"Well, do you?" he asks, looking around the restaurant.

I glance around the room. Why does this place have to be so romantic?

A waiter arrives with a bottle of wine and pours out a couple of glasses for us.

"I will say something, however," he continues. "We like what we've seen, Brooke. *Live It* and *You: Now* are a great fit. I see no reason why we can't table a contract to form a partnership with you."

A slow grin spreads across his face as I light up with excitement. "Really? Oh, that's fantastic news. Thank you," I say with gusto, my heart racing a mile a minute.

My head begins to spin. I can hardly believe it! Everything I've been working towards for the past year is about to come to fruition. We've wanted to grow the business by expanding into Australia and beyond for so long, and now, with the help of Logan's company, we're going to be able to do it. I'm so happy, I could burst.

"I thought you might be pleased." He sits back in his leather chair, watching me. He raises his glass. "Here's to our partnership."

We clink glasses. I take a deep sip, barely believing the news.

"Our lawyers have drawn up a partnership agreement already, which I'll get to you later today, if that suits?"

"If that suits?" As if it didn't!

He laughs. "I guess it does, then."

"Thank you, Logan." I look into his eyes. "I'm so excited about this. I think it's going to be amazing."

"I do too. You have what it takes, Brooke. You run a tight ship, you've developed a strong brand, and with your drive I know you'll go far."

I flush with pride. "With your company's help, we'll go far," I correct him.

Glowing with happiness, we eat our meal and drink our wine in front of the roaring fire, discussing the details of the agreement. It seems *You: Now* had made up their minds about us before Logan and Brad even set foot in the country, and their presence here merely served to confirm their decision to work with us.

We wander back to the car after Logan has purchased some possum wool gloves for his niece and nephew in Colorado at one of the shops on the main street.

"How old are your sister's kids?" I ask as I drive us with more than a tinge of regret out of Arrowtown and back towards Queenstown.

"They're three and five respectively, although you'd think Sammy, my five-year-old niece, was fifteen." He rolls his eyes.

"Growing up too fast?" I ask, chuckling.

"Yes. She's just like her mother: bossy."

"She must be your *older* sister, right?"

He nods. "You have experience with older, bossy siblings?"

"Oh, yes. My brother, Jeremy, is two years old than me, but you'd think he was my dad with the way he tells me how to live my life."

He chuckles. "That sounds familiar. Any other brothers or sisters?"

"I have a younger step-sister, Grace, and half-brother, Dylan."

"Ah, a complicated family structure, by the sounds of it."

I shrug. "Yeah, I guess. But it works."

"So is it your mom or your dad who remarried, or both?"

I'm not in the habit of telling people I've just met my mother is gone, but I'm so at ease with Logan—like we've been close for years, rather than just the few days I've actually known him—I tell him about my mother's cancer, how my dad remarried soon after she died, the whole sorry tale.

It feels so natural, and by the time I park the car back at the hotel, we've shared our full family histories: the good, the bad, and the somewhere in between.

"I've had an amazing day, Brooke. Thank you," Logan says as we stand next to each other in the lift, heading to our respective floors.

"Me too." I know how very much I have.

Even if my life depended on it, I couldn't stop myself from smiling. Not only have I learned all my hopes for my company are set to come true, I've had an amazing time with Logan.

And, what's more, I've proved to myself I can be around him without acting on my feelings.

"Oops, Logan, we went past my floor." I look at the panel of numbers as we stop at the one above. I lean in to press my number.

"Ah, I thought you might like to come with me, Brooke. I can show you the draft contract," Logan says as he walks out of the lift and turns to face me, holding the door open with his arm.

My breath catches in my throat. It will be just the two of us, alone in his bedroom. *So* not a good idea.

Despite how easy and natural today has been with him, my need for self-protection is screaming in my ear.

Until yesterday, I hadn't even kissed a man in the longest time, let alone become emotionally entangled with one, the way I'm beginning to become with Logan.

Sure, I may had an amazing day with him today, and I know those dissatisfied Girly Bits of mine would love nothing more than to climb into bed with him right now. On the other hand, my brain is screaming for me to protect myself.

And really, what could this be with Logan other than a short fling?

Almost a one-night-stand. He's only in the country for a matter of days. It can't *go* anywhere. He'll fly out, back to his exciting life in sophisticated San Francisco, and I'll be left, regretting what could have been, nursing my bruised and battered heart.

And that's before I even consider what it could do to our business deal.

No, it's dangerous territory.

"I, err, I should go," I stutter, torn between wanting him and knowing going with him to his room right now is possibly the dumbest thing I could ever do.

The lift lets out a loud beep, causing us both to jump. Logan offers me his hand, and without thinking, I take it in mine, as he leads me out of the lift, the doors closing behind me.

I turn and look at them, hearing the lift whizz away to the next floor. Well, I suppose the decision's been made, then. And anyway, we're just going to look at a boring old contract. There's nothing sexy—or risky—about that. Is there?

"All right. It would be great to see the contract. I'm really excited about you." *Eeek!* "Err, it. I'm excited about *it*. The contract, I mean. I'm excited about the contract."

"Me too," he replies with a smile. It's unclear whether he's referring to the contract or to me.

He pulls his key card out and slots it in the door to his room.

We're here already?

Once inside, the door closed behind us, Logan turns to face me, his eyes smouldering. My mouth dries and I swallow hard.

"Can I take your jacket?" He doesn't take his eyes from mine.

"Sure." I slip it off and hand it to him with trembling hands. His fingers brush against mine as he takes it from me, sending a jolt though my body.

I watch him as he puts both our coats over a chair, then walks back until he's standing so close to me we're almost touching. I breathe in his scent, a mixture of his cologne and the fresh, alpine air.

"Brooke," he says breathlessly, looking once again into my eyes.

He runs his hand from my shoulder down my arm. My heart is smacking hard inside my chest, like a couple of World Wrestling Federation fighters in the ring.

"It's not every day I meet a woman like you. Hell, I don't think I've *ever* met a woman like you."

Weren't we meant to be looking at a dry, boring partnership agreement about now? A nice, safe contract to dull these electric feelings we seem to share?

"The contract?" I almost whisper in a last-ditch attempt to resist him.

He smiles at me. "Sure, I'll get the contract. But first, can I tell you how I feel?"

I nod, unable to speak as the WWF fighters continue to duke it out in my chest.

Oh, god. Here it comes. And I just know I won't be able to resist him.

"I respect what you said about wanting to keep our relationship purely professional."

Yes, this is good.

"I've tried to do what you want, Brooke. God knows I've tried." He slides his hand up to my shoulder again, making my skin tingle.

Uh-oh.

"Until last night I knew I was attracted to you, wanted you. But seeing you speak at the seminar, to watch how you captured the audience, to see your passion, your knowledge?" He lets out a heavy breath. "Brooke, you were spectacular." He shakes his head. "I can't fight it. I want you so bad. You have to know that. And I think you want me. Am I right?" The hope in his eyes almost brings me to tears.

Umm, *yes*! Is the Pope Catholic?

He reaches up and runs his fingers gently down the side of my face, sending a shiver of desire through me.

I will myself to shake my head, to deny the strength of the feelings I have for him, but instead find myself nodding in assent, my belly tightening with longing for him.

I think I must lick my lips as his eyes dart to my mouth, a sexy smile twitching at the corners of his own. "Sure, us working together complicates this. But that's all it is. A complication."

I nod again. My mouth is like a ball of cotton wool, the power of speech deserting me once again.

"Love isn't logical, Brooke."

Love? I swallow hard.

"And anyway, once we've signed the agreement, I won't be working with you any longer."

He's got this all figured out.

"But—" I take a deep, steadying breath, ignoring the way my body is humming. I call on what can only be my superhuman strength to break his oh-so-pleasurable hold on me.

I know I could fall for this man—hell, I'm already a little bit in love with him—and I'm scared out of my wits.

"You have to know I want you," I begin and his smile broadens in response. "But I swore off men over a year ago when my heart was broken."

He nods, concern etched on his face.

"I know we can't make one another any promises or anything—" I trail off as I his arms encircling my waist, gently pulling me into him. Concentrating on talking is a step too far for me as his body presses lightly against mine.

"Yes, we've only known one another for a short time, but I think I'm falling for you, Brooke," he mutters into my hair, his voice low and husky, warming my neck with his breath.

He trails gentle kisses up my neck, sending tingles through my body. "Are there any more 'buts'?"

I melt into his arms, my body screaming at me to give in to him. My will to fight my intense attraction for him slips away. I want this man with every cell in my body.

Resistance is futile. Devil Brooke is ecstatic.

He scatters slow, gentle kisses on my neck. His mouth is hot, tender, sending electric shocks through me wherever it touches.

Don't stop, don't stop.

"We can take this as fast or as slow as you want." He stops the neck kissing that's driving me almost insane. "It's up to you, Brooke. You need to know, I want you any way I can have you."

His eyes dilate as he gazes at me, and the intensity of my need for him becomes almost unbearable.

He pulls me in closer, and my body throbs in response. Every part of me wants me to kiss him, to taste him. And then he's touching me, caressing me, and I tighten with sweet, sweet expectation.

I reach up and run my fingers though his hair, pushing my body closer into him as he lets out a moan of pleasure in anticipation. I breathe in his intoxicating scent.

Finally, our lips meet in a soft, gentle kiss, tingling as we touch. It's so light and tender, sending a fresh thrum of desire through me, bringing my nerve endings to attention.

Our kiss becomes intense, passionate, we can't get enough of each other, as our mouths open and our tongues find one another.

Panting, we pull apart for what might have been a few seconds, or perhaps longer: I couldn't have told you had my life depended on it.

"God, Brooke," he utters, breathing hard. I notice his excitement is barely contained in his straining jeans. "You are so, so sexy."

Mercifully, his lips find mine again, and as his hands slide up and down my body, I let out a gasp. The throbbing in my Girly Bits intensifies into an exquisite, demanding need for him.

I take a step back, pulling my merino top off and dropping it on the floor. I undo the buttons of my shirt as I hold his gaze, exposing my lacy bra.

He lets out a breath heavy with desire as he watches my every move.

After a moment, he takes my cue, pulling his sweater over his head, exposing the broad shoulders and muscular chest I caught a glimpse of yesterday at the pool. On instinct I reach over and lightly trace the contours of his muscles with my fingers as I kiss his chest, causing his breath to catch in his throat.

As I lower my hand down his taut belly I reach the tantalizing line of hair leading down into his jeans.

The anticipation of his skin against mine has become the most exquisite torture. I can barely wait to touch it, to feel him deep inside me.

My shirt on the ground, he grabs me and unhooks my bra, his thumb brushing my nipple as I let out a moan. My back arches in response as he caresses my breasts with his hot mouth and slips his hands down my body, reaching inside my panties, sending a sharp wave of desire through my body.

"Oh, god, Brooke." His voice is husky.

He pulls my jeans down and takes one of my erect nipples in his mouth, teasing it with his tongue.

I groan in pleasure as I unbutton his jeans and slip them down his thighs to see just how much he wants me.

We continue to kiss, exploring one another's bodies with our hands and mouths as we tug off our final pieces of clothing. We're finally skin-on-skin, deliciously entwined.

"I want you so much," he says hoarsely between deep kisses, his hands sliding over my body.

"I want you too." I'm unable to contain myself a moment longer. "Now."

He sits down on the edge of his bed, pulling me with him, not taking his eyes from mine. I straddle him while we kiss again, his hand sliding down my belly, playing with me, stroking me, bringing me to breaking point.

I lower myself onto him, slipping him inside me. I gasp in pleasure as he fills me completely up. We move in an exquisite rhythmic motion together. It's deliciously slow at first, increasing in intensity as our bodies respond to one another, the rocking motion bringing us both to the crescendo of our desire.

We stay locked in our embrace, our bodies hot, slick with sweat, both breathing hard as we regain our equilibrium.

He kisses me gently. "Brooke," he says simply.

We make love numerous times that afternoon and into the night, sating our need for one another over again.

Being with him is everything I had hoped it would be and so, so much more.

We come up for air just long enough for Logan to buy more condoms at the pharmacy down the road from the hotel. With his ruffled hair and crumpled clothes, he looks just like he's in the midst of a marathon sex session.

Which, of course, he is.

As I lie in bed—*Logan's* bed—waiting for him to return, I'm shaky but blissful. I think about our day together in Arrowtown, about how he'd got me to eat sweets for the first time in years, and of how his body feels next to mine, in mine. I let out a contented sigh, smiling to myself as that Marcy Playground song, 'Sex and Candy', jumps into my head.

I could stay here for the rest of the weekend, and beyond, happy in my little sex and candy cocoon with Logan.

CHAPTER 10

THE SUN IS DOING its best to creep around the edges of the curtains as I wake up the following morning. I'm momentarily disoriented, blinking as I peer around the room, until memories of the previous night come crashing into my brain.

Oh. My. God. I had sex! With *Logan*.

And it was amazing, even better than I had imagined: and I had imagined it would be pretty darn incredible.

I flush as my body remembers how he felt against me, in me, his hands, his mouth, all over my body, bringing me to the point of ecstasy.

I steal a look at him lying beside me, asleep, naked beneath the sheets. He's on his back, his broad, muscular chest exposed. I watch his slow, rhythmic breathing, not daring to move an inch, lest I wake him from his slumber.

Eventually, I pull the sheets off, climb gingerly out of bed, and tip toe to the bathroom, closing the door behind me.

I heave a sigh of relief. Commando Brooke.

I catch my reflection in the mirror above the sink and am faced with my worst fears: what mascara I once had on my lashes is now lodged below my eyes, reminiscent of an American football player's.

And my hair? Let's just say it's not exactly at its stylish best. My natural curl has forced its way out around the edges of my face where I'd worked up a sweat during last night's, umm, activities, making me look like I'm in a Jane Austen novel. And the rest of it better resembles a pile of discarded straw than a human head of hair.

Not having any of my own toiletries with me, I grab Logan's comb from the bench and smooth it out as best I can, then swipe the smudged mascara from beneath my eyes with one of the hotel's facecloths.

Not quite a beauty queen, but a million times better than a few moments ago.

I spy Logan's toothbrush and pause before squirting some toothpaste onto its bristles. Why using his toothbrush seems more intimate to me than the things we did with one another last night will have to remain one of life's mysteries.

As satisfied as I can be with my appearance, I gaze at myself in the mirror once more. With nothing else to do, a cacophony of thoughts swim around my mind like a group of over-excited kids at a pool party.

What have I *done*?

I slept with a man. And not with just any guy: with *Logan*. With the man who holds my future in his hands.

A wave of ice-cold panic threatens to engulf me.

You're an idiot, Brooke Mortimer, a prize-winning, top of the class, *epic* idiot.

My heart races when an image of him looking at me with so much emotion, so much honesty in his eyes, flashes into my head. He said he was falling for me. He said he's never met a woman like me.

He said a lot of things.

It's just like one of my rom coms. And just like in a rom com, I've fallen for a guy I've known for, what? Three minutes? It can't be. It *has* to be just lust.

Either that or the momentary insanity brought on by Mexican food and successful business deals.

I take a deep breath and raise my chin.

Last night I believed every word he said. I believed him when he said he has developed strong feelings for me, that I'm all he can think about. Because I *wanted* to believe him. Because I feel that way about him.

Now, regarding my reflection in the cold light of day, I question his motives. There are so many reasons why he wouldn't want to start up anything serious with me.

To begin with, he lives in another country—another *hemisphere*, for goodness sake—and we all know long distance relationships don't work.

Then there's the fact he's hot hot hot. He could have any woman he wants. Why choose me? I don't mean to be too self-deprecating or anything, really I don't: I know I'm no supermodel.

It's not logical to me.

I let out a long breath, even though I had no idea I had been holding it.

Did he mean those things? Or were they just the way he felt there and then, in the heat of the moment?

And what does this mean for our business deal? He said his company wanted to sign the agreement with me, go ahead with the partnership. Will he have changed his mind now that he's had me? Will the allure of my company have diminished this morning, now his desires have been sated?

Arrrgh! I want to screech, but I daren't for fear of waking him.

I take a few deep breaths, forcing myself to calm down.

I might be making a mountain out of a molehill. Maybe things will go back to normal today, like we didn't do what we did with one another last night, say the things we said. Like it's just an everyday thing to be told how much an amazing guy wants me. And have the most incredible sex of my life.

It's almost like I'm a virgin, sampling the delights of sex for the very first time, opening a new and amazing world for me.

I shake my head. Hell, it's not like I haven't had sex before. It doesn't have to *mean* anything, Brooke. Plenty of people have sex without feelings complicating things.

Feelings like love.

I swallow, attempting to push down the lump forming in my throat. I know I'm not what you would call a 'one-night-stand-kind-of-girl'—hardly a 'love-'em-and-leave-'em-wanting-more' type—but I can try my best to do this. I'm a woman of the world, after all, a big girl.

Sex is just sex. Right?

Hmm, let's see. I scan my brain. What would Lucinda do? She would be happy she had bedded such a hot guy and simply move on to the next conquest. Another notch in the bedpost.

I groan as I put my head in my hands. I'm using Lucinda Hargreaves as my role model here? I've plunged to a new, horrendous low.

Eventually I decide the best thing—the only thing—for me to do is to collect my clothes, sneak back to my own room, and try not to let last night cloud my judgement about work, *and* about Logan.

I wrap myself in a towel and open the bathroom door. Thankfully, Logan is still asleep. I take slow, measured steps around the room, collecting my scattered clothing as I go.

"Good morning, beautiful," he says sleepily. "Going somewhere?"

Busted.

I straighten up from picking my bra off the floor near the end of the bed and my breath catches as I take him in. He's propped himself up on his elbows, the sheets just covering his taut, tanned belly. He smiles lazily at me, his hair ruffled adorably, looking sexier than I think I've ever seen him.

Why does he have to look so good? *All* the freaking time? It's hardly fair.

I choose to ignore his question. "Sorry. Did I wake you?"

"No, I'm a morning person. I wake up early no matter how late I go to bed. I heard you get up."

A morning person? He's even more perfect than I had thought.

"You didn't answer my question." He eyes my ball of clothes. "Are you leaving?"

"I, err—" I begin, looking down at my clothes, which are suddenly as heavy as a pile of stones in my hands. "I thought it might be for the best?"

I hadn't intended for it to come out as a question. Looking at Logan lying in the bed we shared last night, I'm not so sure I can channel Lucinda.

He regards me quizzically, sitting himself up fully. "Why? What do you mean 'for the best'?" he asks.

I hug my clothes into my chest as I look around the room, working out how best to answer him, as I bite my bottom lip.

"I thought maybe last night was, you know, just some fun. I thought, you know, I should, umm, go."

Smooth, Brooke.

"Fun? Yeah, I think you're right. It sure was fun." He shoots me a cheeky grin. He pats the bed next to him. "Come, sit."

I comply, putting my crumpled clothes down at the end of the bed.

"Are you okay?" He frowns and I have to resist the urge to reach up and smooth the lines away.

"I don't know." Inexplicably, I might cry.

"Brooke." He takes a deep breath. "If you want to go, I won't stand in your way."

I nod. He looks at me with such sincerity I'm ashamed of the fact I tried to run out on him while he was still asleep.

He reaches over and touches my hand. "I don't want you to leave."

I look up into his eyes as my stomach does a flip. "You don't?"

He shakes his head. "Not in the slightest. Last night was—" he begins as a fresh smile spreads across his face. "Brooke, you're an incredible woman. I thought I'd made my feelings for you clear last night: I'm falling for you. I think we have the beginnings of something special here. Don't you? The last thing I want to happen right now is for you to leave. Believe me."

Relief floods through me. I smile sheepishly at him. "Me too," I admit. "About falling for you. And leaving."

I knew I wasn't the one-night-stand type.

"Well, then," he says, a glint in his eye. "You had better loosen that towel off and get your hot ass back into bed with me right now before I rip it off myself."

A jolt of electricity courses through me as my grin spreads from ear to ear. "Be my guest."

He moans as he pulls the covers back, revealing just how much he wants me in bed with him.

My Girly Bits wake up as he tugs my towel off me, allowing it to drop to the bed.

"Get in here." His voice is low and thick with lust.

I slip into bed with him, feeling the exquisite warmth of his body against mine once more. I kiss him, tenderly at first, until our tongues find one another, my body demanding so much more.

"Mm, minty fresh," he murmurs between kisses, running his hands over my body.

He rolls me on top of him, pushing my legs open with his knee as he kisses me again.

I wonder why I thought leaving this delectable man would ever be the right thing to do.

* * *

"Want some breakfast? I don't know about you, but I'm famished."

"Oh, yes please." I realise just how hungry I am, my stomach rumbling in response.

With breakfast on its way and Logan in the shower, I sit in bed. It's like I'm in some kind of alternate reality. Until yesterday, I'd spent every waking hour since he walked into my life forcing any thoughts about him—other than purely professional ones, of course—out of my mind.

Now, my brain is filled to the brim with him—of *us*—and it makes me so contented, so calm, so happy. It's like we fit, like this was meant to be. I simply can't stop myself from smiling.

Not only that—as if there needed to be more—we're about to sign the partnership agreement I've been working towards for so long, helping me to realise my dreams.

It's like one big, exciting, crazy—and rather raunchy—dream.

Logan has left the draft partnership agreement on the table, so I pick it up and have a leaf through. It all seems very standard to me, and reflects what we had discussed: I sell *You: Now* half of my company in return for their financial and logistical support in tackling the Australian markets first, then moving further afield in the longer term. In effect it positions *Live It* as the Australian face of their company: exactly what I wanted.

As I begin to go cross-eyed from all the legal jargon, I reach for my phone and notice I've missed calls from Stefan, Alexis, and Grace. I check my messages and listen while Stefan asks where I am; Alexis tells me she has some exciting news and asks me if I've managed to keep my hands off Mr American Love God (if she only knew the half of it); and Grace asks me to give her a call.

I write a quick text to Stefan, telling him I'll see him at the venue soon, then slip down the bed, under the covers. The rest of the world can wait while I luxuriate in Logan's and my wonderful, new world.

Logan pokes his head around the bathroom door as steam puffs out into the room. "I've got to go meet Brad in a few minutes. Will her Highness be arising any time soon?"

A smile spreads across my face. "Her Highness wishes to bask in the memories of last night, thank you very much."

He approaches the bed, leans down and kisses me sweetly on the lips. "Well, they don't just have to be memories. I'm at her Majesty's service at, say, three o'clock?"

"It's a date."

* * *

Floating along inside a gorgeous bubble of joy, I'm showered, dressed, hair tamed, and heading to the *Live It* suite when I notice Stefan approaching me.

"Brooke. I need to talk to you," he stage whispers out of the corner of his mouth.

"Sure. What about?" I ask, smiling contentedly. Nothing can bother me today.

He pulls me towards the lobby. "Let's go for a walk. Outside."

He looks so serious I could giggle. "Sure." I smile at him, not moving.

"Can we just go?" he asks in agitation.

"All right. Keep your hair on." I prod him in the belly.

"What's got into you today?" he asks in alarm.

"Nothing." I do my best to suppress the giggle threatening to erupt.

He shoots me a quizzical look before turning on his heel and stomping towards the lobby.

Once outside, he looks around us to check no one is within earshot as we slow our pace a full block from the hotel.

"Stefan, what is it?" He's acting like some kind of spy in an action movie.

"Okay. We can talk now. It began with a conversation I had with Brad this morning over breakfast," he begins, speaking quietly. "He started out asking me about our attendance numbers and what our attrition rates were, as I'd expect him to. So far so normal. Then when I moved on to talking about our short-term plans, he kept circling back to our numbers."

"So? Our dropout rates are phenomenally good. You know that. He must simply want to understand the numbers more clearly. It's not surprising, Stefan. We *are* negotiating a partnership contract with them. Relax."

We're very proud of our attrition rates at *Live It*. Any course will have attendees drop out within the first day or so, but we lose only a small fraction of ours over a seminar. From what I know, that's not something *You: Now* can boast.

"But he kept persisting with it, Brooke. He wanted documentation on it, and then went on to ask in detail how we attract the amount of business we get."

"It all seems perfectly normal to—"

Stefan cuts me off. "Just let me finish. Please. There's more. The next thing, I'm leaving the Men's by the conference room, and I spot Brad and Logan talking in one of the alcoves. Brad seems fired up, and Logan looks so angry."

I raise my eyebrows at him. Okay, Stefan, now you have my attention.

"They haven't seen me. I move a little closer to them so I can hear what they're talking about."

"You *spied* on them?" I ask disbelievingly. And a little impressed.

"Wait until I tell you what I heard and I think you'll agree it was well worth it."

"Go on."

"I missed exactly what Brad said, but I can tell you Logan wasn't happy with him. I heard him say they need to 'reassess the situation'. Brad seemed pretty pissed off with him and said he was going to call Geoff."

"Geoff?" I ask in surprise. "Geoff Friedlander?"

Stefan nods, looking grim. He crosses his arms.

Geoff Friedlander is the founder and CEO of *You: Now*. Logan and Brad might be the guys on the ground here with us, but Geoff Friedlander is nothing short of *Live It*'s god: what he says, goes.

Brad threatening to call Geoff suggests someone—either him or Logan—wants to make a big change.

"Did you hear anything else?" Anxiety begins to tighten across my chest.

"No. But I got the distinct impression Logan wants to do something dodgy, and Brad was trying to pull him back into line."

I'm stunned into silence, my mind racing like a Formula One car around the track. Could Logan do that? Could he spend that incredible night with me, say all those amazing things, then get up in the morning and renege on our deal?

No, of course he couldn't.

"Stefan, I wasn't going to say anything yet, but Logan has given me the partnership contract to review. He assured me they have every intention of signing it with us."

"He has?" Stefan asks in surprise.

"Yes. Why would he do that if he didn't mean to agree it?" It's basic logic.

He shrugs. "I don't know. He's a slippery bastard, that one, and I for one don't trust him. Haven't since I laid eyes on him. You shouldn't trust him either. He could have any number of reasons to do it."

I leap to Logan's defence. "He's not a slippery bastard. He's a decent guy. You've taken some weird dislike to him and always think the worst of him."

He taps his foot. "Is it signed?" he asks, ignoring my accusation.

"The contract? Ah, no. It's a draft contract, you dingbat. We have to negotiate it with them before anyone will sign it."

He raises his eyebrows and shoots me a look suggesting he thinks I came down in the last rain shower. "When did he give it to you?"

I clear my throat, remembering how I'd read through it, naked, while lying in my post-coital haze in Logan's bed. "Err, earlier today."

I shift my weight from foot to foot, hoping Stefan doesn't sense my mounting discomfort.

"What time?"

"A couple of hours ago, I think." Jeez Louise. He sure is persistent today.

"Huh!" Stefan replies, making me jump. He begins to pace.

He's certainly taking this whole spy thing pretty seriously.

"I overheard Brad and Logan arguing thirty minutes ago. Logan might have intended to enter a partnership with us when he gave you the contract, but after talking with Brad about our numbers, he clearly changed his mind. That's why he said he has to 'reassess the situation'. Brooke, don't you see? I think he wants to steal our company."

I laugh out loud. "That's preposterous."

"Is it, Brooke. *Is it?*" He narrows his eyes at me. "You only think your precious Logan McManus wouldn't do anything to harm your company because you've got the hots for him."

I open my mouth to protest, but no words come out.

"Open your eyes, Brooke. He's up to no good."

"Okay. Let's say for argument's sake Logan was doing something he shouldn't. Why don't you tell me exactly what you heard Brad say."

"Brad said he didn't like what Logan was planning to do and he was leaving to call Geoff about it. Brooke, he was so angry."

He didn't like what Logan was planning to do?

"Brooke, I heard Brad tell Logan he would lose management backing if he went ahead with it."

Lose management backing? For what? My head begins to spin.

"I trust Brad—I definitely *don't* trust Logan."

I drum my fingers against my chin as I attempt to create a picture of what's going on.

"Let me get this straight. You're saying Logan gave me the partnership contract, probably to distract me and make me think we were on track, even though he never had any intention of signing it with me. Meanwhile he's plotting and planning something else, which could very well be something to hurt our company in some way. When Brad gets wind of this he confronts him about it, they end up having an argument, after which Brad leaves to call the big boss."

"Yes, that's *exactly* what I think happened," Stefan replies with venom.

"Do you think Logan has the green light from Geoff Friedlander?"

"I don't know, but I hope to hell he doesn't."

I search my mind for evidence of Logan's duplicity and come up short. After last night and all the things we said? I can't believe he would do something like this: not to me or to my company.

But it *is* possible. I know it is.

And there's no smoke without fire, right?

Cold, sickening dread slithers down my spine. Could Logan have done this to me? Could he have said all those things to get me into bed and meant none of it? Not a word?

I wrap my arms around my body, my heart racing as a tight knot grows in my belly.

Yes. He could.

I swallow hard as my bubble of joy is well and truly popped. I'm exposed, used, mortified. I allowed myself to trust him, to open my heart to him.

I'm a fool.

"Brooke? What are we going to do?" Stefan asks, watching me

closely.

Do? Curl up into a ball and hide away from the world? Never let another man within ten feet again? Oh yes, I've learnt my lesson this time. No. More. Men.

Gradually my confusion and hurt is replaced with anger. A fiery, explosive anger I can barely contain.

I turn to Stefan. "You want to know what we're going to do? I assure you, I know *exactly* what we're going to do."

I storm off back down the street and into the hotel. I'm on a mission. I'm going to find Mr Double-Crossing American right now and find out what the hell he's playing at.

CHAPTER 11

I STORM INTO THE hotel, thoughts pinging around my head like a machine gun. I'm so angry I could pop. If this were a cartoon, I'd have a face like a tomato with steam blasting out of my ears—a thought that might amuse me, under entirely different circumstances.

I find Logan sitting on a sofa outside the conference room, working on his laptop.

"There you are." I force what I hope is a relaxed, nothing's-on-my-mind smile.

"Hey, Brooke." He looks up at me. His face changes as he regards me with alarm. He closes his laptop.

Doesn't want me to see what he's up to, huh?

"Are you feeling okay? You look a little, err, pink."

"Can we talk?" I ask in a higher-than-usual pitch.

"Sure. Take a seat." He smiles tentatively at me.

Scared I know what you're up to, is that it, Logan?

I glance around, noticing people coming and going from the conference room down the hall. "Not here. Let's go to my room."

He narrows his eyes at me. "What's going on?"

"Let's just go, okay?" I drop any pretence of being relaxed and carefree.

He puts his laptop into his bag, gathers up his things, and follows me to the lift. We stand in awkward silence for what feels like an hour as we wait for the 'ping' announcing its arrival.

We reach my room, and, once inside with the door shut behind us, I spit, "Are you going to back out of our deal?"

"What? Why?"

I can't contain my fury. "Just tell me straight, Logan. Are you backing out of the partnership?" I'm standing with my hands on my hips, glaring at him, hoping to scare him into telling me the truth.

He sighs. "How did you know?" he asks in a low voice.

I'm suddenly faint.

I manage to grab the arm of the chair closest to me and plonk down into it. The room swims around me, and I take deep, gulping breaths as I try to steady myself.

Logan is immediately at my side, giving me instructions. "Put your head between your knees. That's right. Now take deep breaths. It's okay, Brooke. This will pass." He's stroking my back.

I do as he says despite myself, and begin to regain my equanimity.

As I gain control of my faculties, I sit up and abruptly push his hand away. He has the audacity to look wounded.

"Did you tell me we were going to sign a partnership contract just to get me into the sack?" I ask through gritted teeth, wanting to know, but fearing his answer.

"What? Of course not. How can you even think that?" he replies with indignation.

"How can I think that? Let me tell you how." I begin to list them off on my fingers. "You take me out for a romantic meal; you tell me the partnership is going ahead, knowing that's what I want to hear; you bring me back to your room on the pretence of looking over the contract and seduce me; then, you meet Brad this morning to tell him you've had a change of heart now you've got what you wanted." I cross my arms. "That's how I can think that."

He raises his eyebrows. "Is that so?"

"Deny it if you dare," I challenge him.

He shakes his head, grabs my hands and pulls me up so we're standing facing one another. He smooths my blonde hair, cupping my face in his hand.

"Brooke, don't you know that I have your best interests at heart? That I would do anything for you?"

I squirm uncomfortably, denying the excitement my traitorous body feels at his touch.

"I 'got you in the sack', as you put it, because you've been all I can think about, day and night, since the moment I met you. I don't know whether this happens to you a lot, but for me to feel the way I do about you is extremely rare. In fact, I would have to say I've *never* felt this this before. Not even for my wife."

What the—? I balk at him. *Wife?*

He sees my expression and raises an eyebrow. "My *ex*-wife. We divorced a few years ago."

I'm having an internal struggle on a marathon scale. On the one hand I know I'm being cynical, assuming he's some cad who woos unsuspecting women into having sex with him under false pretences, but the evidence Stefan presented me certainly supports that.

I want desperately to believe him, but can't quite bring myself to do so.

A tear escapes and rolls down my cheek. Logan wipes it away with his finger, smiling down at me.

"Brooke, I want to be with you. Not just today, but always."

My breath catches in my throat and I swear my heart stops beating. Standing before me is this man, this handsome, sexy, wonderful man, and I want to believe him, with every fibre of my being.

He kisses me, tenderly. My tears flow as I kiss him back.

He passes me a box of tissues and I wipe my eyes and blow my nose. It sounds a little like a foghorn, making us both laugh, breaking the intense tension in the room.

"But what about your conversation with Brad?" I ask a few moments later as we sit together, holding hands on the sofa.

"How do you know about that?"

"It doesn't matter, does it?"

"I guess not." He takes a deep breath. "We were discussing the fact that I'd given you the contract today, and Brad suggested we take a… a different direction with you."

'A different direction?" I ask.

"Yeah. He thought we might want to establish a *You: Now* presence here in New Zealand, instead of entering a partnership with you."

"Are you kidding?" I'm shocked.

"Don't worry. It's not going to happen. Even if his dad *is* Geoff Friedlander."

Hold the phone.

"What? But his name is Brad Stephenson, not Brad Friedlander." My head spins.

"He took his mother's maiden name when he joined the company. He said he didn't want anyone thinking he was benefiting from nepotism. Not unless it suits him, of course."

"Oh." My mind shoots in multiple directions. Stefan had said he'd threatened to call Geoff. If he did, would Geoff listen to his son's ideas?

"Brad's rants are nothing for you to worry about."

I should have known better: Stefan took an instant dislike to Logan, so of course he's going to think the worst of him. And he doesn't know what we've shared, what we've become to one another. He doesn't know Logan.

I'm a fool to have even entertained the notion he would double-cross me.

"You've got the contract and we want to agree it with you. Have you had a good read through it?" he asks.

"Yes, I have. It looks fine."

"Shall I email it to you so you can forward it to your lawyers?"

"Absolutely." I beam at Logan, feeling significantly lighter.

He opens his laptop and taps. "Done."

"Now, I think I need to prove to you you're not just some one-night-stand to me." He begins to unbutton my shirt.

I instantly thrum with desire as I look down at his hands on my skin. "Two nights, maybe?"

His eyes are electric as I reach up and kiss him. He lifts me into his arms and carries me to his bed.

"What did I ever do to deserve you?" I mutter between kisses as we feverishly pull each other's clothes off.

My hands slide easily down his now familiar, firm body, making his breath quicken as he lets out a groan.

"I don't know," he mutters, between kisses as he flips me onto my back with ease. "But it must have been pretty darn good."

CHAPTER 12

WE'RE STILL LOUNGING BLISSFULLY in bed an hour later, talking about Logan's Hobbit tour, when my phone rings. I notice it's Grace again. I decide I had better answer it: she clearly has something she needs to talk to me about.

"Hey, Grace. Sorry I didn't call you back. I've had things on my mind."

I dart a look at Logan, lying lazily next to me. He flashes his sexy smile and it's all I can do to focus on my conversation with my sister.

"Oh, I'm so glad I've got you." She sounds troubled.

"What is it?" I ask, sitting up, instantly concerned. "Is everything okay?"

"No," she answers flatly.

"What is it?" A million scenarios flood my mind, from the mundane to the catastrophic.

"It's Mum. She's sick, Brooke. Really sick." Grace begins to sob.

"Tell me everything," I reply, frowning.

"She's—" Grace begins, but falters.

"It's okay, Gracie." I try to stay calm while my insides are screaming for her to just spit it out.

I wait for a few moments.

"She's got cancer," she manages to get out, before dissolving into sobs again.

"Cancer?" I ask, almost in a whisper. "How? When?" My mind zips to my own mum, and the cancer that took her from us, all those years ago.

Logan sits up next to me, putting his hand on my arm in concern.

"They told me yesterday," she sniffs.

"What sort?" I ask, not sure I want to know the answer.

"It's breast cancer. They say they've detected it early so she's going to be okay, but Brooke, it's still *cancer.*"

"I know." I try hard to control my own emotions.

First Mum; now Jennifer.

"Tell me everything you know, Grace. From the top."

Grace manages to pull herself together long enough to tell me Jennifer found a lump a couple of weeks ago. She went to her doctor, who sent her for a mammogram and ultrasound. The tests confirmed the lump. She had a biopsy done a few days later, and it showed it is malignant, requiring surgery.

"Did they say what stage it is?" I ask, my mind darting to the worst possible scenario. Mum's cancer was so advanced they couldn't do much about it. I say a quick, silent prayer Jennifer's won't be the same.

"Stage one, but she still needs a partial mastectomy to remove it."

"Well at least that's something. They've caught it early. Why didn't she tell us this was going on?" I'm suddenly angry with Jennifer and Dad for keeping such potentially damaging information from us. "We just had dinner together this week!"

My mind darts to that evening and the way in which I caught Jennifer and Dad sharing looks with one another. I'd put it down to them being so in love—which they are—not that she was awaiting news of a potentially fatal diagnosis.

"She and Dad said they didn't want us to worry about her, you know, after what happened with your mum."

I bite my lip, forcing memories of Mum's dreadful illness out of my mind.

We're both silent for several moments, while I process the news.

"I'm coming home," I say decisively.

"Okay," she replies, sniffing. "I think that's a good idea. Let me know when and I'll pick you up from the airport."

"No need, I left my car there. I'll be over as soon as I can."

I hang up and stare out the window, biting my lip.

"I know it's a stupid thing to say, but are you okay?"

"I have to go." I dart out of bed, heading for my bathroom, collecting my clothes, dotted around the room, along the way.

Guilt sears through me as I hastily dress: if I hadn't been so focused on Logan, I would have called Grace back earlier. I could have been there for everyone by now.

I've been so wrapped up in my own affairs I've neglected the most important people in my life.

Watching me frantically dressing, Logan asks, "What can I do to help?"

"Nothing. Look, I'm sorry. It's my stepmum. She's been diagnosed with—" My voice catches. "With cancer." Tears well in my eyes. "I need to get back to Wellington. Now."

"Of course you do. I'll tell your team you've had a family emergency and have had to head back."

"Thanks."

I do a final check of the room, ensuring I haven't missed anything, and then head to the door. I turn back to say goodbye to Logan, realising with a start this is an actual 'goodbye', not just a 'see you soon'. It's come about too soon.

"Logan. This is not how I wanted to end things. Leaving like this. I'd hoped we might have more time. You go in the morning, don't you?" I look into his eyes. Sadness envelops me.

"Yes," he replies, looking downcast. He kisses me gently, and my body aches for him. "Take care, Brooke." He holds me to him. "And... well... it's been incredible."

I look into his brown eyes for one last time. A lump rises in my throat.

"It has. I only wish—" I'm unable to find the words.

"I know," he says kindly. "Me too. I'll call you later tonight."

"That would be nice. Thanks."

I'm so torn between wanting to be with this incredible man and my need to be with my family. But I know I have to go.

"'Bye, Logan."

I turn away from him and head out the door, holding in my tears as I prepare to face whatever life wants to throw at me back home.

* * *

That afternoon, and a large pit of worry later, I'm back in Wellington, pulling up outside Dad and Jennifer's house.

I burst through the front door, calling out to everyone. I find Jennifer in the kitchen. She's chopping up sweet potatoes for the evening meal, looking like she doesn't have a care in the world.

"Brooke, hi! What are you doing here?" she asks, looking genuinely pleased to see me.

I rush over to her and collect her in a hug, forcing her to drop her knife to the bench in surprise.

"Ah. You've heard," she says as I hold tightly onto her. She pats my back, saying, "There, there, it's all going to be fine."

She's the one with cancer and she's comforting *me*?

I pull away from her. "Is it? How do you know?"

She smiles gently at me. "Because I just do, that's how."

Here's this woman suffering from cancer and there's nothing I can do to help her, to protect her. I feel so helpless.

"Here." She pulls me in for another hug.

"Why are you reassuring me? *You're* the s-s-sick one, the one w-w-with c-cancer," I blub, holding onto her for dear life.

"You're upset, and that's okay. Just let it out."

As if I needed permission, another sob escapes. "But Grace told me you have to have surgery. Where I come from, that's serious."

"Shhh, shhh," she soothes until I let go of her to wipe my eyes with a tissue from the windowsill.

For a girl who prides herself on keeping her emotions under wraps, I sure have been letting them out on parade a lot these past few days.

Dad walks into the kitchen, holding a basket of spinach from their veggie garden, followed closely by Dylan.

"Brooke. How wonderful to see you. Aren't you meant to be in the South Island, brokering this big deal of yours?" he asks, placing the basket on the bench and giving me a hug.

I look in wonderment from Jennifer to Dad and back again. "Why are you both so *calm*?"

"Ah, that's why you're back." He darts Jennifer a knowing look and smiles at me. "Because, kiddo, worrying isn't going to make this better," he replies in his pragmatic fashion. "We need to stay positive, for Jennifer and for all of you."

I walk over to Dylan, who's looking even more moochy than when I saw him at dinner last week, and give him a hug.

"I'm fine," he snaps, pushing me away. He's clearly not. I let it slide.

"Did you know about this?" I ask him.

He shakes his head. "Nope. Not until Grace told me."

I glare at Jennifer and Dad, as my anger rises like lava in an erupting volcano. "Why didn't you tell us? We have a right to know. Can't you see that finding out this way makes it so much worse?"

"We didn't want to worry you all," Jennifer replies. "We thought it best I get the tests done before we tell anyone, to understand what we're dealing with here. We would have preferred to tell you all ourselves, but Grace beat us to it."

"Rightly so!" I'm indignant on her behalf. "Where is Grace, anyway? I thought she'd be here."

"She's gone out to let off some steam. We thought it best," Dad says. "She was pretty upset."

"Oh. How serious is this?"

"Let's all sit down, shall we?" Dad suggests.

"Good idea," Jennifer agrees.

We all pull out chairs from the kitchen table and sit down. I prepare for the worst.

"You have to tell us everything. No glossing over details or leaving anything out."

"Sure," Jennifer responds, smiling that calm smile she's had plastered across her face since my arrival. "I was doing my routine breast check in the shower a while ago, and I found a lump."

Dylan groans. "Do I have to hear this?" He looks like he has a sour taste in his mouth. "I'm your son. I don't want to hear about your boobs."

I smack his arm. "Get over yourself, Dylan."

"Oww-ah!" he protests.

"You were pretty happy to know about them when they were breakfast, lunch, and dinner, Dylan," Dad teases, chuckling.

Dylan looks like he might very well throw up.

How can Dad make a joke at a time like this?

"Carry on, Jennifer," I say, trying to pull everyone's attention back to the real concern here.

"Well, I saw our GP, who sent me off for a mammogram and ultrasound. The ultrasound confirmed the lump and showed I have enlarged lymph nodes in my armpit. But, the only way they can tell it's cancer is from the biopsy I had last week. And that came back positive for carcinoma."

I swallow hard. "Did you have to go under for it? Have an

anaesthetic?"

"No, it's done with a needle," she replies brightly, as though it was nothing, just a walk in the park.

I cross my arms under my own breasts, thinking about having a large needle poked inside one and how freaky—not to mention painful—that must be.

"One of the important things to understand is that it's one of the treatable types," Dad adds.

I nod, feeling worried. "What happens now?"

"I'm seeing my specialist in a couple of days' time and we'll have a clearer idea then."

"But it looks like surgery is the best option, hopefully nothing else," Dad adds, putting his hand on Jennifer's arm.

My thoughts flash to my mother, and the vague memories I have of her during her treatment, weakened and grey, unable to play with me, take me to school, or do any of the other everyday things I took for granted she could do. Tears well in my eyes afresh, and I try to swallow the lump rising in my throat.

I guess the thought of losing Jennifer to cancer has shown me just how important she is to me.

"There she is," Dad says brightly as Grace bustles into the kitchen.

"Hey, sis." I stand to give her a hug.

"Hi, Brooke. I'm so glad you're here." Her eyes are red and puffy from crying.

"Did you have a nice time?" Dad asks.

"Hardly, Dad. I just went to Sam's house to hang out for a while," she replies.

Grace is friends with Alexis's youngest sister, Sammy Jo. She's 'Sam' for short because who wants to be called 'Sammy Jo' outside of the American Deep South? Unlike Alexis and me they became close friends at school, virtually living in one another's pockets. They're still great friends to this day.

"Jennifer was just telling us what's happening next," I say to Grace.

"Yeah. I want to go to the doctor's appointment with her, but she won't let me." She sounds hurt.

"Grace, darling, you have an important job to do," Jennifer says, putting her arm around Grace's shoulders and giving her a maternal squeeze. "And anyway, I'd like to go with just Dad."

Grace slumps her shoulders, looking resigned.

"Now," Jennifer continues, smoothing her skirt and picking up her knife, "Who's staying for dinner? I've made my chicken pie." Her eyes sparkle at us, and a fresh wave of sadness washes over me.

"Chicken pie? Yum. I wouldn't miss one of your chicken pies for the world," I say.

After dinner, Dad walks me to my car.

"Doesn't this seem so unfair to you, Dad? Jennifer getting cancer, just like Mum?"

"I'm trying not to think in those terms. It doesn't help anyone." He has a grim look on his face, and I know the thought has occurred to him, probably more than once.

"You're worried, aren't you?"

"Scared shitless, kiddo," he replies with a grim smile. "But I can't show her that. She needs me to be strong. She needs *you* to be strong, too."

Yes, I've got to be that crab again. I've let my tough shell slip too much in the last few days—with Logan and now with Jennifer—and it's time I hardened up so I can face whatever crap the world wants to throw at me.

* * *

Once I'm home, unpacked, and drinking a medicinal glass of wine on my sofa, I get a call from Logan.

"How are you?" he asks hurriedly. "I've been so worried."

I smile, thinking how wonderful it is to have a man in my life, a man who cares for me. Especially a man like Logan. I've pretty much hit the jackpot with this one. Then it hits me afresh he's leaving the country tomorrow.

"I'm all right. Just getting used to the idea, I guess."

"Do you want to talk about it?" he asks.

I'm so comfortable with Logan I tell him everything I know about what's going on, right down to the ways in which Dylan and Grace are dealing with it.

"And how about you? How are you coping?" he asks.

"I'm trying to focus on the next steps and not think about what might be, you know?"

"That's probably the best way to deal with it right now, honey," he replies and warmth spreads through my belly at his first use of the endearment.

"You know, I didn't get to say goodbye to you properly today. I'm sorry. I want you to know I had a great time with you. The best time with you."

Logan's time with *Live It* is due to end tonight with the closing of the seminar. My heart drops at the thought of him going back to the States, of our time together coming to an end.

"So, when do you fly out?" I don't want to know the answer.

"Well, now we've verbally agreed to the partnership and you have the contract, my work here is done, as the saying goes. Brad and I fly out tomorrow morning," he replies, a little too perkily for my liking.

"Oh," I reply, deflated. Why doesn't he feel as depressed as me about this?

"And I land at eleven-thirty."

"In Auckland?" I assume he's catching his flight back to San Francisco from there.

"No, I don't reach Auckland until Sunday next week."

"Oh. So where are you off to?"

"Wellington," he replies, and I can hear the smile in his voice.

"Really? Why?" I yelp, hardly believing my ears.

"Why do you think? I have a few days' leave owing, and I figured, why not spend it in the world's coolest little capital with this hot babe I've just hooked up with?"

"Nice turn of phrase, you've got there, cowboy," I comment, happiness spreading from my head all the way down to my toes at the thought of seeing him tomorrow.

He chuckles. "Shall we meet for dinner tomorrow night? You pick the place, but it's my treat."

"Wild horses couldn't keep me away."

After one of those long farewells people in new relationships do—the old "You hang up," "No, you hang up" routine—I head to bed, exhausted from the day's events, and excited about seeing Logan again tomorrow.

CHAPTER 13

"OH, MY GOD! YOU slept with him, didn't you?" Alexis cries, her eyes wide, a look of incredulity splashed across her pretty face.

We've met for our scheduled cup of coffee at Astoria, in my opinion the city's best café in a veritable sea of supreme caffeine offerings, and Alexis's eyes are shining as she stares at me, open mouthed.

Is it that obvious I slept with him? Mental note: work on my poker face. It's obviously woeful.

I can't help but smile as my mind shoots to my hotel room in Queenstown and how Logan's hands had felt grasping my back, his mouth on mine, as we moved in rhythmic perfection together, sweat rolling down our faces.

I clear my throat.

"I did," I confirm in a matter-of-fact way.

I mean, she's guessed it and I was pretty sure it was written all over my face anyway. There's no point beating about the proverbial bush here.

The look on my friend's face says it all: horror, concern, and disbelief. Maybe a little bit impressed?

I put my hand up to stop her saying anything, despite the fact the power of speech appears to have deserted her.

"I know I said I'd never do it, that my relationship with Logan was strictly business. I know. But what I didn't reckon on was how I would feel about him. And how he would feel about me." A smile spreads across my face. "He's *so* amazing, Alexis. He's kind, smart, and thoughtful. He's totally driven and really successful. Not only that, we have so much in common. And he's *so* hot. You know, you've met him."

It's a little like I'm justifying a murder here.

By now my level-headed friend has crossed her arms and I suppress the almost overwhelming urge to continue to blabber on about how wonderful Logan is. Instead, I decide the best thing—the only thing—to do is sit tight and wait for her reaction.

What I don't expect is how *long* she keeps me waiting. She just sits there, arms crossed, looking into my face, evidently processing the information I've imparted.

From anyone else this could seem like a ploy to make me uncomfortable, but I know Alexis well enough to know she likes to think before she speaks—a very rare quality in this day and age.

It could be because she's the eldest in a large family of Irish Catholics. With four sisters and one brother—the poor sod never stood a chance—there was so much highly opinionated chatter going on in the family home, she told me she would just shut up until everyone had run out of steam.

Finally she speaks. "You know, Brooke, I totally get it. He's cute, he's clearly your type, and yes, I agree with you, he's hotter than Hugh Jackman." She pauses. "Well, not quite." She smiles.

I know how much she fancies Hugh Jackman. I feel the magnitude of her compliment.

I laugh nervously, expecting the 'but'.

"But."

Ah, yes, there it is.

"Have you thought about the impact this could have on your working relationship? I mean, you've just told me how likely it is you'll be working closely with his company now, and office romances can end badly. And then where are you? Not only that, but he's powerful, right?"

"Yes, he is." He's one of the senior executives of the company, and has worked for them for years. "That said, he's in mergers and acquisitions, so effectively his work with *Live It* is done now. My contact with the company will be with another division altogether."

"But he's on the leadership team, right?"

I nod.

"Do you think they'll choose you over him if your relationship goes tits up?" It's clearly a rhetorical question; she answers before I have time to draw breath. "No, they won't. You yourself said there's a lot at stake here, Brooke, and I know how important your company is to you. All I'm saying is, please be careful."

She reaches across the table and rubs my shoulder. Alexis is an amazing friend: she's loyal and caring, and not afraid to say it like it is.

Even if what she says is the last thing you want to hear.

I take a deep breath. "Look, I know all those things. I know my rational brain is screaming at me right now. But the heart wants what the heart wants, right? And my heart wants Logan. Alexis, he makes me feel so incredible, in a way I haven't felt since Scott. *More* so than with Scott, even."

Scott. The man I fell for hook, line, and sinker. The man who reciprocated by stomping on my heart with his expensive tennis shoes.

"You have to believe me, Alexis. It's different this time. *He's* different. He's definitely not Scott Wright, that's for sure. And I'm not going to rush into anything. I'm going to keep the work thing separate and just see where our relationship goes."

She stands and gives me a long hug. "I want you to be with a great guy, Brooke. Hell, you deserve it. I just want you to be careful with this one. Promise me?"

"I promise," I reply, giving my best impression of a girl-scout salute.

Alexis laughs. "You're a total dork, you know that?"

"Yep, but I'm a dork who's getting some," I reply with a cheeky grin and a wink.

"Hey, you know what he is?" she asks. "He's your 'heartbroker'."

"My what?" I ask, puzzled.

"He came here to broker a deal with you, right? And what he got was your heart. That makes him your 'heartbroker'."

I laugh. "I hadn't thought of it like that." A brief chill runs down my spine. "But don't say that. It sounds too much like 'heart*breaker*'."

Let's change the subject. "Anyway, enough about me. What's your exciting news?"

She raises her left hand, displaying the largest diamond ring I think I've ever seen up close. I can't quite believe I've missed it: it's the size of a small planet, possibly Pluto—No wait, Venus, since Pluto got downgraded.

"Oh, my god!" I screech. "You're engaged? And you let me blab on and on about Logan all this time?"

I jump up from my chair, almost knocking the coffee cups from our table onto the floor, and give her a hug. She proffers her hand and I take it, inspecting the ring. "Oh, Alexis, it's stunning."

Alexis can't wipe the smile from her face. "I know. Can you believe it? He asked me on Friday night and I was just bursting to tell you."

"I can, and I do," I reply. "You're the perfect couple, and he adores you. Of course he wants to marry you."

She flushes with pleasure.

"Now, tell me all about it."

"We went for a hike up Mount Kau Kau together. On the way up he was acting so strangely, I started to get concerned for his health, to be honest. Anyway, we got to the top, next to the mast, and he grabbed my hands, went down on one knee, and pulled out this amazing ring." She holds out her hand once again, gazing down at the rock.

I clap my hands together in excitement. Alexis has been with Tim for some time now. They go together like bacon and eggs. You'd be hard pressed to meet two people better suited, or two people more in love.

"You're going to tell me he chose it all on his own, aren't you?"

"He did. I am amazed. He's got such great taste."

"Of course he has: he chose you. Now, tell me how he asked you and what you said, and, well, everything."

Alexis proceeds to tell me how Tim had made a speech about how he couldn't believe how lucky he was to have her, how he wanted to spend the rest of his life with her, and how they should never be apart. And she said 'yes' without a moment's hesitation.

It's all so romantic I think I might actually swoon.

"We don't have a date yet, but will you be my bridesmaid?"

"Of course I will! Are you crazy? Just as long as you don't put me in one of those pink puffball dresses," I reply.

"Never," she replies, widening her eyes and shaking her head. "You and Laura can choose whatever you want."

"Yay, Laura's a bridesmaid too? Oh, we're going to have so much fun!"

"Yes, and my sisters, of course," she adds.

"Of course! We have to celebrate with something better than coffee. How about drinks on Saturday night? You, me, Grace, and your sisters? It'll be the first official bridal party get together."

Logan leaves on Saturday morning, so I know I'm going to want a distraction. A celebration for my dear friend is just the ticket.

"Let's just make it you, me, and Laura. I can do without my sisters."

"Sure." I chuckle. Families might be the most important things in the world, but it's nice to just hang out with your friends sometimes.

My phone beeps and I notice it's a text from Grace. I frown, which Alexis notices immediately.

"What's the matter, babe?" she asks.

I swallow hard and paste on a bright smile. "Nothing. Just work stuff," I lie.

Alexis sizes me up. "Tell me."

"I don't want to burst your bubble," I reply, knowing news of Jennifer's cancer will certainly do that for Alexis.

"I'm a big girl, Brooke. Please, tell me."

I sigh, resigned. "It's Jennifer. She's got breast cancer."

"Oh, my god." Alexis looks shocked.

"I only found out yesterday. She's seeing her doctor this week, so we'll know more then."

"Wow. I'm so sorry, Brooke. Please send her my love." She rubs my hand and I have to hold back the tears. "You've certainly had a big weekend."

Ain't that the truth.

CHAPTER 14

BACK IN THE OFFICE I'm engrossed in re-reading the partnership agreement Logan sent me, translating the crazy language lawyers favour the world over, when Stefan pokes his head around my office door.

"Morning, boss. You free?"

I'm happy to have a break from the legalese. "Sure. Come on in. Did you just get back?"

He sits down on a chair next to my desk. "Yes. Our flight was delayed, but we're back on terra firma now. So, *you* left Queenstown pretty fast. What's the haps?"

As Stefan and I are close, I share Jennifer's news with him.

"Shit. That sucks."

"Yeah, it does," I agree with a bitter laugh. "But at least we've got something we need to focus our attention on right now."

"What?"

Despite having relived Jennifer's health dramas, I can't help a smile from spreading across my face when I think about how our dreams of expansion are about to be realised.

"I spoke with Logan, and he confirmed they want to sign this contract with us. I'm just reading it now before I send it off to the lawyers."

"Really?" He looks dubious. "What about that conversation I overheard between him and Brad?"

"After you told me about it, I got to thinking."

"That Logan's a double-crossing piece of scum?"

116

"Stefan, he explained everything."

"I bet he did," Stefan replies, crossing his arms. "What did he say, exactly?"

"He told me *You: Now* had every intention of entering a partnership with us, and it was actually Brad who was having second thoughts."

He bites his lip, narrowing his eyes at me. "And you believed him, didn't you?"

A blush rises in my cheeks. "Yes, I did, Stefan," I say in a brusque don't-mess-with-me manner. "And here's the evidence." I pass the contract to him. "Why would Logan give me this and mean to double-cross us? It doesn't make sense."

"Harrumph," he replies, taking the contract from me and flipping through its pages.

I lean back in my chair, confident he has no legitimate comeback—other than his irrational dislike of Logan, of course.

"So are we going for it?" he asks.

I nod, smiling. "Yeah, I think we are. But there's one thing I'm thinking of adding."

"What's that?"

"I have my concerns over whether Brad might be able to influence Geoff Friedlander into changing their minds. Did you know Brad is Geoff's son?"

"Really?" he responds in surprise.

"Really. I think not only do we want to get this contract signed as soon as we can, I'm thinking of adding a break clause. I need to clear it with the lawyers, but I know my dad has used them in his property development business in the past."

"What will it do for us?"

"It will mean if things don't work out with *You: Now* we can separate from them and keep the *Live It* brand. Which of course is very valuable to us."

"So it's a self-protection clause?"

"Yes, a kind of 'get out of jail free' card, I suppose."

"Sure, but this isn't Monopoly, Brooke. Couldn't they could use the clause too?" he asks.

"Well, yes, sure. They'd never sign the contract if it was all going to benefit us and not them. Think about it, Stefan: if they decide things aren't working out, I can buy back my fifty per cent interest from them and we'll go back to the way things were."

"Are you sure about this, Brooke?"

"Look, we pursued *You: Now* because we want to break into the Australian and Asian markets, right?"

He nods.

"With their help, I'm positive we can crack those markets, and if we do, it's a win-win situation."

"And if we don't?"

"If we don't, then *Live It* is still the number one personal development company here in New Zealand," I reply with satisfaction.

"But they still own half of our business."

"Yes. I know it's not perfect, but we both know this is the best shot we have at expansion."

Stefan pauses, considering the information I've shared with him. "Well, you're the boss. And whether it was Logan or Brad, one of them was unquestionably trying to screw us over. And I'm still not convinced it was Brad."

"It'll all be irrelevant once this contract is signed, Stefan. Now, I want to get this out to the lawyers this morning, so go and do something useful, will you?"

"Sure thing, boss," he replies, smiling. "And Brooke? Congratulations."

* * *

"You look particularly beautiful, tonight," Logan says as he holds the restaurant door open for me.

"Why, thank you, kind sir." I walk past him and into Boulcott Street Bistro, one of the city's best and longest-standing fine dining restaurants.

"Nice choice." I look around the room appreciatively.

"Thanks. I have a good adviser," he replies, taking my coat.

I wonder who his adviser could be. They've managed to pick one of my all-time favourite restaurants. "Who?"

"Oh, just a little bird. I need to protect my sources."

I let out an easy laugh. "I wouldn't want to put you in a compromising position."

He raises his eyebrows at me, and we share a look, my Girly Bits pricking up their ears. "Later," he murmurs into my ear, before we turn to follow the maître d' to our table.

"Legal say they haven't seen your contract amendments yet," he comments once we've had our first sip of wine, a sauvignon blanc from the Marlborough region in the South Island.

"No. Our lawyers are still working through it. They've promised to expedite it, so I should have their comments in the next day or two."

"Excellent." He smiles at me across the table. "So we don't have to talk about work at all tonight."

"Exactly. What have you been up to in my fair city today?"

"Oh, I've had an awesome day. I started with a run around Oriental Bay where I stopped for a coffee at a place with a great view of the city. Then I had to do some work, so went back to the hotel to do that. Then I went to The Weta Cave and did the tour again."

He flashes me a broad smile and I chuckle, shaking my head at him. He had been to The Weta Cave, the movie effects workshop responsible for films such as The Lord of the Rings and The Hobbit, on his first trip to Wellington before we went to Queenstown.

"What?" He looks both indignant and amused in equal parts.

"You're such a Tolkien geek, aren't you?"

"Loud and proud. You should come. It's awesome. You get to see how they work."

"Sure," I reply, thinking how enjoyable it would be to share Logan's passion with him. "That sounds like fun. Even though I'm more of a rom com kind of girl."

Our waiter interrupts us with an outline of the dining offerings and, once we've both ordered, conversation flows again.

"How many chick flicks have you actually seen?"

"Excuse me, they're called 'rom coms', not 'chick flicks'. And I've seen a few." I don't want to admit to the full extent of my obsession.

"Chicks," he says good-humouredly, shaking his head.

"Well from the perspective of a 'chick', as you put it," I begin, using air quotes, "what's not to love about a romantic comedy? Cute guy? Check. Nice clothes? Check. Happy ending? Check. Perfection."

"You see that's exactly what I don't like about them. They're so predictable. You know the guy will get the girl in the end. Why bother watching it?"

"I'll tell you what: I'll stick with my movies, and you can stick with yours. Deal?"

"Deal," he replies, finding my hand on the table with his, our eyes locking.

My heart clenches.

The waiter delivers our meals, breaking the spell. As we eat we talk about a wide variety of things, until I pluck up the courage to ask about his ex-wife.

"I married my college sweetheart, straight out of school. A lot of our friends were doing it at the time, and it seemed logical that we would too. We had the big white church wedding, got the house with a mortgage the size of Texas, then settled down into spending the next fifty years together."

"What happened?"

"Reality bit, I guess. I woke up one day and realised I wanted something different. We'd built this world for ourselves—hanging out with other married couples like us, doing home improvements at the weekend—but it kind of felt like we were just playing at being married. I guess we were too young."

"Some relationships formed when you're young work out, though. My friend, Laura, married her high school boyfriend. They're still together, got three kids, living in marital bliss."

"I'm not saying they can't work if you get together young, just it didn't work for us."

"So you left her?"

"We left each other. She hadn't wanted to admit it, but she was feeling the same way too. We split up about seven years ago now, when I was twenty-seven. We're still friends, not that we see each other much. She's married with a couple of kids, living in Oakland across the Bay."

"Seven years is a long time. There must have been someone else?" I ask.

"Of course. I'm not a monk. A man has needs, you know." He raised his eyebrows at me suggestively.

I force a light laugh, pushing unpalatable images of Logan with other women out of my head.

He reaches across the table, taking my hand in his, looking suddenly serious. "But there hasn't been anyone who comes within a thousand yards of you, Brooke."

My heart expands. "Me too. I mean I haven't met anyone as

wonderful as you."

He grins at me, both of us revelling in our feelings for one another.

The waiter appears at my elbow, popping our bubble. "Everything to your liking?" he enquires.

Logan releases my hand as we both lean back in our chairs. "Yes, great, thanks."

As the waiter leaves, Logan rolls his eyes at me. "Talk about breaking the mood. Anyway, what about you?"

"What about me what?"

"Any juicy skeletons in your closet?"

"*I've* never been married,"

"I know," he says matter-of-factly.

"You do?" I ask in surprise.

He chuckles. "There's this thing called social media. You might have heard of it even way down here." He shrugs with a glint in his eye. "I checked you out."

"You did?" I'm flattered.

"Yeah. And if you have been married, you've managed to keep it pretty secret."

"No, never married. But I did live with someone. An American guy, actually. We broke up just over a year ago."

"I see. Got a thing for us Americans, do you?"

"Well, if I do, it's entirely subconscious," I reply, laughing. "But I've well and truly moved on."

I'm struck by the realisation I have in fact moved on, and Scott is now only my ex. It's so liberating.

After our delicious meal, Logan and I stroll through bustling Cuba Mall hand in hand, ensconced in our own little bubble.

We reach his hotel and my body begins to buzz, knowing what's to come. Without saying a word, he leads me to his room, closing the door behind us as I take off my coat.

We both know we want the same thing from each other, and neither of us needs to ask.

Unlike our first feverish encounter, he undresses me slowly, taking his time as he kisses my face, then my neck, and down my chest to my cleavage, easily pulling my dress over my head.

"Oh, Brooke." His voice is husky as he unhooks my bra, caressing and kissing my erect nipples, causing goose bumps to spring up all over my body.

A deep, strong thrum for him runs through my body, settling between my legs. I'm aching for him.

And then I slip off his jacket and unbutton his shirt, kissing his firm, toned chest as I work my way down his delicious body.

I unbuckle his belt and slip my hand down inside his jeans. He's ready for me, and he lets out a deep groan as I caress him, our tongues finding one another in a deep kiss.

Some time later we fall asleep in his bed, arms wrapped around one another, awakening with a knock on the door heralding our early room service breakfast.

As I eat my bacon and eggs, sitting next to him in bed, both dressed in our hotel-issued white towelling robes, I'm so happy, so calm.

I never want this to end.

"Do I get to see you tonight for a repeat performance?" he asks as I kiss him goodbye, knowing I'm about to do the humiliating 'walk of shame' in last night's clothes back to my place. "The things you do to me, Brooke Mortimer..." He shakes his head, grinning, a sexy sparkle in his eyes.

I kiss him slowly on the lips. "Just try and stop me." I curse the fact I have a job I need to go to. But then, if I didn't have that job, I never would have met this incredible man.

As I turn to leave, he grabs my hand. "Hey, I hadn't mentioned it, but I love that you didn't hesitate to get on a plane and come back to see your family on Sunday. Even if it did mean leaving me there."

"Well, they're important to me. You'd do the same, I bet."

"I would." He grins at me. "They would love you, by the way. Especially Mom."

"Really?" I ask, flattered. Wow, he's already thought about me meeting his family?

"Oh, yeah."

"I'll see you tonight, then." I grin from ear to ear like some crazed idiot.

I wander towards the lift, floating in my love bubble, feeling like the luckiest woman alive.

CHAPTER 15

TWO DAYS LATER I'M brought down to Earth with a sickening thud.

"I'm scheduled for surgery next week," Jennifer says down the phone.

"Oh." I sit down in my office chair. "When? Where?"

"At Wellington hospital on Tuesday morning. I'm having a partial mastectomy and removal of the lymph nodes the cancer has spread to."

My practical side kicks in. "Right. I see. What do you need? Is Dad taking time off to look after you? I will if he can't."

She laughs lightly, and I'm struck afresh at how relaxed she seems to be about this whole thing. "No, thanks, Brooke. You're a sweetie. Your dad will be there for me. But a visit afterwards would be more than welcome."

"Of course. I'll be there. Shall I come with you to the hospital, before the surgery?"

"Oh, no. You have to work. It's in the morning."

"Jennifer, you forget: I'm the boss. I can do what I like."

She laughs again. "Really, there's no need. I'll see you once I'm in the ward, after the surgery."

"All right then," I reply, resigned.

She's so chilled out about this you'd think she was going for a pedicure, not surgery to remove a cancerous tumour. She's either in total denial or the most level headed, unflappable person on the planet.

My phone beeps. It's the lawyers on the other line. "I have to go. I'll come and see you at the weekend."

"All right, darling. Take care of yourself. Oh, and I want to know all about this man you're seeing, too."

I instantly blush, caught off-guard. "Man?"

"Oh, don't play coy with me, Brooke Mortimer. Grace told me."

How did Grace know about Logan? But then I put two and two together and realise Alexis must have told her sister, Sammy Jo, who would have told Grace, who then told Jennifer.

People may talk about the 'six degrees of separation', but here in New Zealand it's more like half a degree. It's practically a village where everyone knows your every move.

"Okay. I will." I accept defeat, as I surge with pride that I have a special someone Jennifer wants to know about. It makes a nice change for me.

I've missed the call from my lawyers, so call them back as soon as I've said farewell to Jennifer. They've given the okay to the contract and have included the break clause I wanted. I instruct them to courier me a copy to sign before I pass it on to Logan.

I feel a cocktail of emotions once I've hung up.

This is it: do or die.

* * *

That evening Logan and I are in the kitchen at my townhouse in Thorndon. I sign the partnership agreement and hand it over to him with trembling hands. It's hard to relinquish full control of my company—my baby —even if doing so means we can pursue new markets *and* I get a much-needed cash injection.

He pulls a bottle of champagne out of a cooler bag he'd secretly stashed under my kitchen table when he arrived.

"But your company hasn't signed the contract yet." I look dubiously at the bottle of chilled Bollinger in his hand.

He takes a pen out of his laptop bag and signs the contract, too, instantly sealing the deal. "I'd say we just have."

I stare at his signature on the page, almost as though I can't believe what he's done. Clearly as a company vice president he has signing authority, but it didn't occur to me he would sign it here and now.

"Even with the addition of the break clause?" I question, my brow creasing.

I had shown Logan the clause before we sent our version to his legal department, and he'd been confident they would accept it. In fact, he was all for it.

"It's all good, Brooke. Relax. We want to partner with you, remember? Now, where are your champagne glasses? Let's crack this baby open."

I open a cupboard above the bench and pull out two crystal flutes Dad and Jennifer gave me for my twenty-first. Logan's calm, happy mood is infectious, and I find my tension about the contract slip away, replaced instead by a rush of excitement.

"To the beginning of what I know will be a successful partnership," he toasts, raising his filled glass.

I raise mine and we clink. "Yes, to new adventures and successes."

I grin broader than a Cheshire cat. Logan's company is about to help us take on the world.

"I'm really happy for you, Brooke. You deserve this."

"Thanks," I reply, still beaming. "It's going to be a lot of work."

"It is. But you're not a woman to shy away from hard work. Are you?" He puts his glass on the bench and taking me in his arms. "You're confident, strong, and driven. As well as unbelievably sexy."

He kisses me and I melt like an ice cream on a hot day.

"Tell me, what do you think you'd do if you didn't run your company here in New Zealand?"

What? Where's this coming from?

I stiffen in his arms. "Umm, I don't know. Why?"

He shrugs. "No reason. I just wondered if you have any other passions, anything else you might want to pursue."

"I guess there are lots of things I'd like to do with my life, but not right now."

I shift my weight, uncomfortable. This is a very weird line of questioning, especially straight after I've signed a contract with his company.

"Yeah, me too. I love what I do for *You: Now*, but I'd like to do other things some day. I think you and I are quite alike in that way: we're adaptable and could do any number of different things."

"Hmmm." I'm still trying to work him out. I shouldn't read too much into it; it's probably nothing.

My phone buzzes on the kitchen bench next to me, interrupting our conversation. I get a short, sharp shock when Scott Wright's name flashes up on my screen with a photo of him and I together, happy and smiling, on a beach in Rarotonga.

Why on this sweet Earth would my ex be calling me? And, more to the point, why didn't I delete that photo—hell, his entire contact details—when I kicked him out?

I flip my phone over so our smiling faces are no longer staring up at me, turning my attention back to Logan: a far more enjoyable prospect.

"Anyone important?" Logan asks as I take a sip from my glass.

The champagne, combined with the excitement of agreeing the partnership contract, has begun to make me a little giddy.

"No," I reply with a light chortle. "No one important."

And I know I mean it, one hundred per cent.

Later, I snuggle up to him in bed. "I can't believe you're leaving tomorrow."

"I know. It's come around so fast, right?" he replies, stroking my head.

We're lying naked in bed together, my head resting on his chest. I can hear each breath he takes, his heart beating strong and steady. He smells and feels amazing, and I'm not in the least bit ready for this to end. Not yet.

Perhaps never.

"Yes, it has. Too fast." Sadness stings,

We've had the most wonderful, intense week together. Since our time in Queenstown we've eaten out at some of Wellington's best restaurants, run around the city's sparkling bays together, wandered through the Botanic Gardens, picnicked in The Dell. And, of course, we visited The Weta Cave together: my first and Logan's *third*, time.

We've spent every night together, never getting quite as much sleep as a doctor might recommend as optimal for one's health, but waking up each morning satisfied and thoroughly contented nonetheless. It's been utter bliss.

A knot forms at the pit of my stomach as my thoughts turn to the coming week. I don't want this to end. Not only will Logan be gone, I'll have to face Jennifer's surgery and everything that goes with it. It's undeniably grim.

"I've been thinking, honey. Why don't you come visit me? It's just a twelve hour direct flight, and you'd love San Francisco."

I raise my head, anticipation rising in my belly as an instant smile spreads across my face.

"That would be so great. Are you sure? I mean long distance relationships don't have the best track record, you know."

Did I just label what we have as a *'relationship'*?

I backtrack. "Not that this is a relationship, per se, or anything. You know, we're just two people hanging out. Right? We don't *owe* anything to one another or anything like that."

He regards me questioningly. "Is that what you want? For this to be a casual thing? 'Because I didn't get the impression you did."

What I want? Is he *kidding*? He's the most amazing man I've met in my entire life, and I've told him I want a fling. When in reality I want the works with him: marriage, kids, the whole shebang.

I swallow hard, wondering how best to answer. On the one hand I'm aching to tell him how much he means to me, how much I want to be with him. On the other, making myself vulnerable like that is the most frightening thing I could imagine. I'm just not sure I could take the rejection from him if he doesn't feel the same way.

"I, err—" I stammer, biting my lip. "I don't know."

Thankfully, he saves me. He looks deep into my eyes. "Brooke, I'm falling in love with you."

I swallow hard, my heart squeezing. *He loves me?*

I reach up and grab him around his neck, planting a kiss on his lips. "Really?" I squeak, almost not trusting my ears.

"Yes," he laughs. "The time I've spent with you has been the best time of my life. Brooke, you have to know how I feel about you. This isn't just a fling for me. And I hope it isn't for you, either."

All week I'd been dreading what would happen once Logan left, denying how strong my feelings for him are. The cleanest and easiest thing to do would be to let him leave and just be done with it. Call this a fun fling and move on with our separate lives. That's the sensible thing to do, the rational, level-headed thing.

But, as I said to Alexis, the heart wants what the heart wants. And my heart most certainly wants Logan McManus. With great big, shiny bells on.

A tear trickles down my cheek as relief floods through me. Since I broke up with Scott I've been denying myself even the possibility of a relationship with a man. And now I've let my barriers down, I've found someone twice the man Scott was.

And not only that, he loves me.

"I love you too, Logan," I whisper.

"You'll come and see me then?"

"Just try and stop me."

"That's what we'll do," he says eagerly, causing me to smile from ear to ear. "You can visit me then I can come back here to see you. That way we could see each other every month."

My heartbeat quickens at the prospect of being with him again, of having an actual relationship with him. "That would be so wonderful."

"I'm going to Eastern Europe at the end of the month, so come and see me afterwards. We won't be together for a month, but it will be worth the wait."

"Okay. I'll book something." I'm so happy I could pop. We're in love!

"I don't want this to end, Brooke." He leans down to kiss me again, this time more intensity.

"Me neither," I murmur, happily submitting myself to his kisses, my insatiable desire for him rushing through my body once more.

* * *

The following morning we reluctantly shower and dress and Logan packs his bag.

"Here." He holds out a small package. "I got something for you. Call it a memento of our time together. And a sign of what's yet to come."

I take the package from his outstretched hand and unwrap it quickly, pulling out a solitaire diamond necklace I look at in disbelief.

"Allow me?" He takes the necklace from me as I sweep my hair to the side for him to do the clasp. "Beautiful."

I turn to the mirror above my chest-of-drawers, regarding my reflection, my hand instantly reaching up to touch the sparkling diamond.

He wraps his arms around my waist from behind, regarding my reflection in the mirror. "I want you to know how much you mean to me. That I'm serious about us. This is a symbol of my love."

I flush with delight. "Thank you, Logan. Thank you so much. It's so beautiful." I turn towards him and pull him in for a kiss.

He chuckles gently. "I'm glad you like it."

"Wait right there." I dart into my closet, pulling out the gift I'd bought him. I return a moment later holding it out to him. "It's not in the diamond necklace league, but I hope you like it."

He opens the gift, pulling out a framed shot the bungy jump photographer took of us mid-descent. We're clasped together, screaming our heads off: Logan looking ecstatic, me looking exhilarated with perhaps a hint of panic in my eyes.

"Where it all began." He holds the photo in his hands. "I didn't think you wanted a copy of this. I mean we kinda left the bungy place pretty fast, didn't we? How did you get it?"

"It was easy, really." I laugh at the huge gulf between our gifts. "I rang them and ordered a copy."

"It's going on my desk at work. Thanks, Brooke."

I look at my watch. With a jolt I realise we need to get Logan to the airport. "We've got to go."

Once checked in, I walk Logan to his gate where boarding has already begun.

"I hope your stepmom's surgery goes really well."

"Yeah, me too."

He takes my hands in his. "You know this isn't goodbye, don't you?"

"I know." I smile up at him. Oh, my—he's gorgeous. "I'll book something for the weekend of the fourth."

He looks down at me, his eyes filled with what I now know is his love for me. "Meeting you has been the best thing to happen to me."

"Me too." I know it to be true with all my soul.

We hug, kissing one another one final time.

"I love you, Logan."

"I love you too."

He picks up his hand luggage and walks towards the security checkpoint. I hug myself with my arms as I watch him leave, willing him to turn around once more. He does so with a smile and a short wave, and I have to fight back the tears as I watch him hand over his boarding pass and disappear around the corner.

CHAPTER 16

IT'S TEN HOURS AND thirty-seven minutes since Logan left—yes, I'm counting—and I've dragged myself out of my bed to meet Laura and Alexis for a drink. My body had demanded some serious sleep once Logan had gone, having been deprived during the past couple of weeks thanks to our rather fantastic nocturnal activities, so most of my day has been spent in the land of slumber.

Laura, Alexis, and I have settled into a table at Hummingbird, a chic restaurant in downtown Wellington. Laura reaches into her bag, pulling out two light blue envelopes, handing us each one. "Take this as a clear threat: you had both better be there."

I take mine and pull out a birthday party invitation. "Oh, Laura. A cocktail party? How fun."

"I know. I can't wait," she replies, eagerly.

"Thanks, Laura. Tim and I will definitely be there," Alexis says.

"Me too. On my own, that is." I feel a sting of sadness Logan won't be there with me. He's barely left the country and I'm already experiencing the pain of a long distance relationship.

"Great! I figure if we have to turn thirty, we may as well do it—" she pauses.

"What? In style?" Alexis asks.

"Drunk," she pronounces with a wicked glint in her eye.

"Thirty? Laura, please don't mention it." I bury my head in my hands.

"Turning thirty isn't bad," Laura protests. "It's just a number."

"It's fine for you. You have it all worked out," I reply.

Alexis nods. "You do. Great husband, gorgeous kids."

Laura beams. "I guess. You do as well. You're about to get married, Alexis, and you run your successful business, Brooke."

I don't know what it is about turning thirty, but it feels like a significant watershed moment. I'm standing at the edge of a high cliff, about to jump and—if I had done what I was meant to have by now—I would have my career, husband, and family as a safety net, ready to catch me. I might have my career sorted out and have fallen in love with Logan, but I have a long way to go.

"Let's see your beautiful ring again, Alexis," I say, deciding a change of subject would be helpful about now.

Needing little encouragement, Alexis extends her left hand with pride and Laura and I 'ooh' and 'ahh' over its sparkling beauty.

"Have you set a date?" Laura asks.

"Not yet. We're too busy basking in the excitement of the engagement, I guess." She looks like she could practically brim over with joy, and I'm so happy for my dear friend. "I don't want it to be too long, though."

"What's the rush?" Laura asks. Her eyes widen. "Any *other* news you want to share with us?"

Alexis laughs. "I'm not pregnant, if that's what you're asking. But I'd like to be. *After* the wedding. Can you imagine my mother if I had a baby 'out of wedlock', as she would call it. Blimey O'Reilly, she would go ballistic!"

Being from a large Irish Catholic family having a baby exactly nine months after your wedding day is acceptable. Anything less? Well, let's just say Alexis's life wouldn't be worth living.

I laugh. "She would send a personal letter to the Pope, having you excommunicated."

"Exactly," Alexis replies. "It's *so* not worth the family grief. We're going to do it in the traditional order."

Laura turns her attention to me. "So? How about you, missy? Any news?"

"We've agreed the contract and I am now officially moving *Live It* into new markets." I beam with pride, thinking about how my plan has come off.

"Oh, yay!" Laura exclaims as Alexis says, "How fantastic."

"Thanks. I'm so excited about it. But you have to keep it to yourselves for now. I'm not announcing it to the team until

Monday."

"Mum's the word," Laura replies. "You must have been working hard on that over the last week or so. I haven't seen or heard from you."

"Umm, yes. Really hard. I've been putting in long hours, umm, securing the, err, deal." Even I can tell I'm thoroughly unconvincing.

Alexis bursts into laughter and I blush every shade of red. "Some deal."

"What?" I try to appear indignant.

And fail.

Laura's eyes dart between Alexis and I. "The deal isn't all that you've been up to, is it? I can tell." She assesses me through narrowed eyes and I squirm under her gaze. "And you know about it too, don't you, Alexis?" she accuses, Alexis looking sheepish in response.

Finally, I can almost see the light bulb blaze above her head as she exclaims, "You've had *sex*, haven't you, Brooke?"

Several people at neighbouring tables turn to look at us, their attention piqued, and I'm tempted to slip under the table.

"Laura!" I berate through gritted teeth.

"Deny it if you like," she challenges, sitting back in her chair, folding her arms.

"How did you know?" I ask in disbelief.

"I didn't. But ha! I was right," she replies, a satisfied look spreading across her face. "You can't hide anything from me, Brooke Mortimer. I know you too well."

"You may as well confess," Alexis chimes.

"Is it the American guy we met at the restaurant? The one you're doing that deal with? Logan something?"

I blush instantly at the mention of his name, confirming Laura's suspicions.

"Good work," she replies, impressed. "He was cute. Way to go having a fling with a totally hot guy. And no strings attached, either. Good for you. He's back in the States now, is he?"

"He stayed for an extra week. *For Brooke*," Alexis adds.

"Really?" Laura widens her eyes. "Tell me everything."

I flush with pleasure as I tell Laura about everything: from our bungy jump kiss through to our declaration of love for one another.

"Needless to say, I have a *lot* of work to catch up on now he's gone. Oh, and, he gave me this." I touch my diamond solitaire necklace. I had been wearing a scarf, so I pull it off in order to show the necklace to its best advantage.

"Oh, my god, it's gorgeous!" Laura exclaims.

"It is. Lucky you," Alexis adds. "He must be so into you."

"Either that or he's stinking rich," Laura adds.

"I think he does okay." Actually, I have no idea whether he's rich. It never occurred to me to ask. Come to think of it, I didn't ask him a whole lot of things.

"I'm going to see him next month in San Francisco, then he's coming back to Wellington the following month."

I'll put together a list of all the things I need to know about him then.

"So you're doing the long distance thing?" Alexis asks, raising her eyebrows.

"Yes." I feel a surge in confidence at our ability to make it work. "We are. We're in love." I grin from ear to ear.

"Wow!" Alexis exclaims. "Really?"

"Yes." I flush with joy at the thought of Logan. "I wasn't looking for it. It just happened, you know?"

I catch Alexis dart a look at Laura out of the corner of my eye.

"Sweetie, I'm so happy for you. But this is moving pretty fast," Laura says.

"How long was he here? Was it two weeks?" Alexis asks.

"Twelve days," I reply, suddenly struck by how short a time I've actually known him. And how fast our feelings for one another have developed.

I've never really believed in love at first sight, but I'm now a happy convert, kicking my cynical butt to the curb.

"Sure, it's not long, but that doesn't matter. I've never felt like this about anyone else. *Ever.* It's like we're meant to be."

"But you're just starting to get to know each other in that time," Laura says, shaking her head. "It's the lust phase."

"I remember that," Alexis comments, smiling wistfully. "Loads of sex, anywhere, any time."

"That was a long time ago for me and Kyle. Bliss." She sighs.

Clearing her throat, Laura gets back on track. "Are you sure it's not just lust, Brooke? I mean, he's hot and you hadn't had sex in a long, long time."

"Don't rub it in," I protest.

"She's right," Alexis adds, nodding. "It's very easy to confuse love with lust when you meet someone new."

"Come on you guys. It's not like things had died down there or anything. I know it's fast, but when you know, you know."

I smile to myself. I *know* this is love. I *know* Logan is the one. It's as simple as that.

"And anyway, we don't all have the luxury of meeting our future husband at the tender age of fifteen, you know, Laura. Some of us have to take what we can get."

Why do I have such stick-in-mud friends?

"Can you please be happy for me? You wanted me to meet someone, to fall in love. And now I have."

Sensing they're pushing me too far, Alexis tries to placate me. "Babe, we're so happy for you. Really. You're an amazing woman and you deserve every happiness. We just remember what happened with Scott and we don't want you to go through that again."

"You were a total wreck when you broke up with Scott. We want you to be with a great guy, one who will make you happy."

I smile at them both, touched at how much they care. "Logan *is* a great guy. You have to believe me. I can see how you might be concerned. Hell, I was. But it feels different with him. I can't quite put my finger on it. It just . . . feels right."

"Well if you ever have any problems with him, just let me know. I've got a brother or two who could help you out," Alexis jokes.

"Thanks," I reply, laughing. "Oh, and speaking of Scott, just to show you how over him I am, I'm thinking of meeting him for a drink."

"You are?" Laura asks in surprise.

"Yes. He called, said he was coming to Wellington for a while and wondered if I'd like to catch up."

"Hmmm," Alexis says, clearly considering this new information.

"And you know what? I feel like I can see him and be absolutely fine about it, knowing I've found someone who leaves him for dust."

"Cheers! I'll drink to that," Laura says, raising her half-empty glass. "Here's to moving on."

"To moving on," I repeat. Thinking about Logan I add, "And to finding happiness."

CHAPTER 17

"GOOD MORNING, EVERYONE." I'M standing in front of the *Live It* team in the boardroom, dressed in what Stefan refers to as my 'kick ass' suit—a sharp, tailored Trelise Cooper number—my new diamond necklace sparkling at my neck. "I have an exciting announcement to make."

I'm facing a small sea—probably more of a pond, really—of eager faces, including our senior trainers, who have come in for the meeting.

"As of today, *Live It* is officially in partnership with *You: Now.*"

The news is met with cheering and clapping, and I lap it all up, basking in the success of our initiative.

"What this means is a lot of hard work. We entered this relationship with *You: Now* so we could break into new markets. And that's exactly what we're going to do, starting with Australia."

I had received an email from Geoff Friedlander's executive assistant, advising they were sending someone from their marketing team over to New Zealand next week to get the ball rolling. They seem as keen as we are to get started on this new adventure, which suits me just fine.

"Before we start all that hard work, I think we need to celebrate. Drinks at The Tasting Room on Friday night, if it suits everyone?"

There's a general murmur of approval in the room.

"First round's on me," I add to further cheers from the assembled masses.

After people have wandered back to their desks, Stefan walks over to me, giving me a high five.

"Awesome news, boss."

"It is, isn't it?"

We walk together into my office.

"They went for the clause, the one that allows us to get out of the deal whenever we like?"

"They sure did. But of course I'm hoping we won't ever have to use it. It's just a safeguard."

"Of course."

"You'll be spending a fair bit of time with this *You: Now* sales and marketing person. And they're not messing about with this. Apparently she arrives next Tuesday."

"Bring it on," he replies, happily.

I grin at him as I reflect on how much work we've put into achieving this goal, and how good it feels now we have.

"What's her name? I'll check her out online."

"Oh, it's—" I scroll through my emails until I find the relevant one. "—Lana Tomkinson."

I'm secretly relieved they're not sending over another good-looking man. If Logan's and Brad's time here is anything to go by, people at my company could well do without the distraction.

"Cool. I'm on it." He turns to leave my office.

"Thanks. You're the best."

"You know it." He grins cheekily. "And, hey. I'm glad that whole Logan and Brad argument thing was just a storm in a teacup."

"Me too," I reply. "Me too."

* * *

Later that day I arrive at Dad and Jennifer's place for dinner. I'd offered to bring takeaways to save them having to cook, but Jennifer insisted, announcing she was serving her famous chicken cacciatore, a Mortimer family favourite.

"Hey, Jennifer."

I walk through the front door and straight into the kitchen, giving her a hug. She hugs me back quickly before returning her attention to her cooking.

"Lovely to see you Brooke," she replies.

Is it just my imagination or does she say that a little fast?

136

My stomach does a flip-flop as I think about her impending surgery, and I'm finding I have to work hard at staying positive and bright right now. I need to keep my shit together: for me, for my family, and especially for Jennifer.

The excitement of falling in love with Logan and signing the partnership contract has provided me with a welcome distraction. Now it's almost D-Day, though, I'm becoming increasingly worried for her.

"You're just in time for dinner. Any later and you'd have missed it. Imagine that?" she says in a ridiculously bright tone.

I regard her with uncertainty. Her eyes are shining, wider than usual, lending her an almost feverish look I haven't seen before. It's unsettling.

"Well, what are you standing there for? Go and call the others. Go on." She hurries me out of the kitchen.

"Sure. Whatever you say," I reply, then pause before I add, "Are you okay?"

"Me?" She looks at me as though I've just asked her the most outlandish thing. "Yes, of course I am. Why wouldn't I be?"

"No reason." I back carefully out of the kitchen. "Where are they?"

Without looking up from her cooking, she replies, "Grace and your Dad are in the living room and Dylan's probably in his bedroom. He's been even more of a monosyllabic teenager than usual this week, that boy."

Teenagers are a law unto themselves, and Dylan sure does seem to have bought into that whole awkward, moody cliché lately.

"Well, what are you waiting for? Dinner's not going to get eaten by itself."

I turn and hightail it away.

I walk through the rabbit warren of their house, opening the door to the living room. I notice Grace and Dad sitting quietly on the sofa together. She's holding a box of tissues, which, by the looks of their puffy eyes, they've both been utilising.

"Hey there." I go straight to them.

"Brooke," Grace says in a wavering tone. She stands to hug me, Dad joining in after a moment.

"It's going to be all right, girls," Dad says.

"Ib it? How boo doo doe?" Grace asks before blowing her nose.

I grab the cane rubbish bin next to the sofa, and she drops her used tissues in it, darting me a grateful look.

"I don't know," Dad replies. He looks crestfallen.

A shot of worry runs through my chest.

Dad shakes his head. "All I know is Jennifer is strong and determined to fight this. We have to support her, we have to love her."

Tears sting my eyes. "I just saw her. She's a bit... out of sorts tonight."

Dad gives a grim laugh. "She's been a bit manic for days. She won't admit to being worried about tomorrow, though. She keeps saying she's fine and I shouldn't fuss. I have to, though. She's my wife." His voice cracks.

Sadness shoots through me as I regard Dad with fresh eyes. He lost his first wife to cancer, and now he's having to go through it all again with his second. Life can be so cruel.

"She asked me to come and get you for dinner. It's ready."

Grace nods, taking a steadying breath. "I'll just clean myself up. You go ahead."

I walk down the corridor to Dylan's room and knock tentatively on the door. "Dylan, dinner."

There's no reply. I knock again. "Dylan," I say, louder.

Still no reply. I steal myself to face the teenage disaster of his bedroom and crack the door.

"Dylan! It's dinner time." I push the door open and take a couple of steps inside.

His room is dark and dingy, with piles of clothes on the floor and posters of bands I've never heard of on the walls. But what hits me between the eyes is the distinctive smell of marijuana hanging in the air.

Dylan is lying on his bed with his headphones on, nodding his head to music as he air drums to the beat, breaking occasionally to drag on the joint in his hand. He has yet to notice me.

"Dylan!" I shout, shutting the door behind me, reasoning there's no need for anyone else to have to witness his illegal, brain-stunting activity right now. They've got enough to deal with.

He finally notices me, ripping off his headphones and looking at me in surprise. He stubs out his joint on a saucer, pushing it behind his prostate body as he tries to arrange his features to look innocent of any wrongdoing.

"Too late, mate." I shake my head at him.

"What?" he says, his hands in the air. "I'm just burning some incense."

I laugh. "You can't pull that one on me. I was the queen of 'incense' when I was your age."

"You were?" He regards me in disbelief, seeing his boring older sister in a new light.

I pull the curtains and open the window to air the room.

"Hard to believe, I know, but once, many years ago, I too was teenager." I smile weakly at him and he relaxes as he realises I'm not about to rat him out to his parents.

"You're not going to tell Mum and Dad, then?" Hope flashes across his eyes.

I sit on the bottom of his bed, levelling him with a firm stare. "Not this time, Dylan. But don't do it at home again, okay?"

"Okay." He looks thoroughly relieved.

"And you know that crap is bad for you, don't you?"

"Yeah. It's not like I do it all the time, you know? Carl got some from his brother and this is the first time I've really tried it."

I regard him with doubt. "Next you'll be telling me you didn't inhale."

He has the decency to look abashed. "Well, no. But I don't do it all the time."

"Just as long as you don't. And you were lucky it was me who caught you and not your mum."

He shivers involuntarily. "She's been kind of crazy lately."

"Yes, she does seem a bit anxious today, that's for sure. How long has she been like that?"

"Oh, a few days. That's why this is good." He nods at the makeshift ashtray. "I needed some chill time."

"Well, she's about to go through something big tomorrow morning. She's nervous. It's completely understandable."

"She's got this weird look in her eyes, though. Like she's going to knife someone."

I guffaw. "That's rather specific, Dylan."

"A guy at school knifed someone, and he had the same look." As though that explains it.

"Really?" I'm shocked. Things might have been rough when I was a teenager, but the only knives we used were verbal. "Hey, I wouldn't worry. I don't think she'll be knifing anyone any time soon."

He smiles at me, but I can see the sadness in his eyes. "Do you think she's going to be okay?"

"I do," I reply with considerably more conviction than I feel. "She's a tough old bird, that mother of yours."

"*Ours*," he corrects me.

Wow. Out of the mouths of babes.

I look at Dylan and realise for a teenager, he's pretty clued up. Jennifer may not be the woman who gave me life, but she's been there for me through thick and thin, through bullies and braces, through best friends and boyfriends. She's loved me unconditionally—she still does—and I know she always will.

Yes, she's my mother. I love her so much it hurts. And these last weeks have shown me just how important she is in my life.

"Ours."

I smile and he smiles back at me.

"Anyway, I came to tell you dinner's ready." I stand up.

He swings his legs over the side of the bed. "I'll be right down."

I walk to the door, then turn to face him. "I get that you're going through some stuff right now, but you need to be careful. Bad stuff can happen when you mess with drugs."

He grins at me and I'm struck by how handsome he's becoming. It can be hell navigating through your teenage years, but the light at the end of the tunnel is close for him, and I'm confident he'll turn out just fine. "Sure, sis."

Dylan follows me into the dining room where Grace, Jennifer, and Dad are already sitting. Jennifer has pulled out all the stops tonight. She had mentioned she was cooking chicken cacciatore but has also cooked elaborate vegetable dishes and no less than three different types of carbs to go with it: a pasta salad; roasted kumara, potatoes, and carrots; and a large bowl of sticky rice.

It's a truly carb-tastic feast.

I'm going to have to work extra hard tomorrow morning to run it all off. As the saying goes, a moment on the lips is a lifetime on the hips, and I'm not exactly blessed with the naturally skinny genes Grace and Dylan got. It can be exhausting, quite frankly, but the alternative doesn't thrill me.

"Now, eat up, eat up," Jennifer instructs, her voice going almost nuclear, her eyes wild.

"It looks great," I say, as Grace, Dylan, and Dad repeat similar positive things.

There's no mention of the looming surgery tomorrow morning, and, other than Jennifer's frenzied insistence we finish everything on the table—I've mentally added another three kilometres to my morning run—the evening goes well enough, all things considered.

By the end of the meal I'm so full I could roll down the hill to my Thorndon house.

"Are you feeling a bit better about things now?" I ask Grace as I stand at the basin, washing the endless dishes Jennifer's feast created.

"I guess," she replies unconvincingly.

I give her a side-on hug and she hangs her head.

"Are you visiting her after?" I ask.

"I'm going to spend the whole day at the hospital. Sod work."

"But she's adamant we don't come," I protest. "We need to respect her wishes."

"No way. I want to be there, so I'm going to be. End of story."

I smile to myself in admiration of Grace's conviction, resolving to be there with her tomorrow myself. "Me too. Sod work, as you might say."

She gives me a grateful, damp kiss on the cheek. "She goes in at nine."

"I'll be there."

* * *

Early the following morning my phone rings, waking me from my slumber. I get a thrill when I see it's Logan.

"Hey, honey. How are you doing?" he asks as soon as I answer.

Tears sting my eyes at the sound of his voice. "I'm all right, I guess."

"Convincing."

"I'm a bit over talking about it, to be honest. I just want the surgery done now. How about you? I need something to distract me. Tell me about all the fabulous things you've been doing in San Francisco today."

"I've been sitting in my office, looking at the beautiful view, thinking about you most of the day, actually."

A smile creeps across my face. "That sounds like a pretty unproductive thing to do. But I like it."

"What can I say? I'm a man obsessed."

"You certainly have good taste, I'll give you that," I tease.

"I did do one thing, though. I booked my flights to Eastern Europe. I go Monday."

"How long are you away?"

"It should be about a week, all going to plan. Unless I meet a woman I fall in love with and decide to stay on, that is."

"You'd better not," I warn.

After saying our reluctant farewells I get out of bed, preparing myself to face whatever the day brings. I'm considerably lighter, knowing Logan's thinking of me, even if he is ten thousand kilometres away.

CHAPTER 18

I ARRIVE AT THE hospital the following morning just before nine. I'm met by the entire family, waiting nervously outside the pre-op ward. Only Jeremy is missing from the Mortimer clan this morning, and he has the rock solid excuse of living on the other side of the world. Even so, he did call last night.

"Hey, everyone." I hug each of them. "What are you doing standing out here?"

"Morning, kiddo," Dad says quietly. "Jennifer's in with the doctor right now. I thought it best we give her some space. Sleep well?"

"Ah, no. But it doesn't matter." I had spent a fitful night, bizarre and unusual thoughts pinging around my head, until I had finally fallen asleep sometime in the wee hours. "How is she today?"

Dad smiles. "She's doing okay."

"Yeah, less whacko," Dylan adds, rolling his eyes.

"Dylan," Dad reprimands as Grace nudges him.

"What?" he protests, arms out, shrugging. "It's not like you didn't all think it."

"She has had a lot on her mind," Dad concedes.

Dad's phone rings. He looks at the screen. "I have to take this."

"Sure, Dad," I reply. I turn to my sister. "How are you doing, Grace?"

She lets out a deep sigh and attempts a smile as tears well in her eyes. "I'm okay."

"That bad, huh?" I give her a long hug.

"I'll be better once this is over."

"Yeah, we all will."

I look over at Dad and notice him pacing from left to right as he talks hurriedly into his phone. He looks so stressed he could explode in spectacular fashion at any moment.

A few more minutes and a kilometre or more of pacing he returns to our little group.

"Bloody work," he says by way of explanation.

"What's up?" I ask.

"Bloody Sydney Garrett's poached my best guy."

Sydney Garrett has been his long time property development rival. They've come up against one another on numerous projects in the past and there's not exactly a lot of love lost between them. And that's putting it mildly.

"I can't believe he would do that to me. Not now." His mouth forms a thin line. I can tell he's working hard to contain his emotions, to appear strong for his family when we need him most.

The doctor approaches us. "Gosh, there's certainly a few of you here," she comments, taking in Dylan, Grace, Dad, and myself. We're all standing, huddled anxiously together. "You can go in. We're just about to prep her."

"Thank you, Doctor," Dad says.

We gather around Jennifer's bed, Dylan hanging back from us all. She's dressed in the unattractive regulation hospital gown, her hair pulled back, her face pale but otherwise serene: quite the opposite from her almost feverish appearance last night.

"What are you all doing here?" she asks, taking in the large group gathering at the end of the bed. "I told you not to come," she scolds, shaking her head, her face nevertheless breaking into a smile.

"Brooke, darling, come here," she says, her arms outstretched.

I obey, giving her a hug and kiss.

"How are you doing?"

"Actually, I'm doing great." She looks surprised herself.

We heave a collective sigh of relief as it becomes clear she's back to normal.

I let out a little nervous laugh. "Good. You're going to be fine today." I sound considerably more positive than I feel.

"What did the doc say, darling?" Dad asks her, swapping places with me.

Grace stands nervously beside me and Dylan looks down, kicking his feet.

"She talked me through the procedure and told me they'll be in to prep me soon. It all sounds pretty straightforward, nothing we haven't been told before. I told her I'm ready for it."

Grace raises her eyebrows, shooting me a look that says, "Yeah, it's only *cancer* surgery". I dart her a sympathetic look. Jennifer may have come to terms with what's happening to her today, but the rest of us continue to struggle with it.

The curtain is pulled open with a screech, causing Grace and me both to jump and for Dylan to almost stand up straight, abandoning the slouch he is so dedicated to these days.

"Hi, Moira. Welcome to the madhouse," Jennifer says to the nurse.

"It's like Grand Central Station in here," Nurse Moira comments, looking around us all.

Jennifer beams.

Nurse Moira looks for a way through the narrow space to Jennifer. With an exasperated look on her face, she says, "Righto, you lot. Time to get your things and head out. We've got a procedure to prepare for, here."

She's a no nonsense kind of woman, with her hair in a ponytail pulled so tight, an image of her face dropping a good few centimetres when she loosens it pops into my mind. Despite the tension in the room, I let out a muffled laugh at the thought and realise I'm only a hair's breadth from hysteria.

"I love you, Mum," Grace says, her voice wavering as she gives Jennifer a peck on the cheek.

I follow suit, pulling her in for a ginger hug. I'm hit afresh by the enormity of the day, and my eyes well with tears. "I love you, too, Mum." I try out my new name for her.

She regards me with momentary surprise, before her face creases into a beautiful smile, her hand on mine. "I love you too, Brooke."

My tears spill down my face.

"Yeah, ditto," Dylan mutters, peering at Jennifer through his straggly fringe before sloping out of the room.

Pulling myself together, I turn to my siblings. "Let's head out. Give Dad a moment with her, okay?"

"Don't you worry about your mum," Nurse Moira says to me quietly as I shimmy past her. "She'll be right as rain."

"Thanks. Please take care of her for us. She's precious cargo."

I glance back at the woman sitting in the bed, smiling cheerfully at Moira, and am hit by a mix of emotions: concern and sadness, but most of all love.

She's my mum, pure and simple.

* * *

"The surgery went very well, very well indeed," Doctor Chan says, smiling at us.

We've been waiting in one of the sparse hospital waiting rooms while Jennifer's been operated on, and we all jump to our feet—even Dylan, who doesn't seem to do anything with speed these days—the moment the Doctor walks into the room.

"That's great news," Dad replies, letting out a sigh of relief.

We hug one another in relief, glad the waiting is now over.

"What happens now?"

"Right now she needs to rest," the doctor replies. "Once she's recovered from the surgery in about a month, she'll need to start radiation therapy to give her the best chance of a full recovery."

"And is that it?" Grace asks, hope in her eyes.

"No. The type of cancer your mum has is hormone receptor-positive, which means she'll have hormone therapy too. But that's further down the track."

"Oh." I'm struck by the fact the surgery is only the first step in her treatment, and that she has a long road to full recovery. A very long road.

"How long will all that take?" Grace asks.

"The radiation therapy will be for five to six weeks and she'll have to have it every week day."

"She's aware of all of this. She knows what she's in for," Dad says. "She's strong. She'll be able to cope, especially with our help."

I nod grimly as Grace hugs herself, looking forlorn, and Dylan kicks the ground.

"Someone will let you know when you can go in to see her," Doctor Chan adds before she turns to leave.

"Thanks, Doctor," Dad says. "For everything."

She smiles and nods at us before leaving.

* * *

A few days later, with Jennifer safely ensconced at home and Dad fussing over her, I take my team to The Tasting Room, a lively bar in Wellington's restaurant- and bar-packed Courtenay Place, to celebrate the partnership deal.

"To new and exciting beginnings." I raise my glass.

The whole *Live It* team is there and the atmosphere is one of excitement and expectation for the future.

The small group echoes me, sipping their respective drinks.

Jocelyn collects me up in one of her maternal bear hugs. "You must be stoked, love."

"I am, I *so* am. It's everything we wanted, and now it's about to happen."

I know I'm grinning from ear to ear, but what with being in love, signing this agreement, *and* having Jennifer come through her surgery with flying colours, life is pretty darn good. "Can I pour you a glass of bubbles?" I ask, noticing Jocelyn's cradling a Coke.

"No, I'll just stick with my fizzy. Ta, love."

I smile, thinking if Logan were here I would have to act as translator.

As though reading my mind, Jocelyn asks, "Have you heard from Logan lately?"

"Logan? Ah, no," I stumble, lying poorly.

She gives me a crooked grin. "Oh, you can't slip a fast one by me, Brooke. I know you have eyes for him. And he does for you, too."

We have more than *eyes* for each other. I dither over how to respond.

"Did you bonk him?" she asks with characteristic candour, and I spurt out my mouthful of drink onto the floor, thankfully missing my colleagues by a whisker.

A look of guilt must flash across my face, as she answers her own question with a grin on her face. "Oh, Brooke. You did. You corker."

I'm unable to suppress a laugh at this woman I think of as a mother, congratulating me on having sex.

"He's a looker all right, that Logan. And a keeper, I'd say."

"He is. Please don't mention anything, Jocelyn. We want to keep it quiet. At least until the partnership is set up properly."

"Mum's the word." She taps her nose.

"What are you two gossiping about?" Stefan asks. He wraps an arm around each of us, providing me with a reprieve.

"The contract, of course," Jocelyn replies immediately. I flash her a thankful look.

"I'll drink to that," Stefan says, taking a deep gulp of champagne. "Boss, we have to hold a Sydney seminar first, got it?"

"Why?" Although I already know his answer.

"All those gorgeous boys over there, of course, waiting for us to fix them." He smiles lasciviously.

Jocelyn shakes her head at him. "Stefan, you're like a bitch in heat."

"And that's a bad thing, how?" he asks her, arching one eyebrow.

She shakes her head. "Ooh, would you look at the time?" She looks at her watch. "I've got to rattle my dags. My granddaughter's school play is on tonight and she'll have my guts for garters if I miss it. Bye, loves."

She downs what's left of her Coke and gives both Stefan and me a kiss on the cheek.

"Bye," we both say as she farewells the rest of the team and heads out the door.

I order another bottle of champagne for the troops, thankful the *You: Now* buyout of fifty per cent of my business is about to provide me with a decent injection of cash.

We're a small, close-knit, hard working team: treating them to the occasional drink is but a small token of my indebtedness to them.

After we've polished off the second bottle I announce I'm going to head home. It really has been quite a week, and I'm suddenly exhausted.

"I'll go with you," Stefan says as we put on our jackets.

"Thanks. I would have thought you'd have somewhere fabulous to be on a Friday night."

"Oh, I do." He holds the door for me to walk through. "But I'll walk with you on my way."

"You are generosity itself," I jest as we dodge the hordes of revellers congregating in Courtenay Place.

As we round a corner I stumble over a prostrate figure slouching against the wall, kicking him or her in the leg by accident.

Stefan shoots out a steadying arm and I flash him a grateful look.

"I'm so sorry," I say. "I didn't see you there. Are you okay?"

The prostrate figure raises its head.

I rear back in shock. "Dylan? Oh, my god! What are you doing here?"

I squat down next to him, brushing the hair from his face. He stinks of cheap wine and cigarettes.

"Brooke? Hey, Brooke. Look everyone, it's Brooke," he slurs to no one in particular.

"You know this street kid?" Stefan asks with more than a hint of distaste.

"Yes. And he's not a street kid. He's my kid brother."

"Eeeugh," he replies in revulsion.

"Don't be such a princess, Stefan. Help me get him up." I hook one of Dylan's arms over my shoulder. "We need to get him out of here."

Stefan leans down and begrudgingly hooks Dylan's other arm over his shoulder, holding his scarf over his mouth in protest at his stench.

"I know. He stinks. I get it," I say in irritation as we stagger down the side street, Dylan's head lolling about like a bobble head toy. "My car's just down there."

We reach my car after having nearly dropped Dylan a couple of times, and I open the passenger door. Stefan helps me deposit Dylan gingerly in the seat as I buckle him in.

"No vomiting, mister." It's more of a hope than an instruction.

"Sure, no problem, sis," he slurs. "No vomiting. Got it." He raises his hand in a salute, poking himself in the eye. "Ow!"

Shaking my head, I close the passenger door and turn to thank Stefan, who is brushing himself down in disgust.

"Does he do this a lot?" he asks.

"What? No. He's just a kid. I've actually never seen him drunk before."

"Well, sweetie. I'm going to leave you with *this*." He points through the window at my brother before giving me a quick hug.

"Have a fun night." I get into my car and flash Dylan a nervous look.

"I'd say 'you too', but I have a feeling my night will be considerably better than yours." He nods at Dylan who is now sound asleep, his head on the side with drool dripping out of the side of his mouth.

Nice.

I turn the ignition and drive bleakly through the streets. It's not a good idea to take Dylan to Dad and Jennifer's place—not with what they're dealing with right now—so I head to mine, grateful it's just a short drive.

As I pull up in front of my townhouse, I begin to wonder how I'm going to singlehandedly get Dylan out of the car and into my house.

The best—the only—approach is to wake Dylan up and get him to walk as best he can with my support.

"Dylan," I say once I've opened his door. "Dylan, I need you to wake up."

He responds by snorting loudly, rolling his head to the other side.

"Dylan!" Louder this time.

He stirs. "What?" he asks in irritation.

"I need you to wake up. We have to walk to my place, and I can't lift you on my own."

"No, don't want to. Go away."

I decide brute force will have to be deployed, so I unbuckle his belt and give him a decent prod.

"Ow-ah!" he yells, looking in my general direction, unable to focus.

I pull on his arm. "Let's go. Now." I use my best 'don't-mess-with-your-big-sister' tone.

He surprises me by swinging one leg and then another out of the car and I pull him up by his arms. He appears to be steady, so I support his weight on one side as we stagger to my front door.

Just as I'm trying to reach into my handbag to get my keys to open the door, he appears to forget how to walk, and drops to the ground, bringing me tumbling down with him. I land in a bush as he bursts into uncontrollable giggles, and then promptly passes out.

Great. It was hard enough getting him to stand from a sitting position, let alone a fully horizontal one.

I clamber out of the bush, pulling twigs and leaves from my hair. I pull out my phone and dial Grace's number. She answers within two rings and I heave a sigh of relief.

"Hey, Brooke. What's up?" She sounds like she's at a party or a bar somewhere. Whatever she's doing, she's having a significantly better evening than me.

"I need your help."

I explain the situation and she answers my prayers. "I'll be right there."

I sit patiently next to Dylan, brushing the hair out of his eyes. Only a few moments later, Grace arrives with another girl.

"Oh, thank god." I straighten up. "You got here quickly."

"We were at a party a few streets across," she replies, regarding at Dylan. "Look at the state of him." She squats down next to him. "Dylan, it's Grace. Are you okay?"

He looks at his sister and smiles. "Grace!" he says, sitting up, looking more sober than he has all evening. "Hi, Sammy Jo," he adds, looking at Grace's friend.

I blink at Sammy Jo, shocked by her appearance. She used to be a good-looking girl, like a younger version of her gorgeous older sister, but now she looks like she might have actually *swallowed* her gorgeous older sister. She must have put on half her body weight.

"Oh, Sammy Jo. Hi there. I err, didn't recognize you," I say.

"Hello." She looks at her feet.

I watch her, wondering what's happened to her self-assurance. She and Grace have been close friends for years, and she's always been so confident and out-going. The woman standing in front of me now seems almost her polar opposite.

"With three of us, this should be a breeze," Grace says. I have to admire her optimism.

"You take one arm, I'll take the other. Sammy Jo, you go behind him and catch him if he falls," I instruct.

With teamwork and a touch of brawn, we manage to get him inside. I lead him to the sofa and quickly put a bucket from the laundry on the floor beside him: if he's this drunk some of it is bound to come back up at some point. I really don't fancy having it pebble-dashed all over my soft furnishings.

Afterwards, the three of us stand in the kitchen, talking in hushed tones.

"Where did you find him?" Grace asks.

"Courtenay Place. He was propped up against the wall outside a bar, looking pretty much the same as he does right now."

"Has he done this before?" Sammy Jo asks.

"No," I reply at the precise time Grace replies, "Yes."

"What? Really?" I ask in surprise, turning to Grace.

She sighs. "He's been doing this sort of thing a bit lately. I think he's got in with a bad crowd at school. I've been worried about him for a while, but he won't talk to me about it. He just says all the guys are doing it and I need to just chill out."

"Well, he *is* a teenager. Most of us get a bit wild."

"I didn't," Grace replies.

"No, you were the ideal child, Grace," I tease. "I did it. Got up to all sorts of bad things."

Unlike me, Grace never rebelled, never did things she now regrets, both of which I did in spades. I guess she just didn't have anything to rebel against.

She could be the poster-child for the well-adjusted, balanced offspring of a complicated family. If there is ever a magazine dedicated to how to successfully produce a child out of the rubble of failed relationships and untimely deaths, Grace would be the cover model.

And centre-fold.

I shudder, thinking how I want to protect Dylan from doing the sorts of things I did as a teenager. I know I was as wild as I was because I was dealing with my Dad focussing on his new family, but Dylan *is* the new family. I don't see what he's rebelling against.

"Anyway," I continue, "I'll text Dad to say Dylan's decided to stay with me tonight. Do you girls want to hang out or are you going to head back to your party?"

The women look at one another. "Shall we head back?" Grace asks Sammy Jo.

She shrugs. "If you want to. I guess."

"Sam, you're virtually blinding me with your enthusiasm," Grace replies good-humouredly. "How about we just head back to your place and hang?"

Sammy Jo's face instantly lights up. "Sure."

"Want to borrow a movie?" I offer. "I've got loads."

I direct them to my DVD library by the TV. "Take whatever you like."

"Oh, my god, Brooke. You have every rom com known to man— and woman," Grace comments, returning with a large selection.

"I'm working my way through a list of the top one hundred," I reply, embarrassed.

I put a glass of water on the table next to the now snoring Dylan.

"Why? Not enough romance in your life? Oh, but you have that new boyfriend, don't you? The American, right?" She elbows me playfully and warmth spreads through my belly at the thought of him.

"Yeah, I do." The perpetual grin I get whenever I think of him is plastered across my face. "His name is Logan. He left last weekend. I'm going over to see him soon."

I feel a surge of excitement. I've booked my flights and have already begun to plan my wardrobe for the trip, including a new slinky number I purchased at a high-end lingerie shop during the week for our, umm, nocturnal activities.

"That's awesome, Brooke. I'm so happy for you."

I glance over at Sammy Jo, still perusing the DVD shelves. "What's going on with Sammy Jo?" I ask Grace quietly. "She's, err, not herself."

"Yeah, I don't know," she replies, looking over at her friend. "I guess she's just missing her boyfriend. He left Wellington and they've been doing the long distance thing for a while now. I'm not sure it's working out that well."

"Oh." My mind inevitably darts to Logan.

She takes in my expression. "Not that I don't think long distance relationships *can* work, of course. Just she's not coping too well with it."

"Wow, Sam, you've certainly got a lot of movies there," Grace says, eyeing the pile Sammy Jo has in her hands.

"Is it okay with you?" Sammy Jo asks.

"Sure," I reply, smiling. "Take as many as you want."

I haven't felt the need to watch them as often as I had been. I guess these days I'm living my own romantic comedy.

And just like in the movies, I know exactly who I'm going to end up with.

CHAPTER 19

"MORNING, SUNSHINE." I OPEN the blinds in the living room, allowing the watery early morning light to shine through.

In response, Dylan emits a guttural, almost animalistic grunt as he rolls away from the light, burying his head in one of my scatter cushions.

I had left him to sleep last night's overindulgence off on the sofa, covering him up with a couple of spare blankets to keep him warm before I headed to bed.

I spot the bucket on the floor. It's empty—impressive.

"Here." I put some ibuprofen and a fresh glass of water on the coffee table in front of him.

He rolls over with reluctance, shielding his eyes with his hand.

"Do you have to have those open?" he croaks, squinting in the morning light.

"Yes. I'm off on a run. You need to wake up and face the day."

"Sure, sis. Any moment." He sounds unconvincing as he rolls over again and buries his face in his pillow.

I smile as I close the front door behind myself. Today isn't going to be much fun for him. He's going to feel much like a rat died on his tongue while someone whacks his head with a baseball bat.

Just your standard hangover, then.

Hopefully he'll remember this the next time he decides to drink with his so-called 'friends': the ones who abandoned him, passed out, on the side of the road.

I arrive back at my house forty-five minutes later to find Dylan has vacated the sofa, steam from the shower creeping under the bathroom door.

"Put the fan on," I yell through the door before heading to the kitchen to make my daily green smoothie of kale, avocado, banana, and blueberries, with a handful of mint thrown in for taste.

About ten minutes later as I'm sipping my smoothie and I reading the Saturday morning paper, Dylan slinks into the kitchen. He's wrapped in a towel, wet hair dripping down the sides of his face.

"Hey." He looks abashed.

"Hi. You look a lot better than you did last night."

He takes a seat opposite me. "Yeah, sorry about that. Did I do anything embarrassing?"

"That depends on your definition of 'embarrassing'. If you're like me and you call being found by your sister slumped up against a wall, plastered, rambling almost incoherently 'embarrassing', then, yeah, I guess you did."

"Oh." He pales. "Where was I?"

"In Courtenay Place. Don't you remember me finding you?"

"Ah, no."

"Nothing? What's the last thing you remember, then?"

"Umm. I guess it was when we were up Mount Vic. Jono had bought some beers with his fake I.D. and we'd met these hot chicks." He grins. "I remember getting it on with the one with the big—" He pauses, embarrassed, belatedly realising who his audience is.

I raise my eyebrows at him. After not wanting to think about your parents ever, ever having sex, hearing about your sibling's sexual shenanigans ranks a close second.

"Err, anyway, I know they all came into town with me, but that's the last thing I remember."

"Some friends," I comment darkly.

"Nah. They're all right."

"You think? They left you lying on the ground in the city last night, drunk out of your skull. If I hadn't found you, who knows what would have happened to you? You'd have ended up in a cell for the night. I don't imagine that would be very much fun."

He swallows, nervous. "They wouldn't do that to a teenager, would they?"

"Absolutely."

"Oh," he replies. "I'm glad you found me, then, sis."

I offer him some of my smoothie as I pour some more into my glass, and he almost gags at the sight of it.

"I told Jennifer and Dad you decided to stay with me last night. I didn't mention why."

"Thanks. They would kill me if they knew." He shakes his head. "Ow. That hurts." He raises his hand to his head.

"Right. Here's the deal. I won't breathe a word of this to them if you tell me what's going on."

"What do you mean?" he asks, looking as innocent as an angel, wings fluttering in the celestial breeze. "I just had one or two too many."

I shoot him the look every older sibling the world over uses on their younger family members. He cowers in response.

Ah, the power.

He looks down at his hands. "I dunno," he shrugs. "Stuff."

"Care to elaborate on 'stuff?'"

"No." He crosses his arms.

"Look, I know your mum—" I correct myself, "—our mum is going through a difficult thing right now. But you heard the doctor; the surgery was a success. Now she just needs the hormone therapy and some radiotherapy. I know it'll be rough for her, but things are looking better than we thought they might. And she seems to be doing well."

"Yeah, I know." He hangs his head.

"Dylan, it's going to be okay," I say softly, putting my hand on his arm.

He takes a heavy sighs, looking across at me. "Yeah." He bites his lip.

I search his face. "There's something else, isn't there? Is it school? Friends? A girl?" I raise my eyebrows at him. Maybe he's in love? Lord knows people can act pretty strangely when they're in love.

"Nah. They're all sweet." He narrows his eyes at me. He looks like he's making up his mind about something. "It's you. You and Grace."

"Me and Grace?" I ask in disbelief.

"Yeah." He pauses, gathering his thoughts. "Nah. It's me."

I frown and wait for more.

He sighs. "In comparison with you two, I'm a total screw up."

"No, you're not!" I protest.

"Let me finish, okay?"

I nod.

"Grace is Mum and Dad's perfect daughter."

I nod. "Sure." She is pretty perfect, even to my older sister eyes.

"And you've got your big company and all. Dad thinks the sun goes out when *you* sit down."

My heart goes out to him. The poor kid feels so inadequate compared with his older sisters, he's drowning himself in alcohol and drugs. Never the best choice, no matter what your age—or reason.

Dylan absentmindedly takes a sip of the smoothie. He spits it out in disgust. "Yuck! What's in this thing? It's rank."

"It's good for you." I chuck him a cloth to wipe up the drink. "And a whole lot better than the cheap wine you stunk of last night, that's for sure."

He has the decency to look abashed. I pour him a fresh glass of water.

"Thanks." He takes a gulp.

"Dylan, you have to remember both Grace and I are a lot older than you. We've had time to work things out."

"I know. You're ancient." He shoots me a half grin.

"Thanks a lot." I hit him on the arm.

Jeez Louise. I'm only twenty-nine.

"But you always did well at school, you went to university, blah de blah. You did all the 'right things'. I've got no idea what I want to do with my life. You? You always knew. And now you've got all this." He gestures with his hands and we both automatically look around my house.

Wow, that's the longest sentence I've heard come out of my little brother's mouth in months.

I clear my throat. "Dylan, I was the biggest mess when I was at school. I got in with the most self-absorbed, nasty group of bitches to ever attend high school, I drank, did drugs, got up to things that would make your hair curl."

"Too late," he replies, smirking as he points at his curly mop.

I smile at him, shaking my head.

"You should get your facts straight before you take the time to rebel against something, you know." I give him another punch on the arm. "Seriously, though. Don't sweat it. You're going to turn out just fine."

"That's easy for you to say. You don't have to spend your life living up to you."

* * *

I drop Dylan off at home later in the morning, checking in on Jennifer in the process. I reiterated my promise not to mention a word about his recent nocturnal activities to either her or Dad on the proviso he clean up his act. I'll be keeping my big sister eye on him from now on, that's for sure.

On my drive back home I marvel at the irony of it all: I acted out as a teenager because I believed my parents' attention was being solely directed towards Dylan to my detriment. Now he feels like he can't live up to this image of me he's built in his head.

It just goes to show; we all get our panties in a twist about one thing or another.

As I walk through my front door, throwing my keys on the side table, my phone rings. It's a Face Time call from Logan.

"Hey, handsome," I answer as I get myself comfortable in my favourite chair.

"Hey, yourself." He's looking particularly delectable today in his work suit, much the way he did the day we met. It reminds me how much I wanted him from the moment I laid eyes on him.

It's Friday afternoon in San Francisco, hence the suit, and he looks like he's still in the office.

"How are you doing?" he asks.

I relay the details of my team drinks and bumping into the prostrate Dylan—literally—the night before.

"And you know what's weird? He's getting himself all tied up in knots because he thinks he could never live up to me. Like I'm this perfect, over-achieving sister our parents adore."

Logan shrugs. "Well, you are."

I smile. "I'm just as screwed up as the next person. And anyway, my point is I used to get myself upset as a teenager over *him*."

"There is a certain circularity to the equation, yes."

I laugh. "You sound like Doctor Spock, or Sheldon from The Big Bang Theory."

"I think you should be rather glad I'm neither of those two," he replies, raising his eyebrows.

Just as I'm about to reply he turns away from me to speak to someone else. I wait patiently for him to divert his attention back to me, my mind wandering to what it will be like to see him again when I visit San Francisco next month.

"Sorry about that." He turns back to the screen as he runs his hand through his hair. "It's kicking off here."

"Well if you have to go, then go," I comment, hoping he doesn't take me up on my offer. "You look stressed."

"There's a lot going on, that's all. Do you mind?"

What does he mean, do I mind? Of course I mind! I want to sit and talk and talk and talk, the way we do, basking in my love for him.

Instead, I shrug. I understand how important work is for him, just as it is for me. "Sure. Talk later?"

"Sounds good," he replies briskly, distracted.

"I love you," I coo, as I blow him a kiss. But he's already gone. I feel like a prize idiot, blowing kisses at my phone.

I sit and think for a while. Although things with Logan would be so much easier if he lived in the same city as me, it feels like we've got this whole long distance thing nailed. I'm just as close to him now—even more so—as I did when he was physically here with me, and now we have the excitement of seeing one another to look forward to.

My phone buzzes again and I notice it's my ex, Scott. I've removed the photo of him and me together on the beach from his contact information, replacing it with a much more appropriate shot of Elmer Fudd. I giggle before I answer.

"Hi, Scott. How are you?"

"I'm great, Brooke. How about you?" he replies in his American drawl.

I think about Logan and a smile spreads across my face. "I'm great too."

"Cool. I get to Wellington on Thursday. How about we meet for a drink Friday night?"

"You know what? That would be nice".

"Awesome. Meet you at eight? How about Ancient? For old time's sake."

I pause before I respond. Scott and I spent many evenings together at Ancient Bar and Restaurant, either just us or with friends. It became kind of 'our place'. It certainly has a long list of Scottsoaked memories for me.

I take a breath. I remind myself I'm a new woman now, a woman Scott has no power over. "Sure. For old time's sake. That sounds good."

If I can handle seeing him, I can handle meeting him at our old hang out. That's how much confidence Logan has given me.

CHAPTER 20

TUESDAY MORNING SWINGS AROUND. I'm working in my office when Stefan knocks on my door before walking straight in.

"Ready?"

Lara Tomkinson, the sales and marketing person from *You: Now*, is due to arrive any moment. Stefan has done his homework, speaking on the phone with her several times in the last week, and has accumulated all the information she requested.

I walk with Stefan into the conference room where Jocelyn is laying out coffee cups: after our last American visitor I've ensured we have a pot of coffee at the ready.

"Morning, chook," she chirps. "Big day."

"It sure is, Jocelyn," I survey the room. As everything is in its place, all we need do now is wait for Lara to arrive.

"Hi there, Brooke," I hear a male American voice say behind me and for a moment my heart leaps.

I turn abruptly around, but it's not Logan. It's Brad Stephenson. Brad Stephenson? My stomach does an unpleasant flip.

What is *he* doing here?

My brain seems to have gone into slow motion. Brad Stephenson. Here. In my office. Brad—the man who wanted to steal my company. *Here.*

I gape at him in disbelief.

After what feels like an eternity, I take a sharp intake of breath. If it hadn't been for Logan's intervention, we might all be out on the street by now.

Well, figuratively speaking, anyway.

It's okay, Brooke. You have the partnership agreement in your hot little hand—and the 'get out of jail free' break clause, too. I give myself a mental pat on the back for that one.

"I hope you don't mind, but I saw myself in." He walks over to me, hand extended, looking as though he doesn't have a care in the world.

I narrow my eyes at him. He might look like a happy-go-lucky puppet, but there's something sinister about him.

He's Guy Smiley's evil twin.

I take Brad's hand and shake it. "Guy, err, Brad. Hi. What a... a... lovely surprise," I lie through gritted teeth. I plaster as pleasant a smile as I can muster on my face. "Where's Lara?" I glance around to see if she's lurking behind him. He appears to be alone.

"She couldn't make it, so I got sent here instead," he replies with delight. "Any chance to come back to beautiful New Zealand and see you wonderful folks again."

His smile is so wide, with such perfectly straight, white teeth I almost expect one of those sparkles you see on toothpaste advertisements to 'ping', blinding us all.

Knowing Brad was the one who wanted to do the dirty on us, his sudden appearance is unsettling. Why is he here? Could Lara not come, or has there been a change in agenda?

Maybe Brad approached Geoff Friedlander with his plan, only to be shot down in flames? Logan assured me everything was above board. I trust Logan with my life.

And we *did* sign the contract, after all. It's watertight.

I glance at Jocelyn, who appears as stunned as me at Brad's unexpected appearance. And she doesn't know the half of it.

Stefan, on the other hand, looks like he could pop.

"We're *so* happy you like our country," Stefan replies eagerly, as he steps forward to shake Brad's hand. He darts me an excited look that screams, 'I want this man for dinner!'

He looks like the cat that swallowed an entire pot of cream.

"We're going to be spending a lot of time together, Brad. A *lot* of time." Stefan looks at Brad suggestively and I shrink in embarrassment.

Stefan may be an amazing sales and marketing leader, but sometimes he lets his libido take over.

And, yes, I know, I'm the big fat pot calling the kettle black.

Jocelyn appears to have recovered. "Nice to see you, Brad. Welcome back to Godzone." She smiles up at him.

Being accustomed to acting as interpreter for our American guests, I explain. "'Godzone' is our way of referring to New Zealand. Kind of like it's so special it's God's own country."

"Ahh." He nods, as though it all makes perfect sense to him. "I love it!"

There's an awkward silence for a moment, until Jocelyn interrupts. "I'll leave you three to crack on with it. Coffee's on the bench."

The three of us take our seats at the conference room table. God, I wish I could talk to Logan, find out why Brad's here.

Despite leaving him a number of voicemails, I haven't heard from Logan all weekend, other than a hasty text, apologizing for having to cut our conversation short. I've missed him and could so do with talking to him.

Especially now Brad has unexpectedly waltzed back into our lives.

"Okay, so let's get this thing started!" Brad begins. "I need to get access to some of your files. I need to check a few things, you know, for our records."

Alarm bells shriek in my brain.

"Of course you can," Stefan replies smoothly. "Our casa is your casa."

I cringe at the butchered expression, the cogs in my mind whirring frenetically.

"You can have whatever you need," Stefan continues. "We've got nothing to hide."

"Hold on a sec," I interrupt. "What do you want to see, Brad?"

A shadow passes over his face. "Is there a problem? As equal partner in this operation, I would expect your full cooperation." He pauses before cracking his broad smile again.

Well, *that* was disturbing.

"Whatever you need, Brad. You let me know," Stefan coos.

Brad turns to Stefan. "Thanks. Access to your systems would be a start."

"Sure. Come with me." Both men rise from the table.

I sit, rooted to the spot, as I watch them leave the room. Perhaps Lara genuinely couldn't come and Brad does love New Zealand so leapt at the opportunity to return.

I'm probably just rattled by Brad's unexpected arrival, knowing he was the one who wanted to change the agenda back in Queenstown. Although something doesn't quite feel right to me, I need to put it to the side and work with him.

What's the point in entering a partnership with a company if I'm suspicious of their every move?

I walk out of my office to find Stefan leaning a little too close over Brad's shoulder at his office computer,

"Find everything you need?" I ask.

"I sure did. Stefan's been very, err, accommodating," Brad replies.

I bet he has.

Brad, Stefan and I spend the rest of the morning together, going through our business, sharing any detail Brad requires, as agreed in the partnership agreement. Thankfully, Stefan seems to have his hormones under control for the duration, and we get through a mountain of work with impressive speed.

"Let's take a break, grab some lunch," I suggest.

"That sounds fantastic. I'm famished," Brad says, sitting back in his chair.

We put on our jackets and the three of us head towards the door.

"Brooke, phone for you," Jocelyn calls out, holding her hand over the receiver.

"Take a message, please," I instruct, and continue walking away.

"You'll want to take this one, love. You've been trying to get in touch with this bloke for a while." She gives me one of her winks.

Realising she must mean Logan, I turn to Brad and Stefan. "You two go on ahead."

Stefan looks like I've just given him free license to have his wicked way with Brad. "Sure," he replies. "We'll be just fine, won't we Brad. Just us two guys. Together."

"Yeah," Brad says uncertainly as they walk to the lift together, carrying his briefcase.

That's odd. Why would Brad need his briefcase at lunch?

"Your call's on line one," Jocelyn says, interrupting me.

"Logan?" I'm inside my office with the door shut. Only Jocelyn knows about our relationship at work, and I want to keep it that way.

"I've been trying to call," he says, irritably.

"Oh, sorry. I've had my phone off." I'm a little put out by his gruff tone. "It's nice to talk to you now, though. Where are you?"

"I'm in Estonia, about to board another flight." I hear a muffled announcement over a loud speaker.

"Okay." I'm crestfallen. We haven't spoken in days and now I only get a few moments to talk to him. "I had better get back to Brad, anyway."

"Brad's there? Brooke, I—" he begins but cuts out. "—you."

"What did you say? You're breaking up."

"I—so sorry—have happened—tomorrow—you—" He's making no sense whatsoever.

"Yes, let's talk tomorrow. If that's what you said?"

The line goes dead. I call him back immediately, but, once again, it goes straight to his voicemail. I hang up in frustration. This long distance relationship thing is starting to annoy me. I want him here, where I can see him, where I can talk to him, where I can touch him.

* * *

Stefan, Brad, and I spend the rest of the day ensconced in the conference room, barely coming up for air. Brad is one hard taskmaster, wanting to cover significant ground in a very short amount of time, and, despite my tiredness come the end of the day, I have a begrudging respect for him.

"Here are all the files you asked for." Stefan, hands over a memory stick to Brad as we're packing up.

"Excellent. Thanks." He pockets it before putting on his suit jacket.

Despite a feeling of crushing tiredness, as Brad is our out-of-town guest, I suggest we all go out to dinner together.

"Thanks, guys, but I'm going to catch up on some other work back at my hotel, if it's all the same to you." He smiles that full, white-toothed smile at us and I can almost feel Stefan swooning next to me.

He picks up his laptop, placing it on the table. "Well, thank you both. Have a great evening."

"Good night, Brad. It was great working with you today," Stefan says.

"Drink?" I ask Stefan once Brad has left. "I think we deserve it."

"Yes, please. A big fat one."

Five minutes later we're at our favourite after-work drinking hole.

"That went well," Stefan comments. He takes a sip of his glass of red wine.

"I can't quite believe we got through as much as we did today. Although he did ask a lot of questions that didn't seem relevant to our partnership."

"I suppose he wants total transparency," Stefan suggests. "Brad's great, isn't he?"

I smile at him, shaking my head. "Really? You think?" I don't try to hide my sarcasm. "I hadn't noticed you liked him."

"I mean at his *job*."

"Of course you do. What else could you possibly mean?" I widen my eyes in mock innocence.

"Okay, he's hotter than his namesake, Brad Pitt, isn't he?" he replies, excitedly with a glint in his eye.

"Brad Pitt? That's a bit old school, isn't it?"

"Sexy is sexy, babe. No matter what the age."

"Well, he doesn't do it for me. And he doesn't play for your team, does he?"

Stefan takes a deflated sigh. "No. But I can fantasize about him, at least."

"Of course you can," I reply indulgently, as though I'm telling a child they can have an extra scoop of ice cream.

I finish my glass of wine. "Right, I had better go. Another big day tomorrow."

"'Night, babe." He gives me a kiss on the check. "I'm going to stay here for a while. Who knows, maybe Brad will come bursting through that door over there and profess his love for me, whisking me off into the night?"

"Stranger things have happened at sea."

* * *

"Where can he be?" I ask for the fourteenth time as I pace around the conference room. "Try him again," I instruct Stefan.

Stefan dials Brad's American cell phone number once more, again hanging up after a few moments. "Voicemail."

It's almost midday and Stefan and I have wasted most of the morning waiting for Brad to arrive.

"I'm going to call the *You: Now* offices in San Francisco," I say agitatedly as I check my watch. "It's still the afternoon there. They might know what's going on."

"Okay. Let me know if you find anything out. I do hope Brad's all right."

"I'm sure he is." But as I head to my office those alarm bells I felt yesterday ring out louder than ever.

I return to the conference room a few moments later.

"Well?" Stefan enquires as I walk in, deep in thought.

"They say they're expecting him back in the office first thing tomorrow."

Stefan asks the very question buzzing around my head. "How can he get from here to San Francisco in such a short amount of time? Isn't it a twelve-hour flight?"

I sit down in a chair opposite him, rubbing my chin in the age-old gesture for thinking. "Unless of course he never had any intention of coming here today." I look directly at Stefan.

"Why?" Stefan asks, shrugging. "That doesn't make sense."

"I don't know." I trace my mind for an answer—any answer—to Brad's sudden and inexplicable departure, the feeling I had yesterday that something wasn't right stirring again in my belly.

"Brooke," Jocelyn says, standing at the conference room door with a worried expression on her face.

"We're kind of in the middle of something here," I snap.

"I can see that, love. I thought you should know. External Affairs has cancelled their seminar."

I stare at her. "What? Did they say why?"

"Something about a letter? And Brooke? There's more."

If I were wearing boots today, I'd certainly be trembling in them. "Tell me."

"Both Innoviss and Gleeson have cancelled too."

I look at her in disbelief. That's all our upcoming government and corporate work for the next couple of weeks. "Why?"

"Sorry, love," Jocelyn replies, a look of concern on her face. "I'll make you a nice cuppa," she adds, backing out of the room.

As if tea could fix this.

"It's Brad." My heart sinks to the floor. "He's done this."

"You're jumping to conclusions, Brooke. He's late, that's all. And yes, it's bad luck those clients have cancelled, but we can talk to them, find out what's going on, see if we can reschedule or something."

Stefan's words echo around the room. I barely register them.

"I'm going to call Logan," I mutter as I rise from my chair and walk like a zombie towards the door.

"*That* double crossing bastard? Why would you want to call him?" Stefan asks with venom.

"I explained what you thought you heard in Queenstown, Stefan. It was Brad who was trying to double—" I stop midsentence.

Oh. My. God.

I turn to Stefan, shaking. "What was on the memory stick you gave Brad yesterday?"

He shrugs. "Just stuff he'd asked for. Success rates, attrition rates, contact lists. That sort of thing." He counts them off on his fingers as though they don't mean a thing.

Hold the phone. "Contact lists?" I squeak. "You gave him all our contacts?"

Tension pings around my head. Stefan gave Brad all our contacts.

"Yeah. What? You said full disclosure, provide Brad with whatever he needs." He sounds like a hurt child.

"I didn't mean give him our *full contact list*," I shout at him, buffeting him with my gale force anger.

I'm suddenly dizzy. I grasp for a nearby chair, landing on it hard.

"Oh, no." I cover my face with my hands, nausea rising in my throat. "He's gone and taken everything."

I look up at Stefan as he shifts his weight from foot to foot.

My world is tilting on its axis.

"How can he have done that? We've signed a partnership agreement, remember? They can't just come over here and take our company."

I heave a deep sigh, trying to steady my growing panic. Failing.

The partnership agreement. I'm *such* an idiot.

When I don't respond, Stefan asks, "Right, Brooke?"

I look across at him, standing there, hoping for reassurance, knowing I'm about to call off Christmas.

"Remember the clause I added?" I ask him dully.

"The one that allows us to abandon the agreement if we're not happy? Yes. Stroke of genius, that one, boss."

"The lawyers warned me it could be used the other way around. But I thought no, they wouldn't do that. There's no reason on this sweet Earth *You: Now* would want to back out of our deal. But what stupid, stupid Brooke failed to consider was that they might use our partnership to gain access to our company information and then steal it, shafting us in the process."

My anger is rising so rapidly I could throttle a kitten. And I love kittens.

"Come on, Brooke. Don't you think you're jumping to conclusions a bit here?" He's speaking hurriedly, turning increasingly pale. "So Brad's gone back to the States earlier than expected. Maybe something's happened in his personal life he had to get back for?"

I enjoy a momentary surge of positivity as I entertain Stefan's idea. Not for long.

It's no coincidence our clients have begun to cancel seminars. I know it as well as I know myself. And there was something about the way Brad behaved yesterday—his almost feverish need to get through as much of our information as we could—that tells me he never intended to return today.

He's got what he wants and he's headed for the hills, leaving us behind with our mouths gaping in utter shock and disbelief.

CHAPTER 21

LATER IN THE DAY I sit in my office, staring at my desk, lost in my thoughts. I've called our lawyers and asked them—pleaded with them—if there's anything we can do to save my company. The answer has been a big, fat zero.

We're screwed. It's as clear as that.

My brilliant idea of partnering with a big American business to conquer new markets has led to our ruin.

There will be no partnership, no access to resources, no move into Australia.

What's more, now *You: Now* has all our New Zealand information, we'll have to compete with them just to retain our existing clients' business. With *You: Now*'s superior marketing muscle, I'm convinced all but a handful of them will waddle off and dive into their slick, professional pond, leaving us high and dry.

My precious brand, *Live It*, will be just a distant memory for them all and we'll be back to where we started, only worse: we'll be competing against the most impressive and successful personal growth business in the world.

And it's my fault.

I've tried calling Logan but keep getting his voicemail. I've left him a hoard of messages, from panicked to resigned, charting my emotional journey.

Finally, I pluck up the courage to call Greg Friedlander.

"Mr Friedlander is not available at this time," his insipid assistant coos down the line at me. "May I take a message?"

"No. This is Brooke Mortimer from *Live* It. I want to speak with him. Now."

"I do apologise, Ms Mortimer, but Mr Friedlander is not available at this time," she repeats as though I'm a sandwich or two short of a picnic.

"I know. You said that!" I grip my phone so hard I think I hear it crack.

"May I take a message?" she asks in the same tone. She sounds completely unruffled.

Perhaps she's used to her boss sending his oiks out to ruin people's lives? Maybe I'm just one of many such callers today. All part of the job for her, I imagine.

I hang up in anger with an "*Arrgh!*" My head might explode, splattering my brains all over the walls.

My phone rings and I grab it, answering quickly when I see Logan's name.

"My god am I glad to hear from you." Relief sweeps over me. Logan will know want to do.

"Brooke. At last. I've been trying to get hold of you for days. The coverage here is—" His voice cuts out, as if to illustrate his point.

"Logan? Can you hear me?"

"—joint decision. It's what's best for—Hello? Are you there? Dammit!"

"Yes, I'm here. What's this joint decision?" I ask, desperate to understand him.

"—while it lasted—"

"While what lasted?" What is he talking about? While the partnership lasted? I'm gripped with fear. While *we* lasted? "Logan? Logan, can you hear me?"

"Brooke?"

"I can hear you. Logan, did you know about this? About the takeover?"

"Yes, I did." I can hear him now, as clear as crystal.

His words hit me in the belly. Hard. "You did?" I whisper.

"I'm sorry, Brooke."

"You're sorry?" I ask incredulously. "You knew." My world tilts on its axis. "You knew."

"Brooke, please hear me out," he pleads.

Not wanting to hear his excuses, his *lies*, I hang up the phone.

I sit staring at the screen in shock.

He knew. Logan knew.

There's a tentative knock on my door. I look up to see Jocelyn standing in the doorway, mug in hand.

"I thought you could do with a fresh brew," she says, placing the tea on my desk next to me.

I force a smile. "Thanks, Jocelyn."

She stands next to me for a moment and I can feel her eyes on me. "What is it?" I ask, when she hasn't left.

"I hope you don't mind me saying, but it's bloody obvious you're not faring so well right now." She has a look of kindness in her eyes.

Sadness, frustration, anger all reach a crescendo and tears well in my eyes, spilling over. "Oh, Jocelyn. It's all gone to crap."

She pulls me in for one of her bear hugs and I let the tears fall freely.

"There, there," she says, comforting me. "It's all going to be okay."

"But it's not," I blubber, embarrassed my tears are wetting her floral blouse.

"Why don't you park yourself down and tell me all about it."

I look at her through my tears, aware in all probability that when the shit hits the fan—which it's about to do on an epic scale—she'll no longer have a job. Perhaps she won't feel quite so kindly towards me then.

With reluctance I tell how her I've messed everything up, how I've lost the business through my own, stupid fault.

She sits back in her seat, taking it all in. "I knew something was up when I saw you storm out of the conference room earlier. Then Stefan had one of his hissy fits over by the photocopier before heading out. But this?" She shakes her head. "This is worse than I thought."

"I know, and I'm so sorry, Jocelyn." Another tear escapes and I wipe it away.

"Well, love, you took a risk and it didn't pay off. But you have to admit it was worth a crack." She smiles at me.

"How can you be so kind when I've just told you I've lost the business and you're going to be out of a job?" I ask, flummoxed by her reaction.

"Oh, chook. There will be other jobs."

She's so reasonable I want to shake her, force her to see what I've done.

"Have you talked to you-know-who?" she asks in a quiet voice.

"Yes." I'm unable to bring myself to utter his name.

"And?" she asks.

I shake my head, not trusting myself to speak.

Jocelyn appears to understand, her mouth setting in a grim line.

"Brooke?"

I turn, wiping my eyes, to see Stefan standing in the doorway to my office. His head is bowed, his arms wrapped around his body, looking like he's just been trampled by a herd of over-excited elephants.

"Come in, love," Jocelyn says to him. "Close the door. No need to spook the troops."

He walks tentatively in, stopping a few feet in front of us.

"Brooke, I'm so, so sorry." His voice quavers.

If he starts crying we'll be a pretty sorry management team, that's for sure.

Part of me is so angry with him right now I can imagine steam coming out of my ears. But I also know what's happened to us is almost entirely thanks to my naivety.

"I know I wasn't the one to hand our contacts to Brad, but I may as well have been," I say.

"I thought you'd be blaming me." He gives me a grateful hug.

I shake my head. "It was my fault, Stefan. I know that. If I hadn't been so greedy, wanting to grow the business, I would never have entertained the possibility of a partnership with those bastards."

He hangs his head. "But don't you see if I wasn't so, err, blinded by Brad, I might have seen this coming?"

I stop in my tracks. "What did you say?"

He shifts uncomfortably. "Just that if I hadn't, umm—" Stefan pauses, darting a look in Jocelyn's direction.

"Oh, don't mind me, chook. I know you're as gay as the day is long. And Brad's a good-looking bloke. I didn't come down in the last rain shower, you know."

Stefan smiles weakly. "What I'm saying is if I hadn't fancied Brad so much, I might have seen what he was trying to do to us."

I swallow hard, his words ringing in my ears. Oh God. He's right. If *I* hadn't been so involved with Logan, *I* might have seen what was coming. He thinks he's talking about himself but he's talking about *me*.

It's my fault—mine and no one else's.

"He would have done it anyway. It's not your fault, Stefan. It's mine."

Relief floods his face. "Oh, Brooke," he croaks.

"Yeah, I know."

I ask them to leave me alone for a moment. As Stefan closes the door behind himself, my scattered thoughts inevitably land on Logan.

I'm such a fool. While I was busy falling in love with him, he was preparing to stab me in the back, running away with my business.

That explains why he pursued me so relentlessly, why he didn't want to just keep our relationship on merely a professional footing, why he wouldn't take no for an answer.

He knew I wanted him, and he played me like a fiddle.

And then there's the way he seemed so happy I'd had a break clause added to the contract.

My god. He must have planned this all along! And I was just the attention-seeking, rom com-loving fool who gladly hopped on for the ride, losing my company—and my dignity—in the process.

I'm nothing more than a hooker who forgot to ask for payment.

Except there's more: he's broken my heart.

I grab at the diamond solitaire necklace I haven't removed since he gave it to me and yank it off, hurtling it across the room as I dissolve into tears.

It's truly been a crap-tastic day.

CHAPTER 22

TO RECAP—IN CASE you weren't paying attention—my world has imploded.

It's like Logan came along and casually dropped an incendiary device or ten, blowing my world into smithereens.

Just three days ago I had a business with a bright future, and I was in love with the most amazing man I've ever met. I was on Cloud Nine, in full party mode. Hell, I was sailing high above Cloud Nine, laughing in its face.

And now? Let's just say I've had better weeks.

It's been two days since Brad did a bunk with our information, ruining us into the bargain.

We've had a letter from *You: Now* confirming they no longer want to "pursue joint opportunities" but we could "keep the successful brand, *Live It*". So very good of them.

I gave the letter the treatment it deserved and threw it with full force into my rubbish bin. I should have spat on it too.

Between us we've rung all our contacts, asking them to keep their business with us while we weather this storm. But clever old Logan, Brad and their cronies got in there first, offering them discounted rates and the promise of fresh blood to meet all their needs.

"Who did you hear from at *You: Now*?" I ask one of my recently departed clients over the phone.

"I'm not sure I should say, Brooke," she replies.

"What difference would it make, Tui? Please," I plead, "just tell me."

"A guy called Brad Stephenson came to see us, but we got a letter before then. Hold on a sec, Brooke. But don't tell my boss, okay?"

"Sure," I assure her, my voice faint.

Brad went to see our clients? We were sitting ducks and he just sailed in, took what he wanted, and sailed on out again. Much like Logan, although Logan took so much more.

"Let's see. It's signed by someone called Logan McSomething."

"McManus?" My voice comes out so faint she doesn't hear me.

Any shred of hope I had left Logan was somehow not involved in this drops like a rock through water.

"Oh." My heart breaks all over again.

"I'm sorry, Brooke. You guys were great, and if it wasn't for the rates we might have been able to stay with you."

"Thanks, Tui. See you around." I hang up.

It's that classic love story: boy meets girl, they fall in love, boy steals girl's company from under her feet.

It should be made into a Disney movie.

I sigh heavily and walk out of my office into the open plan space.

"I spoke with Michael Cray-Smith," Stefan begins. "He's jumped ship too, gone over to *You: Now*. He was very apologetic about it all, yadda yadda yadda. He makes me sick."

I bury my face in my hands.

"What's next, boss?" Stefan's putting a bright face on it.

"Let's all meet in the conference room once we've finished our calls to go over the data. See what we're left with here."

"I'm done," he replies. His words echo around the room.

* * *

Once assembled in the conference room I troll through the information from everyone. Only a small handful of clients said they would be open to staying with us.

"Does loyalty mean nothing to these people?" I shake my head.

"It's tough out there, Brooke. Our services are often seen as a luxury purchase. If they can get good quality work for cheaper elsewhere, they will."

I feel dejected. "Well, at least we still have our weekend seminars. How are the numbers looking, Jocelyn?"

Jocelyn darts a look at Stefan. "I picked this up at the café across the road this morning." Stefan hands me a glossy flyer.

It's an advertisement for a *You: Now* personal development seminar the same weekend as our next scheduled one.

"I'm sorry, Brooke," Jocelyn says, passing me a spread sheet. "It's not looking too bright."

We have a measly number of attendees, only a few who've paid, and just a small fraction of the numbers we usually attract.

"That's all?" I ask, my voice weak.

She nods. "We've been getting cancellations this morning, love."

"Oh." What else can I say? Sure, I could put up a fight, but sometimes you just need to know when you're beat.

And for *Live It* that time seems to be here and now.

"We can take them on at their own game," Stefan says. "What's stopping us from holding our seminar? We have the brand, the market presence. New Zealanders *know* us, they trust us. We can offer a discount for group bookings, put out flyers, get on social media, get the word out there we're still here and we're still the best personal development seminar in the business."

"Stefan, I admire your enthusiasm, but I think we can all see the writing on the wall. We can't compete with this big American company."

"You're giving up," he accuses.

"Yes, I am. Stefan, if we can't make the numbers work for this seminar, how do we pay for this office, our salaries, the venues with no income? We might last a while as we fight the good fight, but that's all it will be: a while."

"You can't just give up!" He storms out of the room.

I take a deep breath. "Look, everyone. I can pay you to the end of next week, and I'll give every one of you the best reference you've ever had, because you've all been—" I'm forced to stop as my voice catches. After a moment, I try again. "You've all been amazing to work with."

People drift out of the conference room, pack up their desks and bid one another tearful goodbyes.

Stefan storms back into my office, not an ounce calmer than when he left.

"Don't do this, Brooke. You *have* to keep fighting."

Stefan hasn't seen how cut throat this business can be. I have. After all, I was the one doing the throat cutting back when Jonathan and I started *Live It.*

People like to latch onto the new, exciting thing. Back then, that *was Live It* and we rode the wave for years. Now the tables have turned, and I know no amount of price-cutting and advertising can compete with the new, exciting, glossy player in town.

Sure, they may come back to us if they don't like what *You: Now* has to offer. But that may be weeks, months, or even years down the road. We can't survive that long.

I also know *You: Now* offers a great product: that's why I wanted to partner with them in the first place.

No, it's over.

"We have to, Stefan. We can't keep afloat like this."

He hangs his head, the anger slipping away.

"You've been the best sales and marketing manager I could ever have hoped for, Stefan, and I want us to always be friends. But right now it's time to say goodbye."

He sighs. "I'll never work for anyone as fantastic as you, boss."

I hug him in close. "I know."

He manages a laugh. "I'll go pack up my desk."

Jocelyn comes into my office a few moments later.

"I hate to ask this, love, what with the business going belly up and all. Are you sure Logan was involved?" Jocelyn asks.

Anger flashes through me at the mention of his name. "Yes. It would appear he knew all about this."

"Well, blow me down. If I'd known he was going to do this to you, love, I'd have told him to naff off. I feel like a right wally, giving him all that inside info. Ooh, I'm so brassed off with him."

"Inside info? What are you talking about?"

"When you first met, I could tell you both had the hots for each other," she begins.

I nod. It's true, despite how it all turned out.

"I hadn't seen you look at a man that way before, love, and I wanted to give you a helping hand. You deserve to be happy, and I thought Logan might be the fella for you."

I nod. You're not the only one, sunshine.

"When you weren't around he asked me things about you, what you like, the places you go, that sort of thing. I thought he was a good bloke, so I told him where you were going for dinner the day you met him."

"You told him I was going to Charlie Noble with my friends?"

I think back to the evening I met Alexis and Laura for dinner and Logan had left with Lucinda.

God, I bet he did sleep with her.

"I did, love. And when you were going to Queenstown. I'm so sorry."

I let out a puff of air. "It doesn't matter now, Jocelyn. What's done is done. And if it's any consolation, I thought he was a good bloke too. More fool us."

"If I ever see him again, I'll have his guts for garters," she says with rage.

I let out a weak chortle. I bet she would. And I wouldn't translate it for him, either. Let him find out what it means the hard way.

"Come on, love. Time to rattle your dags. You can't sit here wallowing all day."

"I know. Onwards and upwards, right?" I force a smile.

"That's the spirit, chook," she replies, and her answering smile is full of warmth.

I walk back over to my desk and begin to organise some paperwork and files, all the while wishing things could have worked out better.

And Logan had been the man Jocelyn and I both thought he was.

* * *

My phone beeps with a reminder and, after searching around my bombsite of an office for several minutes, I finally find it. I'm due to meet Scott for a drink tonight.

I so can't face seeing him right now.

You know when you see your ex for the first time you want to not only look amazing but have your life sorted too: a new man, a new haircut, a fabulously successful career? When I agreed to meet Scott for a drink I had all that.

Or so I thought.

Now, I'm single and jobless. Hardly a launching platform for a 'look-how-well-I'm-doing-without-you' drink with my ex.

I pick up my phone to call him.

He answers on the first ring. "Hey, Brooke. I'm looking forward to seeing you at eight."

179

"Well, here's the thing. Is it all right with you if we take a rain check? I'm swamped," I lie.

Yeah, swamped packing up what's left of my life.

"Oh," he replies, sounding deflated. "I guess. But I was kind of hoping to see you."

I waiver for just a moment, thinking how it would be nice to think about something other than the ruin that is my life right now.

Scott picks up on my hesitation. "Come on. You know you want to. We'll have fun, I promise. Just like we used to."

Fun? Man, I sure could do with some fun.

"Okay," I concede, perhaps against my better judgment. "But just one drink, got it?"

CHAPTER 23

I ARRIVE AT ANCIENT a few minutes before eight, wanting to be prepared for The First Big Meeting with Scott since our break up.

I order a drink and take it to a nearby table, where I swallow a few steadying sips—okay, gulps—before he arrives.

To my surprise, I polish the glass off in just a few minutes. I order another.

As I sit in the bar alone I think about how I had imagined our first get together since our messy break up would go. I would sashay in without a care in the world, dressed in some gorgeous new outfit that accentuated my small waist and slim, toned legs, looking hotter than a toasted marshmallow.

Scott, of course, would greet me with his jaw on the floor as he took in my beauty, confidence, and success.

I would talk about how much I appreciated our time together, and that I hoped he could be as happy as I find myself now, with Logan and my successful business, branching out into new countries.

We would laugh about the old days, agreeing that our love was only ever destined to be short, and that we had learned so much from each other, things that made us better people.

Of course he would confess with tears in his eyes that he still loved me and I would touch his hand in sympathy. "You will love again, Scott," I would offer with kindness, knowing he would never find a woman he loved as much as me.

Ah, but fantasies about how things will go with our exes are sadly just that, and the reality is often quite, quite different.

I take another sip of my chardonnay and am shocked to see I've almost reached the bottom of my second glass.

That one went down well. May as well get another.

As though reading my mind, a waitress approaches my table. I order another glass, and sit, waiting for Scott, trying my best to look sexy yet unavailable: a pretty tall order when you feel like crap, that's for sure.

A few moments and most of my third—but who's counting?—glass of chardonnay later, my breath catches in my throat as I spy Scott pushing through the door, scanning the room for me.

He's wearing his signature slim-fitting jeans, accentuating his long, athletic legs and slim waist, a white T-shirt under a casual black jacket. He looks like a guy from a hair product commercial with his thick, blonde bed-head hair. He's always been supremely confident—some may go so far as to say arrogant, but I couldn't possibly comment—which serves to make him even hotter.

I wave at him, giving him my best 'I'm-over-you' smile, and he grins at me. As he saunters over to my table, a number of women's eyes follow him, which he plays up by running his hands through his hair and flashing them a smile, much to their obvious delight.

"Hey, babe," he says as I stand to give him a quick 'we're-just-friends' hug.

He holds me at arm's length—literally, not figuratively—sweeping his eyes over my body from top to tail and back up again. "You look a-mazing."

Despite myself, a tingle runs throughout my body. "Err, thanks." I look away.

Jeez Louise. He can still get to me, even after breaking my heart. What am I? Some sort of masochist?

At this rate we'll be going all *Fifty Shades* with one another before the night is over.

"What can I get you?" the waitress asks Scott as he takes off his jacket, revealing a tight white T-shirt underneath. It accentuates his professional athlete's physique to perfection.

He orders his beer and sits down opposite me. "It is *so* good to see you, you know?" He pierces me with his eyes. "How long has it been?"

"A while." Of course I know exactly how long it's been since he slept with someone else, broke my heart, and I kicked him out of our home. But I'm not about to let on to him.

"You look good." I take another sip of my chardonnay, enjoying the buzz it's giving me. "Life's treating you well?"

"It is, actually. I'm here to meet with some investors. I'm getting the tennis resort up and running. Brooke, I'm realising my dreams." He beams at me, thoroughly proud of himself.

When we were together he had big plans to set up a tennis resort in New Zealand's 'winterless north', the area at the tip of the North Island boasting the best weather in the country—ideal for tennis, of course.

"Good for you." I feel a tinge of sadness when I think about the demise of my own business. Since I certainly don't want to go into *that*, I say, "Tell me all about it."

He waxes lyrical about his plans, telling me where his tennis resort will be located, how many courts he plans to have, and he hopes to open it within the coming year.

"I'm so glad you agreed to meet me, Brooke."

"Me too," I reply, and I mean it. It feels so good not to be dwelling on my company or Logan right now. And the wine has given me the best buzz.

"Really?" He's suddenly anxious. "I thought you hated me."

"Hate you? No. Maybe I despised you for a while, but that's all gone. We're good." I smile hazily at him.

Relief floods his face. "You don't know how much I've wanted to hear you say that."

He moves a little closer. "Brooke, babe, I want you to know I never meant to hurt you the way I did."

I study his face for a moment, remembering how it felt when he admitted to having the affair. The alcohol in my system seems to act like a magical elixir, washing any lingering hurt or resentment away.

"I know." I pat his hand. He grabs onto it, fixing me with his gaze.

"Brooke, I still love you. I never stopped. Please, let me back in your life."

I blink at him, barely comprehending his words. "You want me back?"

"Yes," he replies with alacrity. "I do. I want to be with you, to love you again. Like I always have."

To say I'm dumbfounded by his confession has to be the

understatement of the year. I know I was the one who kicked him out, but it was only after I discovered he'd been having sex all over town with my old school friend, Jessica Banks. At the time I thought we were going to be together forever.

While trying to work out how to respond, I absentmindedly raise my empty glass to my lips. "Oops," I utter when I discover there's nothing in it.

"Here, let me order you another one."

With our once attentive waitress nowhere to be seen, Scott goes to the bar to order us another drink.

I watch him walk away. He loves me and wants me back.

I can't quite take it in. Oh, but it's so, so tempting. With everything falling to pieces around my ears, being with someone I know inside out—someone who loves me and hasn't stopped loving me in all this time—is so very alluring.

Although things got pretty messy towards the end, when we were good we were very, very good together.

I can't help but watch his tight, toned butt as he stands at the bar—as do all the other woman in the room—and my mind wanders to how it felt to hold in my hands, squeezing it hard during our frequent love making.

There's an unexpected twinge in my Girly Bits at the memories— and the prospect.

It would be so easy to fall into bed with him tonight.

"What do you think you're doing, young lady?" that pesky angel on my right shoulder asks in my ear.

"She's considering having some fun with that rather mouth-watering specimen of sexy manhood over there. Chill out, will you," Devil Brooke replies. "Go on, look at him. He's hot. And he wants you," she whispers seductively in my ear.

I bang the side of my head in an attempt to shake the sparring Brookes out, making the room wobble unsteadily around me. Man, I can't hold my liquor: I'm such a lightweight.

A lightweight with auditory hallucinations. Wow, I really should get that checked out.

Scott returns with my next glass of wine, which I take from him eagerly, downing several gulps before placing it on the table. I pick it up again, deciding I can save time between swigs if I keep holding it. All that picking it up, putting it down malarkey is just exhausting.

And entirely unnecessary because drinking is so much fun when you do it really, really fast.

He raises his eyebrows in amusement and I grin back at him like a drunken floozy. Which is what I guess I am right now.

"Cheers." He raises his glass.

"What are we drinking to?" I enquire, holding my glass aloft.

"To us?" The corners of his eyes crinkle as he smiles. It's posed as a question but I know, with his supreme confidence, he's certain I will acquiesce.

"Oh." I burst into laughter.

Scott regards me with a quizzical look on his face. "Are you okay?"

"I am fantastic, Scott. Fan-bloody-*tastic*." I take another large slurp from my wine glass. I think I slosh some of it down my front, but decide it's in everyone's best interests to ignore it.

"And I would like to say how great it is to see you again, Scott my old Scotty Scott Scott. My former *loverrrr*. To you." I raise my glass again. "And to your beautiful butt." I giggle. "To your amazing ass." Somebody stop me. "To your gorgeous glutes." *Please!*

Scott flashes me the cheeky grin I know so well from days gone by. "You're toasted." He laughs, shaking his head. "I like it, you know?"

"Maybe. Or maybe I'm just high on life. Who knows?" I shrug as though my current high spirits are a mystery unsolvable by modern science.

He leans closer in towards me and my Girly Bits perk up again. "As much as I'm enjoying this version of Brooke, have you eaten lately?"

I'm too busy watching his lips, thinking how much I want to kiss them, to hear what he's saying. Blah blah blah, it's all just boring old words. I giggle again.

This is turning into the *best* night.

I take an ill-advised slug of my wine mid-giggle, causing me to cough, a bit of wine dribbling out of my nose.

Attractive, I know.

I recover long enough to reply, "Hmmm?" I lick my own lips and bat my eyelashes at him.

"I asked you if you've eaten anything, but I'm guessing not. I'll order some food."

"No, don't do that." I don't want to break the spell. "I have a *much* better idea." I raise my eyebrows at him, parting my lips. "Wanna get outta here?"

Little Devil Brooke is doing cartwheels on my shoulder right now as Angel Brooke sulks, knowing she's lost the good fight.

Scott's face breaks into the crooked smile that used to drive me crazy as he reaches over the table, taking my hand in his and begins to draw circles on my palm. It feels so incredible; all my senses are focused on my left hand.

"I knew you still wanted me."

I barely register his words as my entire being concentrates on my hand.

I want to shout out, "Stop the press! We've discovered a new erogenous zone!"

"I'll go pay."

"Good idea. But can you take me with you? I don't want you to stop what you're doing."

It's tempting to just take him here and now, ripping off his clothes and mounting him on this very table.

It's probably a good thing I don't, however, what with the bar being full of patrons and all. I believe that kind of thing is frowned on—in this country, anyway.

The bill paid and our jackets on, we walk out of the bar onto the street. Scott flags us a cab and we slide into the back together, my heart pounding at the thought of having him.

"Where to?" the taxi driver asks.

Scott looks at me. "Your place?"

I shake my head, thoughts of Logan in my townhouse only a short time ago polluting my brain. "Yours." I force myself to think about Scott instead.

After all, Scott's here with me now, he's made it clear he wants me, and he's unlikely to steal my business after using me for sex. Not that I have a business to lose anymore.

He instructs the driver where to go then sits back next to me, taking my face gently in his hands. Caressing my hair he pulls me into a kiss. It's insistent and deep, sending a course of pleasure through my body, just like it always did when we were together.

"How far are we going?" I ask.

"All the way, I hope."

I laugh lightly. "I mean, how far is it until we get to your place?"

"Oh, umm, it's just the next block. Driver, can you stop there, by the white van?"

He pays the driver and takes me by the hand, helping me out of the car and leading me through a door and up a flight of narrow stairs. The anticipation of having him is almost too much to bear, and I quicken my pace, taking the stairs two by two.

"Hold on." He chuckles. "We've got the whole night, babe."

We reach a door and he pulls out a key. "This is a friend's place. He's away and said I could crash here."

Once through the door he leads me past a small living area with a tiny kitchen, junk scattered everywhere, into a bedroom. The unmade bed almost fills the cramped room, and Scott busies himself with giving it a quick tidy.

I wrap my arms around myself, looking around. I'm struck by the contrast between this place and the plush hotel suite Logan had at The Bolton Hotel on the other side of the city.

Logan. Why oh why do I keep thinking of him? Get it through your thick skull, Brooke: he doesn't love you and never did.

Scott turns to me, slipping my jacket off my shoulders, planting gentle kisses on my bare shoulder, tracing a tantalising path up my neck.

Love the one you're with, love the one you're with, as the old song goes. I just have to forget about Logan and move on with my life, and hot, sexy Scott is just the ticket.

It should be so easy—hell, it's not like Scott and I haven't slept together before—and as the saying goes, the best way to get over someone is to get under someone else.

"Jesus, Brooke," he says huskily as he wraps his arms around me. "You're so incredibly sexy. God, I love you so much. I've missed you, you know? I've missed *this.*"

He leans down and kisses my lips, more tenderly this time, our tongues finding one another as our excitement builds. Those Girly Bits start to hum.

It's a good kiss. In fact, I would go so far as to say it's a great kiss. On a scale of one to ten of kisses, under normal circumstances, I would rate it as almost a full ten.

But these aren't normal circumstances. In fact, these are very far from normal circumstances.

Scott cups my breasts in his hands, letting out a pleasurable groan. "Your body is *insane.*"

I pull away from him, sobering up faster than if I'd drunk a litre of strong, black coffee.

"No. Scott, I can't."

I know with a newfound clarity I can't go there with him. My brain is too clouded with fresh memories of Logan, and having angry revenge sex with Scott—as appealing as that prospect was moments ago—would only lower me to Logan's level.

And I'm better than that.

I grab my coat and turn to leave as Scott chases after me, adjusting his jeans.

"You can't go, babe. Please, stay." He looks desperate and I find myself feeling sorry for him.

I have very recent experience of being in love with someone who doesn't love you back. I know it how much it sucks.

I reach the door and turn to him. "I can't."

All I want to do is head home, curl up under my duvet with a bar or ten of Whittaker's chocolate, and not come out for a week.

Or maybe ever.

"Why?" He trails his hands up my bare arms, sending tingles down my spine. "We were so good together. Don't you remember? I sure as hell do."

As I look at him I know he's right. If he hadn't screwed another woman, ruining what we had, I bet I would still be with him.

But he did and we're not. End of story.

I sigh. "Scott, I—"

He stops me with a kiss, pressing himself against me so my body is pinned to the door. I'll give him points for persistence, that's for sure.

For one heady moment I submit, revelling in the body-tingling pleasure of it. Eventually I push him away, knowing as enjoyable as it would be, it doesn't feel right.

"Scott, please listen to me. I'm in love with someone else."

Logan may be the biggest bastard to walk the face of the Earth, and he may have treated me abominably, but I can't just switch my emotions off: I love him. And I'm going to have to work long and hard at getting over him.

My heart goes thud whenever I think about Logan. I miss him. I miss his smile, his low, mellow voice, his beautiful brown eyes. I miss his laugh, the way his eyes crinkle at the edges when he smiles. I miss his touch, his feel, his heat.

And I wish with every last drop of my DNA I didn't.

"Oh." Scott lets me go.

I put my hand on his chest. "Believe me when I tell you I wish we could do this. But I can't. I'm sorry." I peck him on the cheek and turn to leave.

"Hey," he calls out when I'm halfway down the stairs. "If you ever change your mind, you know how to get hold of me."

I look up at him. "See you later, Scott."

CHAPTER 24

"BLIMEY, BROOKE. IT LOOKS like you fired ten boxes of tissues out of a cannon in here," Alexis comments, looking in disbelief around my usually immaculate living room.

"I guess I could clean up a bit."

I glance at the floor. She's right, there really is an inordinate amount of tissues scattered haphazardly around. With all the crying I've been doing I must be at risk of suffering from severe dehydration by now.

I'm thirsty at the thought, although I have no intention whatsoever of leaving my cocoon on the sofa.

"Are you sick? You sounded dreadful on the phone just now," she asks in concern, sitting next to me on the sofa and placing her hand on my brow. "You don't have a fever, but you look terrible."

I'm still in the fleecy pyjamas I only ever wear when I'm home alone, tucked under my duvet on the living room sofa, usually watching a rom com.

"I'm fine." I know it's an unconvincing lie as tears threaten to flow. Again.

Jeez Louise, how much can one person cry?

I think back over the time since I fled Scott's apartment. With a minor detour to the supermarket to purchase chocolate, I've been enveloped here on my sofa for the best part of two days, closeting myself away from the world. And yes, I've been crying. A lot.

It's like someone pulled a plug out and all the tears I've been holding back since I was a little girl have come flooding out.

Alexis called about fifteen minutes ago to say she wanted to drop off the DVDs her sister, Sammy Jo, had borrowed from me. I'm now regretting answering her call. I just want to be left alone to wallow.

She walks over to the window and opens the blinds.

I'm forced to shelter my eyes under a cushion as the blinding sun comes pouring into the room. "What did you have to do that for?" I ask irritably.

She sits back down onto the sofa next to my prostrate body. "Are you sick?"

I heave a sigh. "No, I—" I begin, but dissolve into hot tears before I have the chance to complete what I was trying to say.

She lets me cry, offering me my final stash of tissues, which I gratefully pull out in clumps.

Once I'm calmer and have somehow managed to stench the flow—perhaps I'm all cried out now? Who knows?—Alexis brings me a glass of water. I'm so parched I scull the lot in a split second.

"What's going on, Brooke?"

I sit up, leaning back against my sofa. I know I look like total crap: my eyes puffy, my nose red, my skin blotchy. I have the headache from hell and my tummy rumbles. I guess several bars of chocolate and a large bag of chips isn't quite enough to eat over a couple of days, even for someone who's been prostrate, wallowing in self-pity.

"You can tell me. I want to help," she adds when I'm not forthcoming.

Even though I know it'll be public knowledge soon enough, I don't want to tell her what's happened: telling her will make it real. Right now I can kid myself it's all just a really, really bad dream.

My phone buzzes and Alexis picks it up and hands it to me. "It's Logan. I'm sure *he'll* cheer you up."

I snatch the phone from her before I hit 'decline' and hurl the phone across the room.

That man deserves so much more than a simple 'decline'.

"What? Why?" she asks, clearly shocked. "What's happened?"

Feeling marginally better, I manage a weak smile. "Quite a lot."

She glances at the phone on the other side of the room. "I'm guessing Logan has something to do with this?"

I nod. "Oh, yes. He wins the prick of the year contest. No, scrub that: prick of the decade."

"Tell me."

And so I do, interspersed with further tears and fits of anger. I tell her about the loss of my company, about Logan's duplicity, about how I've lost everything.

"I just can't believe it." She shakes her head. "Is that it? Your whole business is gone?"

"Yes. We tried to salvage what was left of it, but the numbers didn't stack up. It would have cost more to try to keep the company afloat than to just call it quits. It wasn't worth trying."

"Oh, Brooke. I'm so sorry."

"Yeah," I reply, my voice full of bitterness. "Me too."

"Look, how about you have a shower, freshen up a bit. I'll give this place a spruce up then I'll go to the supermarket and get some real food to make us for dinner." She eyes the empty chocolate and chip packets on the floor.

I nod in gratitude as fresh tears sting my eyes at her kindness.

* * *

I stand in the shower, letting the water flow down my back. I'm downright ashamed at how I've managed to singlehandedly lose the company I created, the company that provided people with jobs and helped thousands on their personal growth. Hiding away has felt like the best thing to do. The *only* thing to do.

As I throw on some yoga pants and a comfy sweatshirt I hear Alexis busying herself in the kitchen. I gaze at myself in the mirror. I'm defying nature by looking somehow drawn and puffy at the same time, my eyes half their usual size. I look a lot like a heroine addict in need of a hit.

Alexis has restored the living room to its usual organization, and the smell of baking lasagne tingles my taste buds, setting my tummy on a new round of rumbles.

"You look so much better," Alexis exclaims as I round the corner into the kitchen. "By the looks of you, you need to eat. And pronto. I bought a lasagne rather than make one. I hope you don't mind?"

I smile to myself. Mind? Is she kidding? Whether the dinner she's cooking me during the lowest point of my life is homemade or not is the very last thing I'm concerned about. "That's great, thanks. It smells so good."

She busies herself with chopping salad ingredients and making a vinaigrette as I sit on one of my bar stools at the kitchen bench. She chats about everyday things like work and her crazy family, taking my mind off the mess of my own life.

"I still can't quite believe Logan was such a dick. It doesn't make sense he would have seduced you just so he could steal your company."

"Well, he did," I reply with venom. "It was always his intention to steal *Live It* away from me. Getting me into bed was just an added bonus for him."

She sighs. "I'm so sorry. What an asshole."

"You've got that right, sister."

"Did he leave you a voicemail?"

In my gloom I'd forgotten he called. I pick up my bruised and battered phone, which Alexis placed on the coffee table in her cleaning spree. Yes, there's a message. I don't even want to hear his voice, let alone what lies he's spun this time.

"You don't have to listen to it, you know. You could just delete it. Here, give it to me. I'll do it for you." She stretches out her hand. I go to hand her my phone.

"No." I pull it back to me. "He's my mess. I think I'll listen to it."

With shaking fingers I dial my voicemail and am surprised there are a host of messages from everyone from Stefan to Dad to Grace and Laura. I finally reach the one from Logan and my stomach does a flip as I hear his smooth, chocolaty voice.

I listen to about as much as I can take—which is only about three seconds—before I throw the phone across the room again, my body shaking with rage.

I'll be amazed if my phone lasts the rest of the day.

"You really need to stop doing that," Alexis says as she collects it up, pressing the 'end' button. "Want to tell me what he said?"

"I got as far as 'I'm sorry' before I couldn't stomach any more."

"I guess that confirms it then. He knew all about it."

"Yep, he sure did."

Alexis walks over and collects me in a hug. "You're going to find someone who deserves you, Brooke. I know you will."

I pull away from her with lightning speed. "Oh, no. No I won't. There's no way on this sweet Earth I'm going near another guy again. I've learnt my lesson well and good this time, Alexis."

Some time later, after we've eaten, I begin to feel almost human again, my tummy's insistent rumblings finally satisfied.

"Hey, I noticed a photo over by your window before." Alexis walks over and picks it up. "Is that your mum?"

I nod at her, biting my upper lip.

In my favourite photo of Mum she's sitting on the beach in a floral sundress, the wind catching her shoulder-length blonde hair. She looks so beautiful, relaxed and happy.

"She was so pretty, Brooke," she says as she inspects it closely. I feel a small wave of sadness as I think of the woman in the picture: so full of life, so full of hope.

Unlike Laura, whom I've known since I was five years old, I didn't know Alexis at school. Although she went to my high school, our paths never crossed.

She picks up another photo, this one of me with Laura when we must have been about twenty-two. I'm dressed in a short, strapless dress, my golden tanned skin complimented by the pale pink of the silky fabric.

"Oh, my god, Brooke. Is this your natural hair colour?"

Embarrassed, I get up and grab the photo from her, examining it critically as I do. I'm smiling at the camera, my arms wrapped around Laura, who looks equally happy, my light brown curls in juxtaposition to her sleek blonde locks.

"Yeah, it is. Pretty Average Joanna, don't you think?"

"No! I think you look amazing. Those curls are gorgeous. I can see some struggling to get free right now."

My hand shoots automatically to my hair and I self-consciously smooth the errant curls down. They spring right back out.

I shrug. "I don't know."

But I do know. I glance at the photo of Mum. I do it because I want to look like her. It seems weird, I know, but in bleaching my hair to her shade I'm keeping her alive, in some small way.

Man, a therapist would have a field day with me.

Alexis hands me the picture and I look down at my smiling face. Perhaps it is time for a change. I know it would only be a symbolic gesture but I sure could do with 'washing that man right out of your hair'.

A new start? Yes, that's exactly what I need to do.

* * *

The following week, I manage to drag myself out of my house to meet Jocelyn at the office to finish the packing and do one final check before handing the keys over to the landlord.

She walks into my office, holding an empty box.

"That's for my stuff, I assume?" I swallow hard. There's something about having to pack your belongings into a cardboard box. It's somehow shameful, the box representing all your failures in the job.

Really, in the end, it's just a box.

"Yes. Here you go." She places the box on my chair. "How have you been, chook?" Jocelyn asks.

"Fine." I know I sound unconvincing.

She pauses, narrowing her eyes at me. "You couldn't have known what that crowd wanted to do, love."

I hang my head. "I added in an extra clause to the contract, kind of a 'get out of jail free' card."

"What a clever thing to do."

"That's what I thought. Until they used it to steal the company."

"Ahhh," she replies.

"That makes it my fault, doesn't it?"

She shakes her head, smiling in sympathy. "I know that's how it must feel, chook. But you didn't know they were going to go pulling this stunt."

"I should have, though, Jocelyn. It was my responsibility to protect the company. Without me, you would all still have jobs."

"Don't worry yourself on that front. I'm a box of budgies. I've already signed myself up with a recruitment agency down the road and the nice bloke, Julian, promised me he'd have me in a new job by the end of next week."

'A box of budgies'? Logan would kill himself with that one. *Arrgh!* I've got to stop thinking about that piece of work.

"That's great, Jocelyn."

"And you know Stefan's gone back to the advertising agency he used to work for?"

"He has?" I ask in surprise. Wow, how long have I been under my duvet?

"So don't you worry about us. We're all right as rain."

I smile weakly at her, wishing I could be as positive as she is about the future.

We continue to sort the office into boxes in silence, broken only when Jocelyn asks me where some item or another should go.

Finally, we're standing at the door together, keys in hand. What's left of *Live It* is now stacked away in boxes, ready to be moved to the spare room in my townhouse.

It's a depressing thought.

"Well, that's it then," Jocelyn says.

"I suppose it is."

She rubs my arm and pulls me in for one of her legendary hugs.

Once we reach the street below, she says, "Take care of yourself, love."

I sniff. "You too, Jocelyn. And thanks. For, you know, everything."

She smiles at me and I turn to walk away.

"Brooke, love," she calls out.

I turn back to face her.

"Logan called me."

I purse my lips, my stomach flip-flopping at the mention of his name.

"He said he's been trying to get a hold of you."

"I know," I reply through gritted teeth.

Logan has called a total of seven times over the last few days, and I've been deleting his messages without listening to them. I don't want to give him the satisfaction.

"Jocelyn, he just wants to come out of all this smelling like roses, like he somehow had nothing to do with it all. I'm not interested in his bullshit."

She nods at me. "He broke your heart, didn't he?"

I look down at the ground, fighting the angry tears springing into my eyes.

She wraps me up in one of her famous hugs. "Oh, love. I gave him a piece of my mind, you know."

"I bet you did." I manage a feeble smile.

That's my Jocelyn: always got my back. I'm going to miss her so much.

"He explained what happened and asked me—"

"Stop right there, Jocelyn," I instruct, interrupting her. "I don't want to hear it. He knew what was going on. He admitted it to me. There's nothing more to discuss."

"But love, he—"

"No!" I say with force. I soften my voice. "Please. No."

"Well, if you're sure?" She looks at me uncertainly.

"I am. He's played you as much as he's played me. And anyway, what's done is done and I'm moving on, okay?"

"Okay, chook. If your mind's made up I'll leave it at that."

"It is."

I get to my car, open the door, and plonk myself down.

I look up at our office. That's it, then: the end of an era, no more *Live It*. I heave a heavy.

What am I going to do with my life now?

CHAPTER 25

I TAKE A DEEP, steadying breath and steel myself. It's now or never.

I've pulled up outside my family's home and am finding it difficult to drum up the courage to get out of my car. I've been putting off telling them what's happened with *Live It*, telling myself I don't want to worry them while Jennifer's going through her radiation treatment. In reality that's only half the reason: I'm so ashamed at how I lost my business.

And how I let a good-for-nothing man walk all over me. Again.

One of the things my dad and I have in common is we both run profitable businesses. Well, *he* runs a profitable business. Me? Not so much these days.

Dad gives me advice and we talk tactics and strategies. I know that my success has made him very proud of me. Telling him I've failed at the one thing he admires me for makes me feel really terrible: like I'm killing off the Brooke he loves and admires, leaving him with the failed Brooke I've become.

I take another deep breath, pushing the front door open. I've brought over some chicken soup and a French bread stick, some flowers, and chocolate brownies: all reputed to be good for the patient in their own, different way.

"That's so kind of you, Brooke, darling. Thank you," Jennifer says as she hugs me gingerly. It's been some time since her surgery, but she's still careful, not wanting to rupture anything.

"How are you feeling?" I ask her. "Here, I'll put those in a vase for you."

"Pretty good, all things considered. The radiotherapy has caused the skin around the treatment areas to be quite sore." She indicates an area on her left breast and under her arm. "Other than that, though, I can't really complain."

Once again I admire her positivity. "I'm sorry to hear that. How long will it last?"

She shrugs. "I don't know. But it's not too bad. I'm not feeling tired, although they say it will come."

"Something to look forward to, then?" I joke, locating a vase in the kitchen cupboard and snipping the wrapping off the flowers.

"Exactly. All part of the fun and games of cancer, I guess." She smiles at me. "And it'll all be over soon. Well, this part, at least."

"Really?" I ask, feeling hopeful.

"My treatment is over in a couple of weeks."

"That's great!"

That went super fast. I guess I've been so busy wallowing in the wreckage of my life I didn't pay enough attention to Jennifer's treatment timeline.

"Yes. Then I'll meet my oncologist and we'll see how things are."

"Oh." The excitement seeps out of me.

She gives me a benign smile. "It'll be fine, Brooke. I know my body, I know I'm healing."

"Of course."

There's a sudden a lump in my throat. You didn't know you had breast cancer: I hope like hell you're right this time.

Dad walks into the kitchen. "Brooke, I thought that was you." He removes his reading glasses and gives me a hug. "How are you? We haven't seen you for a while. Been working on that big, new business venture of yours, I bet."

"Mm," I mumble noncommittally, busying myself with arranging the flowers.

Living in the small city of Wellington, I know they'll hear about it from someone else if I don't tell them, but I haven't quite mustered the strength to broach the subject quite yet.

"How about I put the kettle on and serve up these delicious brownies you brought?" Jennifer suggests. "You two can catch up on all your wheeling and dealing."

"Great idea, darling," Dad replies. "Are you all right to do that?"

She shoots him a 'don't-question-me' look.

"Righto," Dad replies, understanding her non-verbal message perfectly.

Jennifer clearly wants to be treated as normal.

I follow him into the living room as though we're in a funeral procession, which is *so* appropriate: his image of me as a successful business owner is certainly about to buried deep in the ground.

"Come and sit down and tell me the latest." He pats the seat next to him on the sofa.

I hesitate before taking the suggested seat, and prepare to let him down gently.

"Last time we talked you were about to meet with their representative, right? What fantastic plans have you devised?"

He looks so happy, so excited for me, so oblivious to the disaster my life has become.

I hang my head.

"Hey, what's wrong?" He puts his hand on my back in concern.

I look up at him, take a deep breath, and tell him the whole sorry tale.

Of course, I leave out the Logan sex marathon details. There really is some information not designed for a dad's ears.

"Oh, kiddo." He takes me in his arms as my tears make tracks down my face.

"I'm such an idiot, Dad," I say as he proffers a box of tissues. I take them gratefully, wiping my eyes and blowing my nose.

"You didn't see it coming. It can be a dog eat dog world, Brooke. And they sound like a ruthless bunch. You thought you were doing the right thing for your company. It just didn't work out, that's all. I admire you."

"You do?" I question through my tears, thoroughly surprised.

"Of course," he chuckles. "You built a business so good the only way a big international company could break into the New Zealand market was to take you over in an underhand way. You had the whole country sewn up."

I smile despite myself. "I guess." I feel lighter than I have since it happened. It's a nice feeling, one I wish could last. Then reality smashes its way through and I'm defeated once again. "And now I've got nothing."

"I know it feels like that right now. You'll bounce back. I have faith in you."

"What if I don't? I don't feel like I have it in me to start some new company, Dad."

"Well if you don't, you don't. What's the big deal? You managed to do what most people would give their left arm to do: you found a gap in the market, set up a business, and make a huge success of it. Brooke, that's amazing in anyone's books. I know people my age who've been trying for decades to achieve what you managed in just five years."

The wonderful lightness returns. Well, when you put it like that...

He draws me into another hug. "And you know, Jennifer and I love you, no matter what, kiddo."

Tears sting my eyes. "But I always thought I needed to be successful to m-make you happy."

"You did?" he asks in shock. "Oh, Brooke. Where did you get a cock-eyed idea like that?"

I shrug, giving him a watery smile. "I don't know." I snivel, wiping my eyes. "You were so busy with Grace and Dylan but you'd always take the time out to help me with my business. I guess it became our thing. And now it's gone, I'm scared we won't have our special father-daughter thing anymore."

He levels me with his gaze. "You need to understand me when I say we will *always* have our special bond, no matter what. I'm so proud of you, Brooke. That's not going to change because you got duped by some big corporation. You're my girl."

"Thanks, Dad. You're the best."

"No worries." He grins back at me.

After brownies, soup, and a whole lot of tea, I arrive back at my townhouse so much lighter than when I left.

I can't stop thinking about what Dad said to me.

For the first time since I was kid, I feel valued and loved by him in a way I haven't felt since before Mum died. And it's absolutely amazing.

If there's one good thing to come out of this big fat mess it's finding out how much my dad cares for me.

Something perhaps I've known all along, but have been too blinkered to see.

I shake my head dolefully as I think about Dylan. The last time I saw him, after his 'slumped-against-a-wall-semi-conscious-and-drooling' moment, I told him to get his facts straight before jumping to conclusions.

The sweet irony of my words is certainly not lost on me now.

* * *

"I know it's been total crap for you, but please, you *have* to come," Laura pleads.

Although going to a big thirtieth birthday bash—reminding me I'm hurtling towards that age myself at a frightening rate of knots—is about the last thing I feel like doing right now, I don't want to let my friend down.

"I will, I promise." I force a smile across my face.

Like Molly Ringwald in *Pretty in Pink*, I've decided I need to go to Laura's party to show the world I'm not broken.

Shame I won't have Andrew McCarthy there to profess his undying love for me.

But life doesn't imitate rom coms. I've got that message loud and clear.

"In fact, I've just bought some dye to sort out these unsightly roots of mine." I peer in my living room mirror, flattening my hair out so Laura can see the full extent of my hair disaster.

"Yay!" she says, clapping her hands together in her typical seal-like manner. She's so cheerful and optimistic I can't help but feel happier in her company.

"Fancy a coffee?" I wander towards the kitchen.

"Sure. That would be nice," she says. "Come here, my big girl."

This she says to her baby, Sophia, not me. She picks her up out of her port-a-cot.

"She's just too cute." I pinch her gorgeous chubby cheeks. "You and Kyle sure do make a good line in kids."

"Don't we?" She gets that gooey-eyed thing mothers do when they gaze at their babies.

"Would you like a cuddle?"

"Yes, please," I reply as Laura passes me Sophia. I hold her in my arms, breathing in her delicious baby-ness. She coos contentedly, grabbing at my necklace.

"Not broody at all?" she asks, an inquisitive smile on her face.

"Who wouldn't be with this gorgeous girl in their arms?" I look into Sophia's deep blue eyes. She has the longest blonde lashes I've ever seen, framing her eyes like little golden halos.

"Alexis is practically bursting at the seams to have her own now she's engaged. I wouldn't be surprised if she's pregnant before they get home from their honeymoon."

I take a deep sigh.

"Sorry." She takes in my slumped shoulders. "I should know better than to talk about weddings and babies right now. That was dumb of me."

"It's okay, Laura. I'm a big enough girl to know life goes on. Just because I climbed into bed with America's biggest lothario and got dumped on my ass, doesn't mean other people can't be happy."

"Yeah, but you don't need me rubbing your face in it."

"No worries. I'm actually doing a little bit better now."

It's been a while since the implosion of *Live It* and my discovery of Logan's deception. I've had time to get used to it and the pain has begun to dull around the edges.

Up until recently I spent most of my days holed up in my house, mooching around in my sweatpants, and most certainly *not* watching my usual movie line up of rom coms.

Instead, I've been indulging in box sets of *Game of Thrones*. I've been identifying with every victim, hating every cynical, nasty villain. And let's face it; there are a lot of both on that show.

Stabbings? Good. Beheadings? Great. General nastiness, blood, and gore? Fan-freaking-tastic.

Yes, *Game of Thrones* matched my state of mind to perfection.

And now? I'm feeling less bitter, less angry. Life has dealt me a dreadful blow, but I'm ready to start to pick up the pieces and get on with my life.

"Oh, that's so good to hear!" Laura wrinkles her forehead. "I still can't believe Logan did this to you. He loves you. There must be some kind of mistake."

"I love you for your optimism, your faith in the human spirit, Laura. But just because you believe he's a good, decent person, doesn't make him one."

"Maybe." She doesn't look convinced. "Let's get into your wardrobe and work out what you're going to wear to my party."

She pulls anything even vaguely dressy out of my closet, piling them up on my bed. She rifles through them, rejecting most and keeping a few.

"Okay, so I've narrowed it down to these three. With your figure you'll look great in any of them."

She's inadvertently chosen a dress I wore out to dinner in Wellington with Logan.

I point at a black sheath dress lying on the bed. "I don't think I'll wear this one, if it's all the same to you. Bad association."

"Say no more." She removes the offending item, stashing it at the back of my wardrobe. "Now, it's down to these two. The pink will look amazing if you wear your hair down, and the lacy number will make you look like a hot, blonde Kate Middleton."

She holds them both up against me as I look in my full-length mirror. I'm totally uninspired by either of her selections.

Standing behind me, looking at my reflection, Laura lowers the dresses. "You'll be fine, you know. You'll bounce back from this and come back stronger than before. You're one of the toughest chicks I know. You're going to be just fine."

"I know. I'm getting there." Those pesky tears sting my eyes again at her sweetness. Not for the first time, I regret the loss of the hard shell exterior I used to be pretty proud of: it seems to have completely deserted me. Along with my career and love life.

After Laura's gone, I return to my bedroom, pull off my comfy clothes and put on the lacy dress Laura chose. I stare at my reflection and barely recognize the woman staring back. Despite the amount of uncharacteristic junk food I've been downing and lack of my usual exercise regime, I'm looking gaunt, my eyes almost sunken into my skull.

My skin has taken on a greyish tinge, making me look older than my years, and my hair appears frazzled, like I've put my finger in an electricity socket on one of those kids' cartoons.

I smooth my hair down to its ends. In some small, symbolic way, changing my hair colour would mean bidding goodbye to the Brooke I've been for years. The Brooke who built up *Live It* from a struggling start up to a successful business; the Brooke who loved Scott; the Brooke who fell for Logan and lost her company.

My mind made up I slip the dress off, leaving it on the floor in a heap as I climb under the covers and submit myself to the temporary relief that comes with blessed sleep.

CHAPTER 26

"WOW, BABE. YOU LOOK amazing! I hardly recognized you," Laura gushes as she takes my coat, making me wonder how bad I must have looked before.

Yes, I know: pretty bloody awful.

I'm feeling more positive than I have in days. That's not to say I'm about to do cartwheels in the street or anything—especially not in the dress I'm wearing tonight—but I do feel as though the fog I've been floundering in has begun to lift.

She takes one of my newly light brunette curls in her hand. "I know it's a total cliché, but it softens you. Why were you ever blonde? You totally rock as a brunette."

Gone is the poker-straight, high maintenance, *un*natural blonde, replaced by something much closer to the real me. And it feels pretty darn good.

It didn't take me long to talk Rico—my long-standing, long-suffering hairdresser—into making the change.

"With those amazing eyes of yours you're going to look sensational," he cooed to my reflection in the mirror of his upmarket city salon. "So, so sexy. Every man will want to eat you up for their breakfast."

I laughed. "That might be a little ambitious, don't you think?" I replied, annoyed with myself my mind—and my heart—instantly turned to Logan.

Since my transformation at Rico's expert hands, it's taken me a while to get used to it, but changing my look is symbolic of the new me. I'm trying to face the world with fresh eyes.

And hair.

"Brooke? Is that you?" I turn to see Alexis peering at me incredulously. "You look so good!" She hugs me and I breathe in her Dior perfume. "Just like Jennifer Garner. Right, Laura?"

"I was thinking Megan Fox."

I laugh, buoyed by their compliments. "Either way you're saying I look like a beautiful famous actress, so I'm happy."

"Is this a new dress? I don't remember seeing it in your wardrobe," Laura comments.

"It is." I beam as I give them a twirl.

In an attempt to become a new, better version of me, I felt a new party dress was in order. Despite having no income I splashed out on a stunning red dress I saw in a boutique in the city. It's floaty, romantic, and makes me feel incredible, cut into a deep V in the front, fitting my slim, athletic physique to perfection.

I turn to Laura, giving her a peck on the cheek. "Happy birthday, gorgeous." I hand her the present I'd bought the previous day. It's a beautiful piece of blown glass she had admired on a shopping trip we'd been on months ago. Another expensive purchase, but friends like Laura are hard to come by. In the scheme of things, it was well worth the investment.

"Thanks, Brooke," she gushes with pleasure, giving me a squeeze.

"Come with me and get a drink," Alexis commands, slipping her arm around my waist and walking me into the living room.

The room is full to the brim of partygoers, lively music blaring. Alexis hands me a shot glass filled with tequila and a slice of lime.

"Down in one."

I grin at her. "Down in one," I confirm, tossing the liquid back before sucking on the wedge of lime.

"Hey, I feel bad I haven't asked about your wedding lately." She hands me another shot.

We knock them back. Wow, this woman's on a mission tonight.

"That's okay. I knew you were going through some stuff. Talking about my wedding was probably the last thing you wanted to do."

"Hi there, I'm Tim," Alexis's fiancée says as he wraps his arms around Alexis from behind. "Wow. Brooke? I didn't recognize you. You look like you did years ago."

"Thanks. I think." I assume that's a good thing? "Hey, and

congratulations on getting engaged too, Tim."

He unravels himself from his fiancée to give me a quick hug.

"It was about time, don't you think?" They grin at one another and I have to force a fresh wave of misery down.

Dammit! I thought I was doing so much better.

"I'm really happy for you."

"Here," Alexis says, handing me another shot. "I think you could do with one more one of these."

I chug it back, taking a mental note to stop drinking now: the last thing I need is to end up making alcohol-soaked decisions like I almost did that night with Scott.

I notice Lucinda walking into the room, laughing and preening like she's some kind of Hollywood starlet we all adore. "What's *she* doing here?"

"Oh, you know Laura: friends with everyone." She shoots Lucinda daggers.

"That really is an annoying habit of hers," I comment.

Lucinda waves at us, as though we're her good friends, as she hands Laura a present and gives her a hug. She slips her jacket off and hands it to Kyle, Laura's husband.

Oh. My. God. She's wearing my dress!

But whereas it looks slim-fitting and classy with a hint of sex appeal on me, on Lucinda's hourglass frame it's extremely figure hugging, her breasts popping out of it all over the place. With her platinum locks and full red lips she looks positively pornographic as she wiggles her way towards us.

She looks more like she should be the guest of honour at the Playboy Mansion than at Kyle and Laura's suburban birthday bash.

She makes a B-line for us and I shrink into my dress. She walks over and stands next to me, creating a 'who-wore-it-best' moment.

She wins hands down—or tits up.

She looks me up and down. "Nice dress," she murmurs with a crooked smile.

She smooths her own dress down across her belly, pumping her ample assets out as she does so. I swear every man's eyes in the room follow her hands' slow, deliberate progress. She revels in the attention.

"Err, thanks. You too." I know as certain as the sun will rise tomorrow every pair of eyes in the room will be comparing me with this sex siren next to me. And I'm not likely to be the victor.

"Hey, Lu," Tim says, smiling at her like an idiot.

Alexis shoots him a look that says 'put-it-back-in-your-pants-if-you-still-want-to-be-my-fiancée' and Tim does just that.

"Is the dress perhaps a little too small for you?" Alexis asks.

"I suppose some of us just fill it out better than others, that's all." She shoots me a smug sideways glance that makes me want to pull her hair extensions out. One by one.

Lucinda studies my face, recognition dawning. "Is that you, Brooke? My, my. Don't you look like a schoolgirl. What's with the new locks?"

I open my mouth to speak, looking like a fish out of water, unable to think of an appropriately bitchy comment to shoot back at her.

"I think she looks amazing," Alexis jumps in. "So young and fresh and *natural*," she adds with extra emphasis. It goes over Lucinda's head.

"She does," Lucinda replies genuinely. I nearly fall off my heels at the unexpected compliment.

Then I spot a nasty grin spreading across her pretty face. Isn't it funny the way good-looking people can suddenly appear ugly when they're full of anger and spite?

"And I see you got the memo," she adds.

"The memo?" I inadvertently fall straight into her trap.

"To give the field its straw back." She smiles sweetly at me, catching one of my curls in her hand.

"People in glass houses shouldn't throw stones, Lucinda," Alexis states, nodding at Lucinda's platinum locks while crossing her arms.

"Oh, I'm just kidding around. You know that, don't you, hon?"

"Sure." I purse my lips.

"Now, tell me, Brooke. Do you make it a habit of only dating cute American men?" Lucinda asks.

My heart skips a beat as an image of Logan pushes its way into my head.

"Err, no." I laugh nervously. "Why?" I ask before I can stop myself. You're a prize idiot, Brooke Mortimer.

She shrugs, smiling sweetly. As sweetly as a she-devil intent on destruction can smile, that is. "I was at Ancient not that long ago. Been there lately?"

My throat seizes. I know what's coming next.

"I always thought you and Scott made a cute couple. By the looks of you two together, I assume you're back on?"

I let out a puff of air, trying to conjure up a genie to get me out of here at lightning speed.

Needless to say, no genie appears and Lucinda's casual reference to Scott is greeted by an ear-splitting screech from Alexis. "*Scott?* What were you doing with *him?*"

I haven't told anyone about my nearly-sex encounter with Scott—or his unexpected profession of love for me—deciding it's an embarrassment I just don't need to relive.

"I, err—" I begin, blushing every shade of red imaginable. Thank god the lights are low in here.

I take Alexis by the arm, glaring at Lucinda's smug face as I do, walking her away to a quiet spot.

"We had a drink. I had a bit too much and we nearly ended up in bed together."

"*Nearly?* What does 'nearly' mean?" She raises her eyebrows at me.

I'm a naughty schoolgirl who has to justify her behaviour to the principal.

Deciding there's nothing for it but to come clean now, I tell her about how he had told me he was still in love with me and wanted me back; how I had felt flattered; how he had looked so hot in his jeans; and how I had come to my senses once we were back at his apartment.

"Thank god for that. Why didn't you tell me, babe?"

"I was embarrassed. I've screwed my life up beyond recognition. Almost sleeping with my ex just felt like a step too far." I hang my head.

"Oh, sweetie." She rubs my arm.

The music stops and we both turn to see Kyle standing by the fireplace, a smiling Laura looking cute in a 'Fifties-inspired navy dress, by his side.

"As you know, I'm not one for making speeches." There's a general murmur of agreement and a sprinkling of laughter from the partygoers.

"Since it's my wife's thirtieth birthday I thought I'd share a few words with you all." He pulls a battered piece of paper out of his back pocket to whoops from several of his friends.

He turns to face Laura, who looks at her husband with such love in her eyes it almost makes me cry. Again.

He clears his throat, looking at his notes. "Laura," he begins.

"Glad you got the name right!" someone calls out. It's funny because Kyle is terrible with names, often giving his friends nicknames. Which, surprisingly, he seems quite capable of remembering.

I smile as I turn to see who is heckling him with the in-joke. It's one of his good buddies, Ben, a nice guy I knew a little at university.

Hmmm. If Ben's here, then of course his girlfriend, Jessica, will be too. She's the woman Scott had an affair with, the reason I kicked him out. Seeing her would *really* make my night.

I scan the room, oblivious to the speech everyone seems to be finding so entertaining. I spot her standing next to her friend, Morgan. She's wearing a strapless floral dress, her long dark brown hair falling over her shoulders.

Our eyes meet and she gives me a friendly, if tentative, wave. I respond in kind, trying my best to look like I don't have a care in the world. A bit of a tall order right now.

"So, to wrap up. Laura. Babe. You are the love of my life, and I wish you the happiest of thirtieth birthdays."

She beams at him as he looks at her through embarrassed eyes.

"And that's all there is. You can clap now." We all burst into spontaneous applause, some people cheering.

"Oh, one other thing I forgot," Kyle says.

"Good one, mate," another one of his friends calls out.

"Yeah, yeah," he replies good-humouredly.

We all turn as Jessica walks back into the room, holding a cake blazing with candles. We break into song, Laura flushing with happiness.

Once she's blown out the candles she turns to face us all again. "I just want to say a huge thank you to all of you for coming. And to Kyle's mum, who has our three little treasures tonight. I'm having the best time, and I want you all to stay and drink and have fun. I sure as hell am."

People cheer. She holds her hand up and everyone falls silent once more. "I also want Kyle, my wonderful husband, to know how lucky I am to have him and our three amazing children in my life. I don't know where I would be without you."

You would be where I am, Laura. And you wouldn't like it, not one little bit.

There's a series of 'ahh's' from the crowd followed by applause as Kyle and Laura kiss.

She turns to face us and everyone falls silent once again. "This is the final thing I want to say tonight, I promise. Now, I know this night is all about me, as it should be," she says to laughter, "but I'm bursting to share some news with you. Ben? Come over here."

Laura takes Jessica's hand as Ben makes his way across the room, smiling so much he looks like his face might crack, his eyes trained on Jessica. When he reaches her he wraps his arm around her waist, and they share a smile.

I can almost hear my heart go clunk, heading southward, as it dawns on me what may be about to happen.

"These two took some time to work out they were perfect for each other. *Some* of us knew all along. I'm just saying. So?" She looks at them, waiting for one of them to jump in.

They're both smiling widely at one another, until Jess turns to us, "Ben and I are engaged!"

Clunk, clunk, *bang*. My heart hits the floor.

Jessica's friend, Morgan, lets out a squeal of excitement as Laura hugs Jessica. The rest of the partygoers, most of who know the newly-engaged couple well, clap, cheer, and offer their congratulations.

"Isn't it exciting? You know them, right?" Alexis asks.

"Yeah, I do." She's the woman who had an affair with Scott. Great memories.

"Come and congratulate them with me. I don't know Jessica or Ben very well, but I'd love to talk weddings with them."

"Sure." I square my shoulders. Jessica deserves happiness just as much as the next person. After all, she didn't know I was with Scott when she slept with him. He was the love rat, not her.

We walk through the crowd towards the happy couple. We line up behind a group of others, all jostling to offer their congratulations. It's like a frigging royal line up and I'm a mug standing there, waiting to pay my respects.

"Hi, Brooke," Jessica says brightly when we get our turn. "I love your hair. You look amazing. Welcome back to the brunette club." She gives me a light hug.

"Thanks. And congratulations."

"You're so sweet. I really appreciate you saying that." She leans in, adding, "You know, after everything."

I nod at her. "Yeah. Water under the bridge, huh?"

"Water under the bridge."

Ben interrupts our moment. "Hey, Brooke. I haven't seen you for ages. How are things?"

"Oh, fantastic!" I smile as brightly as I can muster.

Alexis shoots me a sideways glance, but what else can I say? I'm hardly going to say 'my boyfriend, who I thought loved me, stole the business I'd worked years to build up, leaving me destitute, jobless, with a broken heart'. Am I?

"You two make a cute couple," I say, diverting attention back to them.

I might have made my peace with Jessica, but I don't need to go back over my recent disasters, just as I'm beginning to pull my life together.

They grin like the lovesick puppies they are as I back away.

"Ow!" a woman behind me shrieks, almost deafening me.

I turn around and notice I'm standing on Lucinda's toes. She's wearing black strappy heels about one hundred inches high—as befitting the porn star she's dressed as tonight—and one of my nude heels is crushing her toes.

"Oops. Sorry, Lucinda." I move my heel away, even though I'm sorely tempted to give it a quick turn before I do.

"Watch where you're going, Brooke. You're so *fucking* clumsy," she growls at me.

I blink at her in shock.

She might be a sex siren, intent on rubbing us mere mortals' faces in her assets—not literally in my case, thank goodness—but I've never had her pegged as nasty.

She pushes past me to get to Jessica and Ben.

"I'm so excited for you both," she gushes, grabbing their hands, oozing sweetness and charm.

I've almost got whiplash from the change in her mood.

"Err, thanks, Lucinda," Jessica replies uncertainly. She turns to me. "Are you all right?" Concern is etched on her face.

"Yeah, thanks." I still feel stunned.

She leans in closer so only I can hear her. "Don't worry about her. She's a total bitch."

I grin at her, nodding. "That she is, Jessica. That she is."

"And what's more, you look *so* much better in that dress."

"Thanks."

The music starts up again and people begin to dance.

I may be trying out this new and improved version of myself, but I think I've had enough of this party. All I want to do now is go home and curl up in my PJ's.

"Hey, are you leaving already?" Alexis asks as I grab my jacket from the mountain of coats on Laura and Kyle's bed.

"Please don't tell Laura. I know I'm bunking out on her birthday party."

"That's okay. She'll understand. Are you okay?"

Am I okay? I think before I answer. I've successfully sported the new 'I'm-over-him' hairdo, weathered a beating at Lucinda's catty hands, and made peace with Scott's former lover. All without falling to pieces. I'm actually pretty proud of myself.

"You know what? I am." I hesitate. "Or at least I know I will be."

I give Alexis a hug and head home, knowing with certainty my future will be better than my past.

I'm Brooke Mortimer: I'm tough, I'm driven, and you can bet your life I'm not going to be beaten.

CHAPTER 27

THE NEXT DAY I wake to the sound of birds chirping their morning chorus in the tress as the sun shines in the sky. For the first time in a long while, I decide to go for a morning run. It's hard work and I'm astonished at how much fitness I've lost in such a short space of time. It's so good to be out in the fresh air, getting my blood pumping around my body.

I'm beginning to feel more like me, less like the shell of a person I've been recently. And man, it feels good.

Every time my mind takes the inevitable path to Logan I force myself to think of something happy—bunnies hopping through sun-filled fields of lavender, that sort of thing—and, for the most part, it's working.

If I sit around too long I get agitated: I need to *do* something. And I've been sitting around way too long. It's time to move on. It's time to leave what's happened in the past right there where it belongs: in the past.

I pick up my phone and dial Dad's number.

"Hey, kiddo. How are things?"

"Good, thanks, Dad. I've got a proposal for you."

"I'm intrigued."

"Well, I've made a decision. I've decided I want to get on with my life. Do something with it, I mean."

"Ah, you want to need to grab the bull by the horns?"

"Exactly."

He laughs. "That sounds great to me. Where do I come in?"

"You know you mentioned a while back Sydney Garrett had

poached Tyler?"

"Yes. How could I forget? Scheming bastard, kicking a man when he's down."

"Have you managed to find a replacement for him? Because I wondered if you would like me to come and work for you for a while? I have the big payout from *You: Now* so I don't actually need a job, but I'm itching to get back out there and *do* something."

Dad chuckles. "That sounds like my girl."

"So?" I wait, hopeful.

"I'm so glad you asked, kiddo. I haven't had the chance to get someone new and I would love you to come and work for me. In fact, I had thought of asking you myself." I can hear the smile on his face.

"Thanks!"

"I've got a load of projects on at the moment, and my priority is—has to be—with Jennifer during her treatment."

"Of course! And I've worked for you enough in the past to know the ropes pretty well. What I don't know I'll pick up really fast, I promise." My excitement rises like a hot air balloon at the prospect of getting back out into the real world.

"I think this is a wonderful idea, kiddo. What are you doing on Monday?"

"Hang on, let me check my calendar," I say down the line. "Well would you look at that? Turns out I'm free on Monday."

Dad chuckles. "Come and see me at my office tomorrow morning at eight and I'll take you through what I need you to do, okay?"

"Sounds great. And, Dad? Thanks."

"See you then, kiddo."

* * *

I arrive at Dad's office first thing on Monday morning with coffee in hand. I've donned my favourite dress and styled my hair into a simple high ponytail. It feels good to be back in the land of the living.

I walk through the door and Dad waves at me, indicating for me to take a seat as he finishes his phone call.

I look around his office, reminded of how I used to spend my summers working here as a teenager, doing odd jobs and admin things for him. It was probably just an excuse for him to give me more pocket money than anything else.

"Hi Brooke." He gets up from his desk and giving me a warm hug. "It's great to have you here. Wowzers, kiddo: I love the hair!"

"Thanks, Dad. I thought I'd go natural for a change."

"It was the right decision. You look great." He collects me in a hug.

"How's Jennifer today?"

"She's doing all right. A bit tired and sore, but her spirits are high."

"That's good. I'll pop in and see her this afternoon." I haven't been to see her for a while, and I'm beginning to feel guilty.

"Actually, I think you might be a bit busy today, kiddo. You do know I've got this new development right now, don't you?"

"The green fields one in Aotea?" I ask, referring to a residential development in one of the city's outer suburbs Dad has been working on for months.

"That's the one. Come and sit with me and I'll take you through where we're up to."

We sit together with a site map of the land and a variety of documents as Dad takes me through the steps so far and what needs to be completed next.

"As you can see here on the project management sheet, we are in the final stages of getting these land parcels ready for sale and these ones for construction." He points at two different areas on the map.

"This is a big project, Dad," I comment, taking as much of the information in as I can. "How many houses are you planning on building?"

"Ten. You can see why I need your help," he comments. "If you hadn't become, err, free, I would have had to employ someone else, thanks to Garrett."

"Maybe it was all a master plan." I smile coyly at him.

I'm making some major progress if I can joke about what I've been through.

"Maybe." He smiles kindly.

"Right. Where do you want me to begin?"

"These land parcels over here are almost ready to be marketed, so there's not much more to be done there." He circles an area on the map. "It's here I want you to focus. I need you to meet with the architect this morning to discuss plans, dates, that sort of thing. They are expecting me at eleven-thirty on site. I'll call them to let them know it will be you instead."

"Sounds good to me. I'll need to head home to get my car first. Who am I meeting?"

"You're meeting my usual architect's sidekick. She's new. Now what's her name?" He searches through his project plan. "Anita McAndrew. That's the one. You'll need to meet her at Lot Twelve. Here's a checklist of the things you'll need to cover off, as well as some notes from our initial meeting." He hands me a file.

"Okay." I take it from him and collecting my things. That name sounds familiar to me, but I can't work out from where. "I'll have a read through at home when I grab my car."

"That's my girl." He smiles with obvious pride in his eyes.

I smile back at him, basking in my newfound assurance I don't have to be the most successful businesswoman in the city to hold his affection.

Shame I had to lose my company to learn it.

* * *

I reach the site at Aotea just over an hour later, wanting to scope it out before the architect arrives. It's a wet, blustery, and unpleasant day—the type Wellington specialises in at this time of year—and I pull my coat hood over my head to protect me from the virtually horizontal showers.

The site has been subdivided and I can see evidence of utilities already in place at each plot. So far so good. I wanted to check the light planes, per Dad's check list, but the low clouds and rain have put a literal—as well as metaphorical—dampener on that idea.

There's only so much battling of the elements a girl in heels can manage, so I give up after about ten minutes in the driving rain, heading to the sanctuary of my car.

Almost as soon as I shut my door and remove my dripping jacket there's a knock on the passenger window. Despite bearing more than a passing resemblance to one of those Sand People from Star Wars, with her hood tied tight around her face and her bespectacled face poking out, I know it must be Anita McAndrew.

I lean over and open the passenger door. "Are you Anita?" I ask as rain drives in through the door and onto the passenger seat.

"Yes. Can I hop in?" A gust of wind blasts her from the side, pushing the door open further.

"Of course," I reply, wishing I'd brought a towel: we could both do with a decent drying off right now.

She grabs hold of the door and pulls it closed as she sits down, water dripping from her coat.

"It's feral out there!" She removes her wet glasses and hood, turning her from Sand Person to human being.

"It sure is. I'm Brooke Mortimer. It's nice to meet you, Anita." I proffer my hand.

She takes it, shaking it with vigour. "I hoped it might be you." A grin spreads across her face. "When Roger, I mean your dad, said he was sending his daughter in his stead this morning, I expected Grace."

I regard her with confusion and a tinge of amusement. She clearly knows who I am, but I can't reciprocate.

"Well, I'm glad it's me then." My laugh is tinged with a hint of nervousness: I'm not really sure how to respond.

"You don't remember me, do you?" Her face drops as she narrows her eyes.

I search my mind but come up with a big fat zero. "Sorry." I shake my head.

To my relief she shrugs, a fresh smile breaking out on her round face once again. "That's okay. I was a couple of years younger than you at the time. You dated my big brother in high school."

"You might have to narrow it down for me a bit, Anita. I went out with a few guys back then."

"I'm sure you did. You were the most popular girl in your year, and so pretty. Not that you're not pretty any more, of course. You're gorgeous," she adds. "I really looked up to you. You were my role model in high school."

She's a one-woman fan club.

"Who's your brother?"

"Steve McAndrew." She beams at me. "I think you were about fifteen when you dated? He's a graphic designer in Auckland now. Married. Happy."

My mind darts back to Steve, cute and lanky in his school uniform. We would get together after school and kiss for hours, adding in the odd fumble over our clothes for good measure. We only dated for a couple of months, but of course it felt like a serious, long-term Relationship Of Significance back then.

"I remember you. You and I used to chat a bit, didn't we?"

"We did. You gave me such advice at the time. I've followed your career, actually."

"You have?" I ask in surprise.

"Yes. You've done such great things. Are you still running *Live It*?"

"Ah, no." I feel the now familiar pang of loss, although not as acutely as I once did. "*Live It* is over."

"That's a shame. I did one of your seminars and got a lot out of it."

"That's good to hear."

"You're working for your dad now?"

"Yes, just for the time being. Until I work out what to do next."

She nods at me, smiling. She has such a sweet expression on her face I'm compelled to share with her what had happened to my company. I omit the Logan part of the sorry tale—I prefer not to have to think about him these days.

"That's so shitty. Poor you. You'll bounce back. Someone like you always will."

I smile at her. "You know what, Anita? You're right. Not about the 'I'm-so-great' bit," I clarify with a laugh, "about the bouncing back bit."

Life isn't over. I will create a new life for myself. Sure, I don't know what it will be right now, but that's all part of the fun.

CHAPTER 28

I'VE BEEN WORKING FOR Dad for over a week now and I am loving every moment. After having spent what feels like an eternity wrapped up in my misery at home, it's so good to be *doing* something, to have a purpose to my days.

Dad's been helpful and involved, not fatherly in the slightest, treating me like he would any member of staff.

We've just finished another meeting with Anita—this time in the dry, sitting at her firm's chic city offices, rather than in my steamed up car—and are walking back to Dad's office together down the city's main shopping street, enjoying the brilliant sunshine.

"I really like her designs, Dad. I think she's come up with something that will appeal to our target market but look and feel different from those of the mill new developments."

"I agree. She's doing a great job for us. Hey, want to grab a coffee?" he asks as we walk past the park in front of Astoria, my favourite café.

"Yes, thanks. That'd be nice."

We sit at a table outside, sipping our coffees, discussing the next steps in Dad's development.

"You have a real knack for this work, you know, kiddo."

"Thanks, Dad. I really enjoy it." I beam at the compliment.

It's true: I held an initial fear I would be reminded too much of my high school holiday jobs as Dad's Girl Friday. But such fears have abated as he's passed me challenging and interesting tasks, trusting me completely.

"What are your plans? I love having you in the business, of

course, though I wonder if you might want to branch out into something else. You did run a successful business on your own, after all."

"Yeah." My mind turns to *Live It*.

Jeez Louise. *Live It* feels a million years away now. Surprising when its demise occurred only a short time ago.

I've stayed in touch with Stefan and Jocelyn, both of whom have scored themselves jobs they love, landing on their feet, much to my endless relief. The guilt of causing them and the rest of my staff difficulty and pain still smarts. I guess it always will.

I think about the work I'm doing with Dad, about how I get to spend time with him, about how much I enjoy the job without the stress of running my own business. Although I don't get to be the omnipotent boss, calling the shots, that no longer seems as important as it once did. I smile to myself as it dawns on me I'm happy doing what I'm doing and I don't want to be anywhere else.

"I'm not sure what I'm going to do yet." I bite my lip.

"Oh?" Dad questions.

"I was wondering. Do you need me to stay on for a while? I like the work."

A smile breaks across his face, crinkling the corners of his eyes. "I'd love you to."

Relief floods through me. Yes, this is the right move for me—for now, at least.

"Thanks." I jump out of my seat to hug him.

"We're a pretty good team, wouldn't you say, kiddo?"

I nod, smiling. I have a sense of happiness I haven't had since before my world came crashing down around my ears. "I do, Dad. I do."

* * *

I'm still buzzing when I get home that night. I walk through the door, dropping my keys on the kitchen bench, and open the fridge to pull out a bottle of wine.

Pouring out a glass I hear a knock at my front door. That's weird: I'm not expecting anyone. Maybe it's Alexis? She said she might pop around.

I open the door, glass in hand, and my heart leaps into my mouth.

Logan is standing on my doorstep, looking nervous as hell.

He stares at me, hesitating for a moment. "Hi, Brooke. Wow, you look different. You look so beautiful." He's tentative, almost breathless.

I stand, rooted to the spot, mouth agape as my brain tries to compute his unexpected presence.

Then hot anger rises, threatening to explode out of the top of my head like a volcano on cocaine.

I fix him with my coldest stare. "What. Are. You. Doing. Here."

It's not a question: it's an accusation.

"I wanted to see you. No, I *needed* to see you. You haven't returned any of my calls. You kind of left me no choice."

He has the audacity to smile at me, as though he hasn't used me and dumped me, causing me more humiliation than any one girl ought to have in a lifetime.

Remembering the full glass of wine in my hand, I hurl its contents at his face, watching with angry satisfaction as he blinks, frowns, and is forced to wipe the wine away with his sleeve.

"How dare you turn up here like nothing's happened? You prick!"

I turn and slam the door, almost breaking the window as I do, hearing the satisfying *whack* as door meets jamb.

My heart is hammering so hard, any moment now it's going to leap out of my mouth.

I drop my glass on the floor. I barely register it smashing against the tiles.

I can hear him banging on the door. "Brooke, please hear me out. You have to. Please."

"I don't have to *do* anything," I shout through the door. "There's nothing you can say I want to hear. You can just piss off back to America, Logan."

He bangs on the door again. "Please, Brooke. Honey. I can explain everything."

"Oh, I bet you can." I cross my arms, drumming my foot on the floor.

"If you just hear what I have to say, I promise I'll leave. Five minutes. That's all I ask."

I try to steady my shaking hands, making white-knuckle fists at my sides. "You can have three minutes."

He lets out a small chuckle. "Always negotiating. Three minutes it is."

I open the door and look at him, my belly flip-flopping again at the sight of him. I almost feel sorry for him, standing on my doorstep, wine splashed across his face and down his white T-shirt.

I force myself to concentrate on his face rather than trail down his body, knowing his wet T-shirt is clinging to his toned chest.

Hey, he may be the biggest asshole to walk the face of the planet, but I'm only human.

He walks through the door and into my house, crunching across the broken glass, and closes the door behind himself. I prepare myself for what's to come.

As he turns back to face me an involuntary shot of desire runs through my body.

Really, Brooke? After all he's done?

"Well?" I ask, tapping my foot in impatience, ignoring the way my Girly Bits are betraying me.

"It's *so* good to see you, honey." He takes a step closer to me.

"Don't! Don't you dare come a step closer," I say, putting my hands up. Thankfully he complies. "And I am *not* your 'honey'."

He looks wounded. Good.

"I know how this looks to you."

"You do?" I ask sarcastically. "Like you slept with me and stole my company, perhaps? Is that how it looks, Logan? Is it? Because that's sure as hell how it feels."

He stares at me before responding. I squirm in my heels. I hold my ground defiantly, reminding myself this man stole my company— my baby, my *life*—after everything I put into it over the years. And he broke my heart.

He shakes his head. "That's not what happened, Brooke."

"Really? Well maybe you would like to put me straight, Logan? Because from where I'm standing, that's exactly what happened." I glance at my watch. "You have two and a half minutes left."

He runs his hand through his thick hair and I'm forced to look away. It's such a familiar gesture, reminding me of our time together. I swallow hard.

It was all a ruse, it wasn't real. Logan never loved me; he was just using me.

"I know *You: Now* has taken your client base over, and all but destroyed your company. Brooke, I am so sorry about that."

"Sure you are. Tell me, Logan, were *we* a part of your take over process? Was that your plan? I'd be so busy falling for you I wouldn't notice the dagger being stuck into my back?"

"It wasn't like that!" he protests.

I'm on a roll. "Oh, really? Who knows? Maybe this is something you do regularly? Maybe you're the resident gigolo? You find a company you want, then you screw your way in so you can grab and run before the sex haze has worn off."

"Gigolo? Sex haze?" He frowns for a moment before his face clears. "No. You've got that so wrong. You and me? We had nothing to do with what happened."

"That's where you're so wrong, Logan. We had *everything* to do with it." Tears sting my eyes and I wipe them away furiously. "You *knew*: you work for the company that stole *Live It*."

"*Worked*. Past tense."

"What?" I ask in irritation.

"When I found out what they were doing, I put it on the line to Geoff. I told him it was either me or you."

His words sink in, and I stare at him. "You quit? Over what happened?"

"I told you all this in my messages. Didn't you listen to them?"

Messages? Oh. All those voicemails he left: the ones I deleted without listening to.

"I even tracked down Jocelyn and convinced her to talk to you, to help you see reason, to explain."

My mind races back to my last conversation with Jocelyn, outside our old office block. She had things she wanted to tell me. I didn't let her.

My legs suddenly turn to jelly as I struggle to breath. Logan strides over, steadying me before I fall.

He wraps his arms tenderly around me. It feels so good, so right.

"Brooke, you *know* me. You think I've done these dreadful things, but I haven't. I would never do anything to hurt you. I quit my job because I couldn't work for a company that would do that to you, to your business."

"But, but—" I take a deep breath to steady myself. "You signed the letters to our clients, the ones stealing our business."

He shakes his head. "It was an electronic signature. I didn't sign any letters." He takes my hands in his, and I look down at them, almost as though I'm watching it all on TV. It doesn't seem real.

"It was never my intention to steal your business. I was sent to New Zealand to assess your company so that we could enter an honest partnership with you. And that's exactly what I did. It was Brad who came up with the idea to dupe you, and it was Brad who did it."

Memories of the way in which I confronted Logan about Stefan's suspicions in Queenstown flood back. Brad had threatened to call his dad with his new plan, and Logan had argued with him about it. Brad was the one who turned up on our doorstep. Brad was the one who took our data, stole our clients. Deep down inside I know Logan is telling the truth.

"You weren't in on it." It's a statement of fact, not a question.

"No, Brooke. Not only would I never do that to you, I'd never do that to anyone. It's not who I am."

A fresh thought occurs to me. "Why has it taken you so long to come here to see me?"

He looks at me in obvious exasperation. "I tried every way I could think of to get in touch with you. You didn't return my calls. You wouldn't listen to Jocelyn. Hell, I even called Stefan, although he hung up on me after calling me names."

I manage a weak laugh.

"I was stuck in Eastern Europe for days, unable to get through to you. Once I got back to San Francisco I confronted Geoff on what he'd done. It was then I put it on the line to him and ended up quitting. I got on the first flight I could out here. Brooke, I needed to see you."

I look into his eyes and something stirs inside me. I believe him with all my heart.

"What about how you asked me what I would do if I didn't have my company? You asked me straight after we signed the contract. The timing seems pretty suspicious."

He shrugs. "To be honest, I was sounding you out. I wanted to see if you were open to other possibilities."

"Why?"

He sweeps one of my errant curls away from my face. "In case you might, I don't know, decide to live somewhere else some day. Somewhere like . . . San Francisco?" He smiles shyly at me and my heart squeezes in my chest. "I was too nervous to come straight out and ask you, in case you said no. Even though I knew how much I loved you, we had only been together a couple of weeks. I didn't want to freak you out."

"Oh." I bite my lip. A tear trickles down my face.

"You and me?" He brushes my cheek with his thumb, sweeping my tear away. "We were something amazing that happened. It wasn't planned. I fell in love with you, Brooke. Almost from the moment I met you."

My throat tightens. "How can I trust you after what happened?" My tears stream down my face. "You broke my heart." My voice cracks, my whole body shaking.

He pulls me in closer to him. "I know." He hangs his head. "I never wanted to do that, not in a million years. Brooke, I quit my job for you. I'm here in Wellington—for you. It's—" he falters, his words momentarily choked. "It's all for you."

I look up into his face, his eyes glistening from unshed tears.

"I want to be with you. Nothing else matters." He leans down and brushes his lips against mine. The kiss is so gentle, so tender. It sends a shot of electricity through my body.

It feels so exquisite, so right. It's like coming home.

He pulls me in close, wrapping his strong arms around my quivering body, and kisses me again, this time more insistently.

"Say you love me, Brooke. Say you want to be with me forever."

As I look into his eyes I know with such clarity of thought no one else will do. I love him with such depth, such strength, it makes my head spin.

"I love you, Logan."

And now I know he loves me.

EPILOGUE

"WHERE DO YOU WANT this thing? Whatever it is," Logan asks, examining the contents of his hands.

A smile spreads across my face as I look at him standing in his jeans and characteristic white T-shirt, smeared with dirt, as he holds my home pedicure tub in his hands.

"Bathroom, please." I look around the room, noting with satisfaction that we're alone. "But first, come over here."

He puts the box on the floor and saunters over to me, sliding his arms around my waist. "I assume this is what you're after?" he asks cheekily as he leans down and kisses me teasingly on my lips.

My body quivers in response, the kiss over far too soon. "You've got it in one." I rub my hands down his taut back grabbing his toned butt. I give it a satisfying squeeze.

"Hey, you two. Break it up. There are others present, you know," Grace instructs as she places a box on the kitchen bench, panting lightly. "We'll never get you moved into this new place of yours if you keep stopping every five minutes to pash."

Logan raises his eyebrows at me, whispering in my ear, "I want to do a lot more than 'pash' with you right now."

"Stop it," I whisper without conviction. Truth be told I could take him right here, right now. "Go. Unpack boxes."

"Yes, Ma'am." He picks up the pedicure tub and heads to the bathroom, flashing me a wicked grin as he leaves.

Grace sighs. "You two are so cute. A little gross, but mostly cute."

I flush with happiness. "You'll have this too, some day."

"Ha! Not likely. Guys my age are all a bit crap."

I laugh. "You'll meet someone. You're only twenty-four. Just give it time."

She pulls and face and changes the subject. "This is a great place." She looks out of the window at the view of Wellington's picturesque harbour. "You're going to be so happy here."

"It is great, isn't it?" I couldn't stop smiling if you paid me.

In fact, I've not been able to stop smiling for months now. It's been almost ten months since Logan turned up on my doorstep, and we haven't looked back. He's moved to Wellington and we've been revelling in our time together, travelling the length of the country and the States too, meeting one another's families and friends, and getting to know each other really, really well.

I've even done a *Middle Earth* tour with him, which I enjoyed. I'm not about to become a fully-fledged Tolkien geek any time soon: I'll leave that to Logan.

Dylan drops a box with a thud on the living room floor.

"Hey, careful with that," I say in alarm.

"Yeah, dufus," Grace chimes in.

"It was heavy," he protests, as though it were a valid reason.

I read the side of the box, where I've scrawled the word 'plates – kitchen'. "I hope for your sake there's nothing broken."

"Nah, it'll be fine. I didn't hear anything break," he replies, skulking back out the door to get his next haul.

Dylan seems to be doing better these days. I hate to say it, but seeing me at an all-time low did him the world of good. I don't think he'll be keeping me on that pedestal so much these days.

Although I could have done without the drama, I guess every cloud has its silver lining.

"This box says 'bedroom'," Alexis says, standing in the doorway. "Is that master or one of the other ones?"

I peer at the contents through the top of the box. "Take it to the bedroom next to the master. We'll be needing that stuff in there before long."

I follow her into the bedroom, passing Logan in the hallway on his way back to the truck. He gives me a little squeeze.

Unlike Dylan, Alexis places the box with care on the floor, straightens up, and grins.

"I can't believe you guys are going to have a baby!" she exclaims excitedly, eyeing my small belly with envy.

"I know. I can hardly believe it either." Happiness swells inside me.

We found out I was pregnant after Logan and I had been together for six months. Although it wasn't in our plan—hell, we were so busy being with one another, we hadn't even thought about a 'plan'—we were both over the moon about it. It felt so right.

We decided my townhouse was too small to raise a family in, so bought this beautiful house in Wadestown, a stylish suburb close to the city. Plus, part of me wanted to start afresh, in a place we could create new, wonderful memories together as a family.

"I'm just hoping I'll fit my bridesmaid dress for your wedding," I add.

"Don't worry, babe. I'll have a tarpaulin made up in silk just for you."

"Very funny."

"Coming through!" Grace staggers into the bedroom with a large box, a lampshade balanced precariously on top.

Concerned she can barely see I take the lampshade from her as she stacks the box next to the one on the floor.

The three of us wander back to the living room. "I'm sorry I can't bring in all our stuff. You guys are amazing. Thank you so much." Tears well in my eyes.

That's the other thing: since falling for Logan and the demise of *Live It* I've gone from being that crab with the tough exterior to a total sap.

I'm not sure I'm overly happy with this new development, but it appears to be here to stay.

"Hi everyone. We wanted to drop by and give you this," Jennifer says, handing me an orchid pot plant.

"And this," Dad adds in as he hands Logan a bottle of Bollinger, my favourite champagne.

"Shame I can't partake," I comment, my hand automatically going to my middle.

"As if we could forget you, kiddo," Dad adds, handing a bottle of sparkling grape juice to Logan.

"Thanks." I let out a laugh. "This orchid is beautiful. Hey, you look great, Jennifer."

Jennifer's treatment was a success, and we celebrated her

remission a few months ago. She has to keep up the hormone therapy for the next four or more years, but she looks strong, healthy, and full of life.

"So do you, sweetheart." She puts her hand on my belly. "How are you feeling?"

"Good, thanks. A bit nauseous at times, otherwise great."

"I still can't believe I'm going to be a grandmother," she replies, shaking her head.

"You'll be the best," I respond, knowing full well she will be.

I'm still working at Dad's company and loving it, although I'm due to take an extended leave of absence in a few months' time of course. He's asked if I would like to become a full partner in the business. Tempted as I was, I decided not to.

Work doesn't come first, second, and last in my world anymore. What does? Love. It turns out, that's all you need.

THE END

GLOSSARY OF JOCELYN'S SAYINGS
(For those of you not from *Godzone*)

Belly up – going wrong
Bloke – man
Blow me down – that was unexpected
Bonk – sex
Box of budgies – happy
Brassed off – angry
Brew – tea
Bust a gut – work hard
Corker – something really good
Chook – chicken, term of endearment
Crack on – get on with it
Cuppa – cup of tea
Dag – something funny
Fella – man
Fizzy – soda
Gave it heaps – tried your best
Godzone – God's own country, New Zealand
Good as gold – great
Good on ya – well done
Guts for garters – make someone pay for what he/she has done
Hard yakka – hard work
Hissy fit – dramatic outburst, usually unnecessarily over the top
Hob nob – talk
Hunky dory – good
Looker – good-looking
Mum's the word – my lips are sealed
Naff off – go away
Park yourself down – sit down
Pike out – quit
Rattle my dags – get a move on
Right as rain – fine
Right wally or wally – a silly person, an idiot
Righto – right, okay
She'll be right – everything will be just fine
Skite – show off

You can't slip a fast one by me – you can't fool me
Stoked – overjoyed
Strewth – oh dear
Suss out – look into something, work it out
Ta – thanks
The hots – sexually attracted to someone
Throw a hissy fit – get upset
Too right – that's correct
Up at the sparrow's fart – up early in the morning
Worth a crack – worth a try
Yank – an American
Yoo-hoo – hello

ALSO BY KATE O'KEEFFE

There are three books and a short story in the *Wellywood Romantic Comedy Series*. They are:

Wedding Bubbles (short story)

Book 1: *Styling Wellywood*

Book 2: *Miss Perfect Meets Her Match*

Book 3: *Falling For Grace*

I hope you enjoy reading them as much as I did writing them!

ACKNOWLEDGMENTS

I wrote my first novel, *Styling Wellywood*, in almost complete isolation, barely telling a soul I was writing it. God knows what my family and friends must have thought I was doing with my time. Consequently, I only had a small handful of people to thank.

In this, my second novel, things have changed a bit. To start with, my friends and family know I'm a novelist these days, so even if I had wanted to write it in secrecy, I would have failed abysmally. Secondly I've become a fully-fledged member of the wonderful world of writers' communities, both virtually and in person. And it totally rocks.

So, who to thank? The biggies have to be my editor, my critique partner, and my beta readers, all of whom have offered me invaluable advice and support. My editor is the fabulously finicky Julie Crengle, who gladly gave up her time to fix my (hopefully only occasional) mangled language and grammatical anomalies. She's also a lawyer and offered advice on that partnership agreement. Julie, thank you so very much.

My critique partner is a fantastic fellow Kiwi chick lit author, Maggie Le Page. Maggie, your sharp mind, strong sense of humour, and ability to create wonderful characters and story lines in your own work has helped me immeasurably in the creation of mine. Thank you.

To my beta readers, Leanne Mackay, Marina Collot, and Nicky Willis: thank you for not only your suggestions but for believing in my novel, even when I had my own doubts. I particularly liked it when you have used the words 'love' and 'your novel' together. I shall be using you again for novel number three.

Thank you to all the wonderful authors of New Zealand Romance Writers, particularly the Wellington chapter. I don't get to attend as many meetings as I would like, but when I do I leave brimming with ideas, enthusiasm, and extremely useful information. I would especially like to acknowledge the wonderful romance author Kris Pearson, whose expertise in hot and racy sex scenes helped me give Brooke and Logan a night to remember. Kris also came up with the novel's cute title, which clicked with me straight away. Thank you, Kris.

The other writers' group I want to thank is Chick Lit Chat HQ, a virtual group of like-minded chick lit authors who support one another through the writing and marketing of our work. Thank you all for gladly offering your time and ideas, especially Tracie Bannister and Whitney Dineen whose grasp of the chick lit world is nothing short of miraculous.

I also want to thank Pete McLennan for his general wonderfulness as well as for his knowledge; my hairdresser, Kate of A Beautiful You, for her advice on Brooke's hair; and the American Cancer Society for information on Jennifer's breast cancer.

Last but most certainly not least, a huge thank you to my husband. You give me the time, the support, sometimes even the ideas, to pursue my passion for writing. I know some days the laundry's not done, the dogs aren't walked, the house is a mess. I want you to know how much your support of my writing means to me. Thank you, you're the best husband I could wish for.

ABOUT THE AUTHOR

I write sexy, feel-good romantic comedies.

I've loved chick lit and romantic comedies since I first encountered Bridget Jones as a young, impressionable writer. It really was a match made in chick lit heaven.

I've been a teacher and a sales executive, but am now content as a mother and writer, madly scribbling all the ideas I've accumulated during my time on this planet we call home.

I live and love in beautiful New Zealand—where my novels are set—with my wonderful family and my two very scruffy dogs.

Sign up for my newsletter at kateokeeffe.com to hear about new releases and more!

CPSIA information can be obtained
at www.ICGtesting.com
Printed in the USA
LVHW090248231020
669617LV00007B/227